# The Magellan Chronicles

## Seas of Conquest
### (Book 2)

A biographical novel series of Ferdinand Magellan

By

Brett Stortroen

The Magellan Chronicles: Seas of Conquest
(Book 2)

Treasure Hill Publishing
Dunedin, Fl, USA

Library of Congress Cataloging-in-Publication Data

ISBN  978-1-957612-04-1

Cover art by Mark Daehlin

For inquiries, please email the author at bstortroen@protonmail.com

4

## By Brett Stortroen

*Mecca, Muhammad & the Moon-God: A Candid Investigation into the Origins of Islam*

*Night of the Dragon: The Saga of Saint George*

*The Magellan Chronicles Series (Books 1-3)*

## Dedication

A special thanks to Thomas Nowaczyk for editorial assistance. His insightful comments were invaluable, much appreciated, and instrumental to the project.

Another thanks to my wife Iris for having patience during the many years of research for this book.

# Maps

# Sail Route to Battle of Diu
(Jan 5 to Feb 3, 1509)

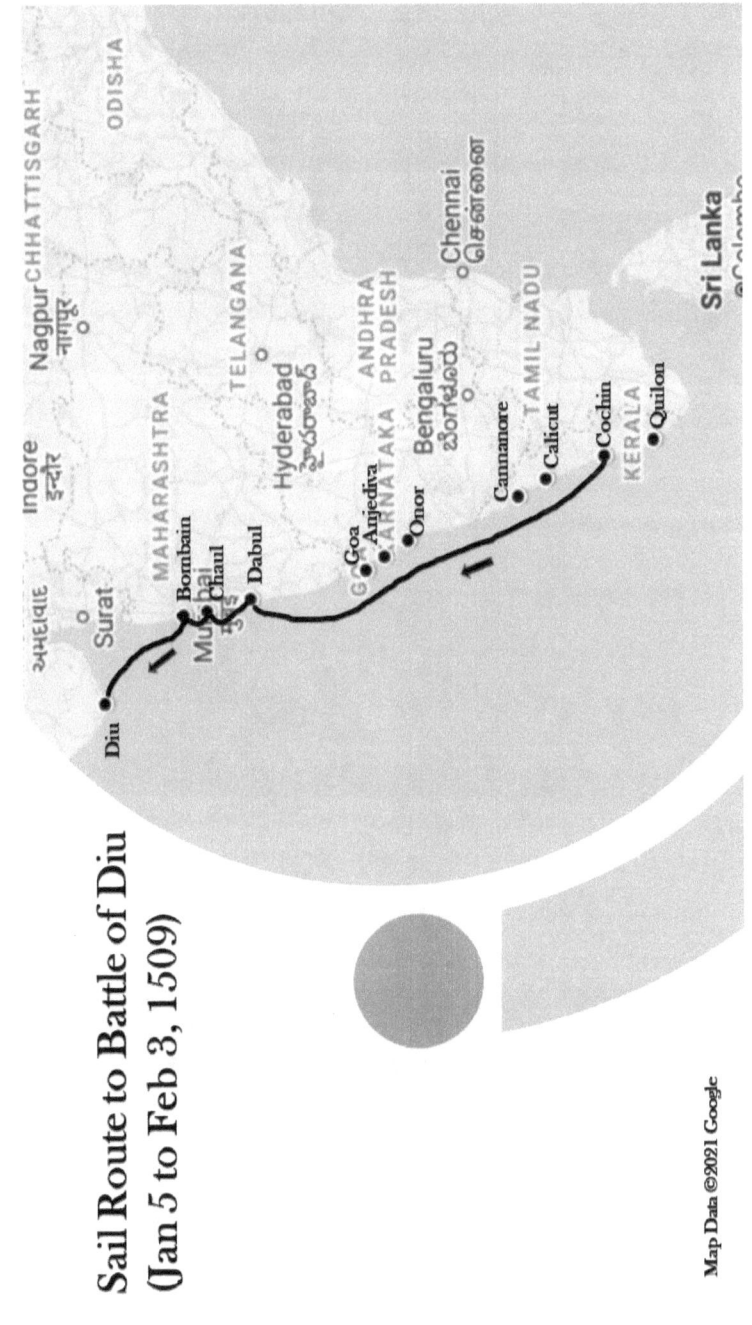

Map Data ©2021 Google

# Magellan's Sailing Route to Battle of Goa (February - 1510)

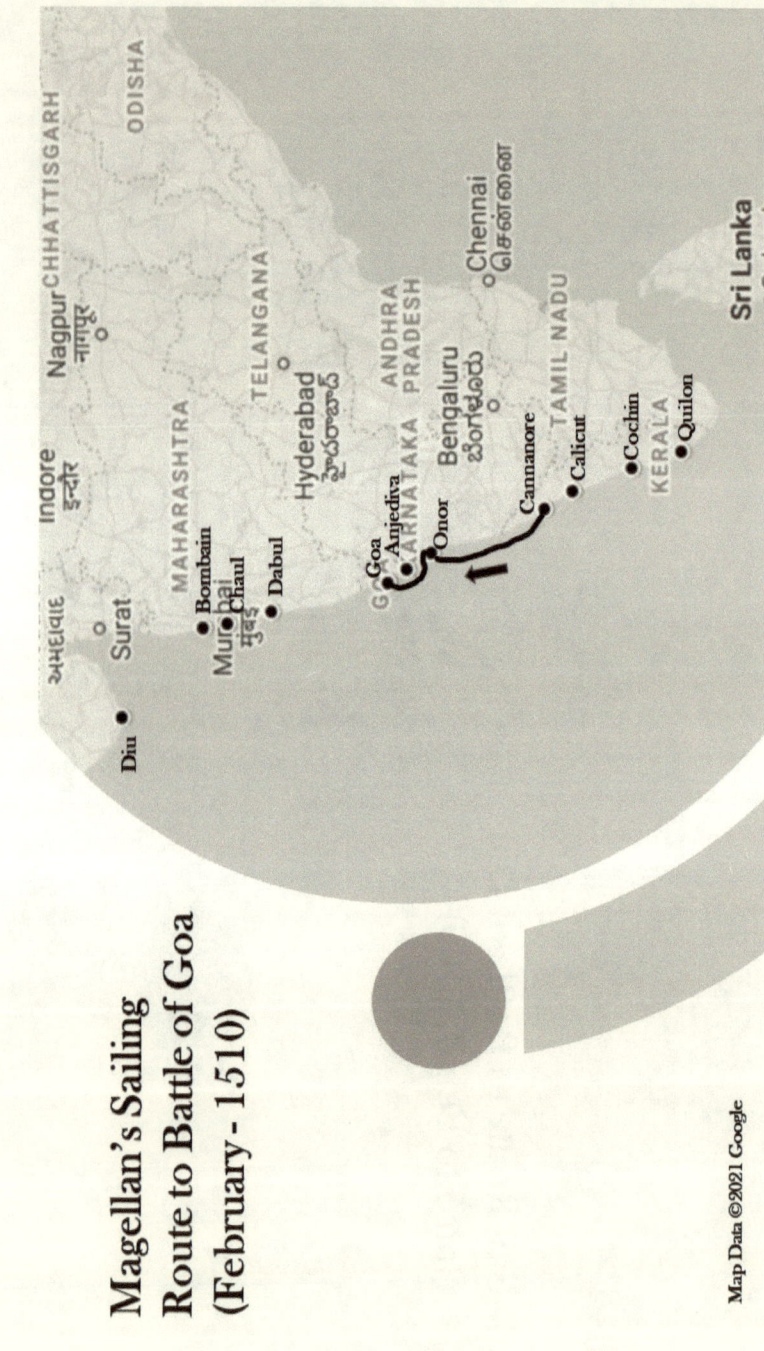

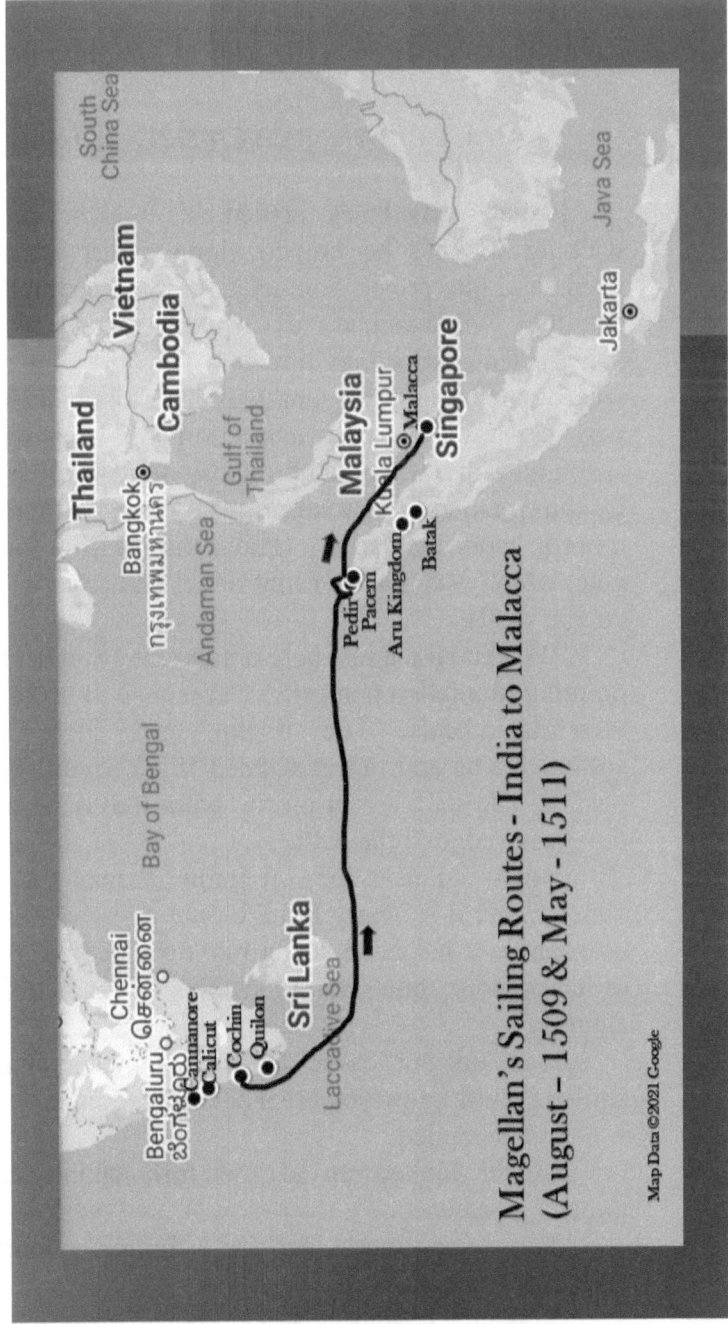

Magellan's Sailing Routes - India to Malacca
(August – 1509 & May - 1511)

# 1

## Cochin – November, 1506

Fernão Magalhães braced his weight upon a walking stick as he limped along a dirt path. His friend and interpreter, Samuel Levi, accompanied him as they approached a square-shaped fortress constructed of coconut timbers. The fort of Cochin was situated along the southwestern coast of India. It was constructed upon a section of land mostly surrounded by water, and slightly south-west of the Cochin mainland. Samuel noticed Fernão's limp was more pronounced as they neared the massive fortress gate, which was made of limestone, and covered with cockle shells.

'We can take a rest here a moment,' Samuel said, pointing to a fallen palm tree. 'You need to make sure your leg heals. The doctor said there were complications and that you need to be careful not to push it.' He took a seat on the palm tree lying along the grassy edge of the path.

Fernão sat near him. 'I know, thanks for your concern, but it is nearly healed, only an issue walking a distance. It has been seven months since the Battle of Cannanore, but now I am finally ready to sail again.'

'I would not agree to look at you,' Samuel smiled. 'But I know you are a determined man.'

Fernão smiled.

Samuel looked up at the fort, taking in its imposing presence.

'This is an impressive fort,' Samuel remarked. 'When was it constructed?'

'You have heard of Captain Pedro Cabral?'

'Of course, the one who discovered Brazil.'

'Yes. He had discovered it on his way to India in 1500. Here, they established the first Portuguese settlement in India. Later, Vasco da Gama constructed the first trading factory. But, after Da Gama departed, the Zamorin of Calicut destroyed it.'

'It was all destroyed?'

'Almost. You must know that we responded to this aggression. Have you heard of Duarte Pacheco Pereira?'

Samuel shook his head.

'Well, he was a famous explorer and cosmographer. In September of 1503, he joined the Albuquerque brothers in reclaiming the remains of the factory and built a new defense—Fort Manuel.'

'The Albuquerque brothers?'

'Yes, naval commanders,' Fernão replied. 'The Albuquerque's and Pereira were all loyal to the crown and determined to protect our interests in India. It was not long before their resolve was tested, for, once again, the Islamic mercantile factions admonished and incited the Zamorin to force us out of India. But Pacheco remained steadfast, always defending against the numerous incursions and overwhelming numbers. His cunning and sometimes daring tactics won stunning victories, both on land and sea. It spread fear into the enemy, even unto kingdoms far abroad.'

Fernão smiled. 'I remember one account during Pacheco's command as it was told to me in the India House. One day, the Zamorin had brought a force of 50,000 of his Nair warriors and a fleet of 280 ships against us. Our forces were only 100 soldiers, 5,000 allied troops from the king of Cochin, and a small naval contingent under the command of Afonso de Albuquerque.'

'How did Pacheco and Albuquerque overcome against such odds?'

'I can give you one reason. Duarte Pacheco had a young mulatto son called Lisuarte. At 20 years of age, he was full of sculpted muscle and skilled in all weaponry, especially the two-handed sword. As Pacheco's vessel drew near Cochin, his son and 20 men launched a skiff. Lisuarte commanded them to row hard and were the first of the armada to reach the causeway, which was filled with hordes of the enemy. He led the charge, cutting and slashing with his two-handed sword with such ferocity and speed that he lost all his men in the throngs of combatants. Duarte Pacheco gave orders to Albuquerque's trumpeters to sound off so that all other units under the captain-major might know where he was in all the chaos. After all present shouted in response, Pacheco rushed into the enemy to find his son. Lisuarte wore greaves on his legs and other heavy armor, so Pacheco had hoped his son would not be wounded. When he and the others located him, they found 20 bloodied corpses strewn about, one of which had been sliced in half. Pacheco was unaware his son had such skills and immediately kissed him on the face. Lisuarte then knelt and confided that he had desired to honor his father by defeating the enemy. Pacheco responded with a hands-on blessing. Once all the enemy had fled or been slain, he brought his son before Captain-Major—Afonso de Albuquerque. As Lisuarte approached, Albuquerque embraced him and said: "God strengthen you in his holy service." Lisuarte knelt and pleaded to be made a knight. The captain-major replied: "We ought to be receiving this honor from your hand, for you have won everything on this field." Albuquerque then knighted him. When the raja heard of these events, he encouraged Pacheco to go home and make more sons like his and begged for Lisuarte to remain as a deterrent against the Zamorin.'

Fernão's tale was interrupted by Francisco's approach.

'Any idea what the viceroy wants?' Francisco asked.

'Only that he requests our presence,' Fernão replied.

The three friends approached the main gate, nodded at two sentries, and entered Fort Manuel. They continued onward to the commander's quarters and entered. Viceroy Almeida and several officers were conversing as they pointed to various sections of a nautical chart.

Fernão cleared his throat as he neared his superiors.

Almeida turned his head and grinned. 'Ah, my brave warrior. Captain Serrão had reported your deeds and injuries. Are you ready for more action?'

'Yes sir,' Fernão replied.

'Very good. We have need to reinforce our positions in Africa. I am giving you command of a *bargantym* once you arrive to Kilwa.' Almeida turned to Francisco. 'You and Magalhães will sail with Captain Nuño Vaz Pereira on board the caravel *Espera* next week. Later, I will inform King Manuel of my decision.'

Fernão's heart raced upon the thought that the King would know of his promotion and would have to acknowledge his abilities to command.

All eyes then turned to Samuel Levi. 'Ah yes, the interpreter. Acquire any sense of these local dialects? The friars have made some progress, but we need more precision.'

'Yes sir.'

Almeida raised an eyebrow. 'Indeed.'

'I had some good fortune,' Samuel said. 'I met some fellow Jews in Cannanore. They spoke a certain Judeo-Malayalam dialect. After almost nine months conversing with them, I am now able to decipher much of the Malabar vernacular.'

'Were you aware there exists a much larger community of Jews here in Cochin?' Almeida asked. 'Some claim their ancestors arrived from the vessels of King Solomon and later, many other exiles arrived during their Babylonian captivity.' Almeida paused in thought. 'We also have learned others arrived here after the Romans demolished the second temple in Jerusalem.'

'No sir, I was not aware so many arrived in India,' Samuel replied, surprised by the revelation.

Almeida looked Samuel over. 'Well, my point is, I need a good interpreter, especially now.' He scratched his beard. 'I propose a deal. You serve three years here in Cochin. Once that time served, you will be a free man and be able to live in Cochin with your kindred, or anywhere you desire. You will have a letter signed and sealed as proof. Does that appeal to you?'

Samuel turned toward Fernão and Francisco, not sure how they would react. But the two both nodded in affirmation. Samuel turned back to the viceroy. 'Yes sir. Thank you, sir.'

Almeida smiled. 'Very well. I will have the paperwork drawn up. For now, you are dismissed.'

The following day Fernão, Samuel and Francisco met just outside of town. 'We might as well explore Cochin before departing,' Fernão proposed. 'The caravel already has enough staff for last preparations.'

'Count me in,' Francisco said.

Samuel nodded and they set off along a dirt road. Soon, a heavily armed man approached wearing a sort of cloth called a *lankoutah*. It was tied around the waist and draped to the knees. All peoples in this region were attired in such manner except the Muslims who dressed in the elaborate Arabian fashion. In one hand, he carried a buckler of ox-hide and in the other, a sharp poignard that glistened in the sun. Fernão had become familiar with these soldiers, called Nairs. They were of the warrior caste, second in hierarchy, just below the Brahmans. All Nairs were loyal to the king and were required to always bear arms whenever they went out, no matter how old, even the old and infirm. If their king died in battle they were also required to die. Nairs abstained from wine, often ate only once per day, and slept on a bare bench. They lived a disciplined life in service to their assigned sovereign.

Fernão regarded them with some familiarity, much like his own upbringing. He himself was trained as a young page in all facets of weaponry. The Nairs were schooled from seven years of age in all athletics such as dance and tumbling, and they could bend their limbs in any direction. Later in their education, a captain of war called a *panicar* would teach them to handle weapons best suited for their skills. Most learned the sword and buckler but others the bow, club, or lance. They honored the masters who had taught them. If a Nair met another Nair older than himself, he would make reverence and give way. Nairs lived outside the towns in fenced off estates. The caste system was heavily enforced. When traveling they would shout at peasants to get out the way. If a peasant did not comply in this customary law and give way, the Nair could strike them dead without penalty. If any peasant by chance touched a

Nair lady, her family would immediately kill her and the man who touched her. This was done to avoid any mixture of the castes. Foreigners were exempt from these caste laws.

As the Nair approached, he made a turn down a narrow path leading through a lush grove of areca palms and surrounded by stones. Fernão watched as black cobras slithered around a snake idol situated in the center of this grove. Nairs reverenced snake deities above all other gods and virtually every household had such devotional groves. It was also forbidden by law for any Nair or Brahman to kill a cobra, for they were considered holy.

The Nair passed along the grove perimeter and approached a medium-sized house made of coconut palm timbers. The roof was thatched since tiles were prohibited for all citizens in Malabar, except for mosques, temples, or for a great kaimal—the equivalent of the Portuguese dukes, and other such titled nobles. These laws concerning tiles were imposed to thwart any resistance to the kaimal's power. The Nair placed his hands on his hips and shook his head in disgust at the white sash hanging from the door latch. He kicked some dirt and walked away.

Fernão chuckled.

'What's so funny?' Francisco asked.

'I heard some things about the Nairs some weeks ago,' Fernão replied. 'They have a strange custom of polyandry.'

'Polyandry?' Samuel asked.

'Nair warriors do not marry and do not know their fathers or sons for they share one woman. A young Nair virgin is deflowered by a Nair who gives her a gold necklace. Later, more Nairs have their time with her and give her various choice gifts. She will achieve greater esteem by acquiring more lovers, some entertain ten or more.'

'What?' Francisco asked. Both he and Samuel looked astonished.

Fernão continued, 'Nair women are supported by their lovers and devote themselves to pleasing their men. Their children are taken care of by her mother or uncles. Nair women may only entertain men of the upper two castes—Nair warriors or Brahman priests. Furthermore, they may never enter town except once per year with their harem of men. It has been understood the king instituted this custom so his warriors would not be covetous and loyal only to himself. Nair warriors have their appointed day from mid-day until the next day at the same time and are required to leave a signal upon the door if occupied. Apparently, in this case, another lover had extended his time with their shared consort.'

'That poor fool, Francisco said. 'Knowing another may still be finishing the deed.'

'Disgusting,' Samuel said. 'But indeed, quite funny.'

'I hear women in these lands prefer to ride on top,' Francisco replied with a grin.

Samuel and Fernão looked at one another and scoffed at this.

'It is true,' Francisco insisted. 'I heard it from several Nair warriors I met back in Cannanore.'

The three of them stood and stared at the house, wondering what exotic customs were being observed that would be considered taboo back in Portugal.

They were soon on their way again, but as the three drew near the center of town they were pleased to find that Cochin was full of revelry and processions of elaborate rituals. 'What is this?' Francisco asked.

'The harvest festival,' Samuel replied. 'Locals call it Diwali and lasts several days.'

'Looks entertaining,' Francisco said. 'Let us have a look.'

They were especially interested with one procession. Elephants with expensive regalia escorted a chariot through the streets. The backs of the elephants were covered with a velvet cloth, embroidered with gold and silver. Bells suspended by chains hung below the belly and ropes intertwined with ornaments were attached all over the bodies. The ivory tusks were protected by kalaps covered with iron and brass rings. In the middle of the great procession of elephants and pilgrims was a chariot decorated with a gold cloth and pulled by two oxen. In the chariot rode an idol with four arms. It was made of gold and vivid colors. Attached to the cart was a long bamboo pole supporting a canopy which shaded the idol. Pairs of young virgin girls danced before it while minstrels played their instruments as they followed. Dancers and jesters entertained along the sides. As the procession neared, a ghastly sight emerged from between the throngs of pilgrims. Samuel's jaw dropped. 'What the devil?'

'Indeed, a devil,' Fernão replied, scowling at the apparition.

Within the chariot, a crane was mounted. From the crane a beautiful young woman was hoisted by two iron chains and hooks fastened to her thighs. Naked from neck to waist and wearing a blood-stained white garment that draped to her knees, she sang and shouted praises to the idol, all the while holding a small round shield in one hand and a bag of lemons and oranges in the other.

Fernão and his compatriots mingled in with the crowd to get a closer look at the bizarre event. All three stared in disbelief as they observed men foaming at the mouth and eyes rolling back in their heads. These men slashed knives and swords at their own shins, thighs, and shoulders. Others threw themselves under the chariot wheels, crushing their bones. Blood flowed into the streets as the wounded and dying offered themselves to their idol with fevered devotion.

'What sort of demons have taken hold of these people?' Fernao asked.

Francisco and Samuel just stared and shook their heads.

Samuel spoke with one of the pilgrims and translated back the response to his friends. 'The woman had prayed to the idol of Vishnu in desire to wed a certain man. She indeed married her desired one and now must honor her pledge with blood.

The three followed the procession to a temple. Upon arrival, the young woman was freed from the bloody hooks and collapsed to the ground. Her husband carried her to a shady tree and placed a wet rag on her forehead, which partially revived her. The temple had three doors and the main door faced the west. In front of the main gate was a flat square stone about three feet high and with three wooden steps all around it. As dusk approached, priests carried the idol in procession around the temple, their own wives following, all the while holding lit oil lamps. After three circumambulations, the idol was set upon the black stone and worshipped. Once all the rituals had been completed the idol was housed in a chapel within the temple. Fernão wondered at the significance of the number three, at the notion that they might have some crude understanding of the triune nature of God. Why else would they have the number—three—imbedded into all their rituals?

Francisco tugged on his shoulder, breaking his thoughts. 'Look, Cochin lights up!'

Citizens had lit oil lanterns and candles throughout the city, flickering lights reflected off freshly white-washed homes, while Chinese imported fireworks lit up the night sky. Revelers gathered in elaborate feasts throughout the city. Fernão wondered how such marvelous displays of visual delight could be co-mingled with such savage heathen idolatry. Each of these idol temples were often attended by 50 to 100 women.

Fernão had heard from the locals in Cannanore as to why so many served the idols in every temple. Much like Varthema's account from the far east islands, all wives in Malabar were expected to burn themselves to death when their husbands died. Obedient women were to utter these words: "See ladies, how much you owe to your husbands for in this manner you ought to accompany them even in death." Once these words had concluded, her relations would give her a pitcher full of oil to set upon her head. She then recites a prayer while facing the east and throws the pitcher of oil into a fire pit below, kindling the flames. Finally, the woman jumps into the pit as her relations throw on more pitchers of oil so that the fire soon consumes her flesh. Most are obedient in this custom of self-immolation. Those who refuse, have their heads shaved by their relatives and are banished from their homes and family. They wander the land in disgrace. If her family wishes to show some mercy, they may send her to a temple to serve. Young women will sing and dance before the idol some hours of the day and the remainder of time work for themselves. He had also heard that when a king has died, as many as 500 women would offer themselves to the fire pits in willful obedience.

Fernão recalled another barbaric practice among a certain sect of holy men in these regions. The men wear about their necks a silk cord, and wrapped in a colorful cloth, which holds a stone about the size of an egg. All the people venerate these holy men greatly because they believe the stone is their god, and which they call Tabaryne. When such a man dies, the family would dig a pit, somewhat deeper than his wife's height, stand her upright within the pit, and fill the grave with dirt up to her neck. Finally, they all would stamp down until the earth was pressed hard, place large stones around her head, and leave her to a miserable death.

'I can hardly believe what we have witnessed today,' Fernão said.

'I hear the festival continues tomorrow,' Samuel said.

'Perfect,' Francisco said. 'We should continue our tour and discover even greater oddities.'

# 2

It was mid-day when the Diwali festival had resumed. As they walked the streets, they encountered an oddity of nature seated upon a bench under a coconut tree. A woman had one leg swollen about four times the size of her other, much in appearance like that of an elephant.

'That looks like it hurts,' Fernão said.'

'I heard from sources it is rarely painful, but many will die of this,' Samuel replied. 'They say about one in five—perhaps more, from all castes, have this disease.'

'What is it called?' Francisco asked.

'They call it pericaes and ask the gods to protect them from, that which nests inside and swells.'

'Why so many?' Fernão asked.

'They believe it's due to the marshy waters frequented along the coasts of Malabar.'

They continued down the street and took notice of a man in the shadows of a building. He was seated upon what looked like a wine cask. But as they drew closer, they stared in revolt, for the man did not sit upon a wine cask but upon his own uncovered and grossly swollen scrotum.

Francisco said, 'Now, *that* looks painful,' my friend.

'The poor wretch,' Fernão said.

They continued onward and encountered another entourage of devotees escorting an idol in a chariot. A second chariot followed with an elaborately dressed man—a kaimal ruler—seated within. Several cows were led alongside, and young women carried gold dishes filled with water. One of the cows let loose a pile of steaming excrement and one of the ladies immediately scooped it into the bowl and stirred it with her hand. She then took a handful of dirt and mixed it into the bowl until a thick paste formed.

Francisco pointed. 'Look! What in the devil is she doing?'

The three stared as the girl climbed into the chariot and spread the cow dung paste along the chariot sides, floor, and seat. She then rubbed some on the kaimal's forehead. Fernão and Francisco looked at Samuel for any possible explanation.

'As you know they highly venerate the cow,' Samuel said. 'I never realized how much so.' He stared off toward the kaimal's chariot. 'The law of the land states that anyone who slays a cow shall be executed.'

Francisco shook his head. 'Incredible. What a waste of such good beef.'

As they continued wandering among the throng of revelers, they encountered several men covered only in loin cloths. They had elaborate metal nets full of hooks attached to their skin and wrapped tight, forcing their bodies into painful contorted positions. Their flesh stretched and bled, yet they remained silent. Many appeared in a trance.

They quickly came upon another oddity; a man sat cross-legged upon a pillar nearly 30 feet tall and staring to the east, motionless and in deep concentration. Samuel seemed mostly non-plussed by the unusual customs, but Fernão and Francisco shared a glance of incredulity.

Later, in the afternoon, they stopped before a building made of timber and stone. A cross was affixed to the top. Fernão found a sense of relief in this, hoping some sort of divine presence in the lands may exist. He climbed three steps made of stone and pushed a large door open. He entered, his companions following, to behold an unorthodox-styled house of worship. Instead of seats, only thatched mats in ordered rows. Fernão walked toward a plain altar, a sweet incense permeating the air. Along the sanctuary perimeter, short inscriptions were carved into the stone walls. He turned to Samuel and pointed to the wall. 'Hebrew?'

Samuel focused upon one inscription. 'This one is Hebrew. *Hear O Israel: The Lord our God, the Lord is one. Love the Lord your God with all your heart and with all your soul and with all your strength.*' He then stood in front of another writing. This one in Syriac, a derivative of Aramaic. *In the beginning was the Word, and the Word was with God, and the Word was God. He was in the beginning with God. All things were made by Him, and without Him nothing was made.*'

Fernão considered the walls of biblical verses inscribed in ancient languages of the near east. 'Interesting, one verse focused upon the oneness and the other upon the triune nature of God.'

Two large books lay open upon the flat altar with lanterns lighted nearby. Samuel compared the two and turned to Fernão and Francisco. 'Incredible. A complete copy of the Tanakh in Hebrew and this other appears to be a compilation of Christian scriptures in Syriac.' Samuel Levi looked over some liturgical ornaments. 'Looks like one of our synagogues back in Lisbon. Odd.'

'Yes, odd,' Fernão said. 'And no idols or images, only scripture verses. And strange that—'

Footsteps echoed through the sanctuary. The trio turned to see a group of men approaching. All were dressed in white cotton robes. Two carried scimitars. The third wore a silver cross necklace, and the fourth had a thin cotton cord of many threads, split in three, which hung from his shoulder and under his right arm. Francisco and Fernão placed their hands upon their black sword hilts. Samuel reached for his dagger.

The man with the cross around his neck raised his right arm. He had a long dark beard, and his red-sleeved white cotton robe accentuated a regal status. 'Peace and greetings gentlemen.' He noticed they had fixed their eyes upon the two warriors with scimitars. 'Please do not be alarmed. Most of us have been trained as youths in the martial arts. We follow the words of our Lord who commanded Thomas and all his disciples: *But now, he who has a money bag, let him take it, and likewise a knapsack; and he who has no sword, let him sell his garment and buy one.*' Many of us serve in the army to protect our own as well as the kings who have treated our people well for generations.'

'Your people?' Francisco asked.

'Forgive me. I must introduce myself. They call me Mar Yaqob. I have come from the land of Persia to help our brothers here in Cochin and the lands of Malabar.'

'How did you come to learn Portuguese?' Fernão asked.

'In my service as a bishop I have studied many languages and met many people from afar.' Yaqob paused. 'In these parts we are called Nasranis, those who follow Yeshua the Nazarene. Many of our people can trace their Christian roots back to the ministry of the Apostle Thomas.'

Fernão narrowed his brow and looked at him. 'The Lord's disciple? Here . . . in India?'

'Yes. He landed in a port town called Muziris, not far from Cochin. His first mission was to the Jewish community, and many were baptized as Christians.'

Samuel was intrigued. 'And how many Jews were here at that time?'

'Thousands from what has been told.'

'And what about the natives of the land?' Fernão asked.

'By the power of mighty signs and wonders, natives of all castes came to the faith. In our community, we accept all who wish to believe, no matter if a high caste Brahman or a lowly untouchable. Eight churches were established before Thomas was martyred in Chennai.'

'And how many Nasranis live in Malabar? Fernão continued to question.

'It has been said 30,000 believers confess themselves as Christians.'

Fernão's mind raced as he remembered the accounts of medieval literature. 'And do they serve King Prester John? Are your warriors in his service?'

Yaqob chuckled. 'Oh my. Our people were asked that same question by Da Gama and the friars. We know nothing of this Prester John but of stories from abroad.' From their expression, Yaqob sensed the Portuguese visitors were quite serious about their quest. 'Well, I have heard rumors of such a king. He lives across the Arabian Sea . . . to the west, in a land called Ethiopia.'

Fernão recalled a rumor he had once heard during his service in the India House of Lisbon. Many years ago, King João II had sent two spies on a top-secret mission to Ethiopia in a quest to forge an alliance with the legendary Christian king, Prester John. Neither spy returned, and the mystery of Prester John remained an enigma. Fernão reflected—*what a shame the Portuguese armada had focused their attention to Africa only as far north as Mogadishu, for encounters with the famous Christian king may now elude them further.*

'Thank you for your candor, sir,' Fernão said, then shifted the conversation. 'We observed some men in peculiar positions; some sitting cross-legged on tall pillars and staring blankly to the east, others in contorted positions in apparent self-mutilation. Can you explain this for us?'

Yaqob glanced over to his colleague who wore the cotton cord and was clean shaven. 'Perhaps it is best that my friend Yosef elaborates. He has great knowledge of Hindu custom, for he was a famous Brahman priest before converting to our faith. He has studied Portuguese under the visiting friars.'

Yosef stepped forward. 'You have encountered those who have sought to obtain supernatural powers for advancing their state of being, in the cosmic cycle of samsara. Yet some of those you have witnessed have loftier goals. They wish to bypass all reincarnations and self-awaken their consciousness . . . their atman . . . or soul, and thus merge with the ultimate supreme being called, Brahman.'

'And what has that to do with their strange behavior?' Francisco asked.

'Those who inflict such pain upon themselves are preparing themselves for intense meditations to come. You see, in order to realize their true consciousness, they must focus their attention either inwardly or upon an external source and thus disconnect from the external universe including their mind and body, only to find their true atman. All those seated on the pillars control their breathing with precise rhythms. Some will focus with great intensity upon an object and detach from their physical and mental existence until they finally discover their atman. Others retreat inwardly to find their consciousness.'

The Portuguese stared at him blankly. Sensing their confusion, Yosef paused a moment to rephrase. 'You must understand, the real self is hidden behind concentric sheaths of three levels of materiality or consciousness. That is to say: The *body* with all its senses, the *mind* with its own automatic faculties of thought, decision and command, and the *advanced consciousness* of deep dreamless states. Behind all this lies the true consciousness of *atman*.'

'You mean our spirit being?' Fernão asked.

'Precisely,' Yosef said. 'Once self-realization is attained, the individual enters a blissful state called Moksha and is thus liberated from all previous karma and future reincarnations. Their atman merges into the oneness of the universal Brahman and their individuality ceases to exist, like a dissolving lump of salt.'

Fernão scratched his earlobe, confused. 'So, let me understand. A spirit is reincarnated over several hundred lives until one finally reaches a self-conscious state of bliss with a universal force known as the Brahman?'

'Well, actually many repeat thousands or even tens of thousands of life cycles before they are liberated from the Samsaric cycles of birth and rebirth.'

'You mentioned karma and reincarnation. Can you elaborate?' Francisco asked.

'Surely. Karma is a transcendent action or cosmic energy from acts, words, or thoughts of people. It is the consequences of good or bad. Thus, one may advance upward in hierarchy if their lives obtain more good karma than bad.'

'So that explains the caste system in these lands,' Samuel said.

'True. For example, I was considered the highest-level status in the human realm, born a man in the Brahman caste. Under this system I could actually lower my position by acquiring more bad karma than good.'

'So, if you were to acquire more good karma then what? Are you not of the highest caste? Is there a heaven you could attain? Or a hell?' Fernão asked.

'Indeed. There are many levels of heavens and hells, and many levels of physical existence. The sage Manu cited 21 levels of hell. Punishments vary in intensity. Some may be burned in hot sand, boiled in jars, or devoured by ravens. The horrors are unlimited in variety and degree. An individual must endure these tortures and acknowledge one's past sins in order to rise one level to the next. Once liberated from the hells one may incarnate into a mineral, insect, or plant; then, further climbing up the cosmic ladder to an animal status of varying levels and finally achieving an incarnation as a human. One must then achieve a final awakening to enter the heavenly realms. Celestial levels begin with the musicians of the gods, then the sages and revered ancestors, next the ordinary gods, and finally the heaven of the creator—Brahma—which is the highest realm.'

The Portuguese stood in puzzled confusion. Francisco scratched his head and stepped forward. 'So how does one acquire good karma as, let's say a rock? Does it just exist as a good rock to later become an ant?'

'Yes, that is the way of samsara,' Yosef replied.

Fernão continued his inquiry, 'So individual spirits or what you call atman will live many thousands of lives until they finally achieve the highest level of heaven, but only to lose their individuality by merging and dissolving into the ultimate being, Brahman? What is the point if one loses their consciousness?'

'Precisely. One reason I accepted the faith of the Christians was because the soul will always continue as an individual while also obtaining a deep closeness with the Lord of the universe.'

Fernão smiled. 'And what of the idols? How many idols exist in India? And why? If the path to enlightenment is simply moksha or self-awareness, why the need of idols?'

The Brahman Christian grinned. 'Nobody knows how many, perhaps many thousands, or hundreds of thousands. Many follow the path of devotion to a particular deity or deities and hope to achieve good karma to climb the ladder of cosmic Samsara until they reach Moksha in that manner.'

'I am still confused,' Fernão said. 'If there is one supreme deity that most Hindus believe as the Brahman, why so many gods?'

'Indeed, some believe in specific personal deities that will lift them upward through the cycles of birth, death and rebirth. Yet, others simply believe the many gods are just facets or attributes of the supreme Brahman. They hold devotion to the deity or aspect of Brahman they most dearly love.'

'Seems like idolatry,' Fernao said, shaking his head. 'And what of these rituals you practice? Why such focus upon the number three?'

'There exists a trinity of sort here but much different than the Christian triune God. This triumvirate is responsible for the creation, preservation, and destruction of the world. Brahma, as—creator, Vishnu, as—preserver, and Shiva, as—destroyer.'

'Seems to be much confusion and mere philosophical conjectures—so many contradictions!'

'Ah. Yes. Indeed!' Yosef said. 'That is why some choose to follow the way of the Nazarene. We teach the holy scriptures to all who will listen. Unfortunately, most stay loyal to the old ways and remain in darkness.' Yosef glanced over to his ecclesiastical superior, Yaqob.

Yaqob stepped closer to Fernão. 'Perhaps you would like to assist us in reaching the lost?'

'It would be an honor and my own desire,' Fernão said. 'Unfortunately, we have already pledged service to our commander.' Fernão looked at Francisco who nodded in return.

'We have orders to depart this week,' Francisco said.

'I am to remain in Cochin. Perhaps I could visit? Samuel suggested. 'I am curious why such early Jewish liturgy exists here in a Christian church. I would also like to improve my knowledge in Syriac.'

'You would be most welcome to visit or stay with us,' Yosef replied.

They talked as the afternoon waned. The Nasranis then escorted the Portuguese out of the church and bid farewell.

Fernão turned to Samuel. 'Perhaps we should bid you farewell as well?'

'It has been an honor,' Samuel said. 'Perhaps, one day you will make it back here to Cochin and find me.'

'Perhaps,' Francisco said. 'If fortune is kind to us all.'

Captain Nuno Vaz Pereira, Fernão Magalhães, and Francisco Serrão left Cochin in November of 1506, on board the *Espera,* on a mission to support operations in East Africa. Upon arriving in Kilwa, riots and disorder broke out, and the captain had to mediate a dispute concerning two claimants to the throne. Fernão assumed his command of a bargantym in Kilwa. It was a large flat-bottomed galley and powered with oars, useful for transporting goods and troops along the coasts.

For the greater part of a year, he commanded this galley, patrolling the coast against incursions from pirates and unscrupulous Moor invaders. Fernão brought supplies and reinforcements to Sofala, the ancient gold trading port of East Africa.

Captain Periera's command in Sofala was brief, for a new fleet arriving from Lisbon under Vasco de Abreau assumed duty. In September of 1507, Fernão then accompanied Captain Pereira on the vessel *Sao Simao* to Mozambique. The coasts of East Africa were full of disease and sickness. It was so prevalent that upon landing they immediately constructed a hospital. Fernão often wondered how his propensity for acquiring wounds in battle seemed to be offset by his almost supernatural immunity from disease, for he always remained in good health in these dangerous tropical zones. He was especially fortunate for this since their stay in Mozambique was extended due to the intensity of the monsoon season.

Eventually, they arrived at Cochin in October of 1507. Upon arrival, Viceroy Almeida gave Captain Periera command of a new caravel that was in the process of construction, the *Santo Espirito*.

Meanwhile, rumors had increased, both from locals and Almeida's trusted spies, that an enemy Egyptian and Indian alliance was sailing south to oust the Portuguese from the Malabar coast of India.

As a precaution, the viceroy dispatched his son, Dom Lourenço, with a small fleet of eight vessels to guard the outposts to the north. The *Santo Espirito* was still in final preparations and could not join the expedition. Missing the opportunity to catch up with Dom Lourenço's fleet, Captain Pereira, along with navigational officers Fernão Magalhães and Francisco Serrão, steered south toward the Maldives in pursuit of other enemy forces. But a mighty storm raged and drove their caravel east toward Ceylon where they remained for a short while. Finally, they sailed back north to Cannanore where they functioned as reserve troops, assisting in patrols along the Malabar coast, and loading cargo.

# 3

## *Chaul – March, 1508*

As Dom Lourenço had sailed onward to Chaul, the Mamluke sultan of Cairo, Al-Ashraf Qansuh Ghawri, had dispatched a war expedition under the command of the governor of Jedda in the Red Sea, Amir Hussain Al Kurdi. The Portuguese called him, Admiral Mirocem.

Admiral Mirocem had sailed to the grand emporium port city of Diu in Cambay with intentions to forge an alliance with the naval commander of Gujarat, Malik Ayyaz, known as Meliqueaz to the Portuguese. He had been a former slave, forcibly converted to Islam and taken to India. During the Ottoman expansion, the strongest and brightest Christian boys were kidnapped from the Balkan countries, indoctrinated with the tenets of Islam, and trained as warriors to serve in its armies. They often served in the Ottoman's elite infantry—the Janissaries corps. Meliquaez had achieved exceptional martial skills and was eventually appointed governor and naval commander under the Sultan of Gujarat, Mahmud Begada. With caution, the calculating Meliqueaz agreed to an alliance with Mirocem to sail with his own fleet of fustas, or small galleys.

Meanwhile, far up the Indian coastline, the Portuguese squadron was plying their time along the banks of the Kundlika River, near Chaul. Dom Lourenço and some men were honing their martial skills with spear throwing. About midday, scouts made out a fleet of ships at sea approaching. One scout yelled out, 'Ships! Ships!'

Dom Lourenço approached his vice-captain, Pêro Berreto and said, 'Good news. Maybe the remaining ships of Albuquerque are returning to Cochin.'

'It must be,' Berreto said.

The crews shouted and waved at the fleet.

One of the fidalgos climbed up an embankment and squinted his eyes while looking out to sea. After a moment, he rushed back to the beach and yelled to his servant, 'Give me my breastplate!'

The crewmen laughed at his panic. Lourenço and Berreto looked at one another and shrugged their shoulders.

'These are not the ships of Albuquerque,' the fidalgo insisted. 'They are not flying the crosses, but the flags of Muhammad! Gentlemen, I pray to God that I alone will be the fool today, and that you will still be laughing in the evening.'

As the fleet neared, red flags with gold crescent moons soon appeared. Warriors clad in shining armor, elaborate turbans, and colored silks stood on deck readied for war. When their trumpets blared, the Portuguese scattered for their weapons.

The allied Islamic force consisted of 1,500 men, 6 large carracks, 6 galleasses—which had guns mounted on a deck above the banks of rowers, and about 40 smaller galleys supplied by the Sultan of Gujarat. The Portuguese only had 500 men who manned a limited fleet of 3 small carracks, 3 caravels and 2 galleys.

Mirocem's naval armada halted at the mouth of the Kundalika River, waiting for Meliquaez's fustas to join the attack. But the Gujarat admiral prudently held his fustas anchored offshore. Nevertheless, Mirocem decided to push onward upriver.

Meanwhile, Dom Lourenço's flagship, *São Miguel,* and the *São António,* commanded by his vice-captain, Pêro Berreto were separated from the fleet midstream. Closing in upon the two vulnerable Portuguese vessels, Mirocem sent a salvo of artillery bombardments and rained down a barrage of arrows. An iron ball shot through the *São Miguel* causing extensive damage to the hull. With a steady barrage of incoming arrows, the Portuguese took early losses; from a roster of 100 men, 30 were wounded.

They responded furiously with a counter assault of crossbow bolts, arquebus, and cannon-fire. Mirocem's vessel was pummeled, bodies ripped apart, and the decks ran red with blood. He decided to retreat. With the tide and sea breeze in his favor, Mirocem passed the Portuguese ships and anchored upriver.

Lourenço attempted another attack to take their flagship. He ordered the boats to tow the carracks toward the enemy, but they did not have any support from their galleys. Mirocem's own galleys then repulsed the Portuguese boats with a heavy onslaught of arrows and forced the Portuguese to retreat. By then it was late in the evening, and both sides pulled back to assess damage, and reorganize.

The following morning, the Portuguese found Mirocem's ships arranged in an odd position, all chained together, with prows facing the river. Gangplanks ran between the ships to move troops where they were needed most. But his fleet was vulnerable since the broadside cannons could not be employed, and if any escape was needed, it would be difficult due to their tight formation. Meliqueaz remained on the open sea, his fleet waiting in reserve.

The Portuguese convened a war council on board the *São Miguel*. All the captains and leading officers were present. Dom Lourneço stood in front of the men.

'We have two choices,' he said. 'Bomb them into oblivion or take their ships as a prize.'

Michel Arnau, Dom Lourenço's master gunner, stepped forward. 'Do not put yourselves at risk, because what you want done can be done without any danger, except to me and my gunners. I suggest we disembark the crews and then I will take my gun crew to sink their fleet.'

Captain Berreto nodded in agreement.

'Your wisdom is sound,' Lourenço said. 'But remember my father was upset when we did not take any prized ships in Dabul. Shall we not have our glory and honor this day by taking over their flagship, even their fleet?'

All in the meeting gave their assent to taking the enemy fleet intact, except Arnau and Berreto. The council came up with a plan to have the *São Miguel* and the *São António* focus on Mirocem's flagship while the light caravels and galleys turned to attack the remaining vessels.

In the early afternoon, with the winds steady and the tides flowing, the Portuguese weighed anchor and sailed upriver, the *São Miguel* leading the convoy. The Portuguese limited their cannon bombardments so as not to damage the war booty. Mirocem's flagship rained down arrows upon the closing *São Miguel*. With only 15 yards to go, the wind subsided. But with their momentum from the current, it was still possible to grapple the enemy ship.

Finding the Portuguese closing near, Mirocem made a strategic countermove by loosening the forward anchors while his crews pulled on the stern cables attached to shore until all vessels were brought up on the riverbank.

The *São Miguel*'s rudder could not compensate. The boatswain's mate decided to drop anchor so they would not drift past their target. The *São António* close behind had to veer off to avoid collision, as did the others following her.

Dom Lourenço rushed across the deck with sword in hand. 'You will pay for this!' he yelled at the boatswain's mate. The frightened crewman leaped off the ship and was quickly killed by enemy fire.

Michel Arnau approached Lournenço. 'Sir, we can still fire our broadside guns and destroy the enemy fleet.'

'No, we take the war prizes!' Lourenço insisted.

Anchored near Mirocem's flagship, more barrages of enemy arrows pummeled the *São Miguel*. Brazenly giving orders from the open deck, Lourenço exposed himself to enemy fire. One arrow grazed his flesh and moments later, a second arrow struck him in the face. Blood flowed profusely as he gave the command to raise anchor and avoid another onslaught of arrows.

Meanwhile, the remaining Portuguese galleys and light caravels were able to board the enemy vessels near shore, and the crews engaged in hand-to-hand combat. Their victory was quick, and four galleys were hauled away as war prizes.

Meliqueaz delayed no longer, for cowardice in the Islamic world would not go unnoticed. He brought his fleet upriver to join in the battle.

The Portuguese were in dire straits; exhausted and running low on gunpowder, with enemy ships bearing down upon them. Another council was hastily assembled, and they decided to make a retreat under cover of darkness. But the Muslims pursued, and one cannon ball slammed into the *São Miguel's* stern, close to the waterline. Nobody noticed water leaking into the rice store in the hold below. The water gushed in, making the flagship difficult to steer. To complicate matters, the wind died down, and the current brought the vessel close to the southern shore, and into fishermen's mooring stakes.

Water continued to gush in, and the weight forced the hull further upon the stakes. Soon the vessel began to list. The pilot went to investigate and found a nightmare situation, the rice and water had mixed and would be impossible to pump out. Dom Lourenço decided to cut the ropes from their galley prize in tow. Mirocem, meanwhile, realized the flagship was damaged and closed in with his two carracks.

Lourenço's able-bodied men now numbered to 30 for defense of the ship. Many more wounded and unable to muster. Arrows rained down upon the decks and cannon blasts filled the air with smoke. The Portuguese repelled two attempts by the enemy to board. A cannon ball severed Dom Lourenço's leg at the thigh. Bleeding profusely and barely conscious, he requested his crew to tie off the leg, then secure him to the mast so he could continue to give orders. Soon after, another cannon ball slammed into his chest, killing him instantly.

The vessel listed further, and the crew knew it was now lost. The men of the *São Miguel* bravely fended off five boarding attempts until a sixth finally overpowered them.

The battle at Chaul could have been worse considering the well-equipped enemy vessels they had encountered. The Islamic alliance lost nearly 700 men and the same number wounded. Many of their vessels suffered major damage. The Portuguese lost their flagship, about 150 dead and wounded; but they returned the rest of their fleet almost fully intact, to Cannanore.

On an early December morning of 1508, Fernão walked a trail along the Cannanore coast leading to Fort Sant'Angelo. More Portuguese vessels had recently arrived, bringing the armada to full strength. Sailors busily outfitted and loaded supplies near the port. He too had been saddened by the news he had received of the Battle of Chaul, and as he reached the top of the hill, realized it was still affecting him, and he knew he needed to shake the feeling off.

Fernão looked up as he approached the gates of Fort Sant'Angelo. Captain Nuno Vaz Pereira stood near the gate attired in proper military dress.

'On time as usual, Fernão,' Pereira said. 'Almeida has called all captains for a meeting.'

The two entered the fort and into an inner chamber. Viceroy Almeida sat behind a desk made of teak wood and the captains of the new fleet gathered nearby, all looking over a navigation chart. He looked up at Pereira and Fernão as they entered. 'Good morning gentlemen. We have been planning for a new mission. I want you to continue your command of the *Santo Espirito*, with Magalhães to serve as your navigation officer.'

'Yes sir,' Pereira said.

Almeida then glanced over to a young muscled mullato dressed in officer uniform. 'Lisuarte, you will serve as a reserve captain.'

'Yes sir,' Lisuarte replied.

Footsteps in the hallway led to a commotion in the doorway and a short stern-faced man with an unusually long nose and a pointed grey beard reaching to his waist, entered the chamber. He was dressed regally in a velvet cloak and cap, a heavy gold chain around his neck, and knee-high leather black boots. Afonso de Albuquerque's commanding presence filled the chamber at once with both awe and dread. Albuquerque acknowledged Lisuarte with a nod, which was immediately returned.

Albuquerque then turned to the viceroy. He cleared his throat and said, 'I have news from the king. Orders to be precise. I am to take over as the new governor of India. I have the sealed papers here with me.'

Almeida gathered himself, tightened up his vest, and responded, 'My term does not expire until next January. You will have to wait.'

The entire room was shocked by the apparent breach of protocol. Fernão turned to Captain Pereira with a look of astonishment.

Albuquerque countered with indignation. 'I see you have taken my mutinous captains under your wing. Four of my captains deserted me in Ormuz: Campo, Costa, Telles, and Nova. You have the nerve to enlist them in your fleet!'

'I have indeed,' Almeida replied. 'They have informed me that you deviated from your orders to blockade the Red Sea and constructed a fort without any ability to maintain an adequate garrison. Furthermore, you commanded your captains to forced labor in this endeavor, all under extreme climate and under the watchful eyes of the local populace, a public insult to their dignity! Did you ever assist them?'

Albuquerque just stared back, stoic, and indignant.

Fernão had not expected this confrontation and watched in some disbelief as the two naval commanders exchanged verbal broadsides.

Almeida continued. 'You refused to take council with your captains. They had written two formal letters with their grievance, which you simply ignored.' Almeida turned to look at one of the captains who appeared to have half his beard torn off, red scabs still healing from where the flesh was pulled away. 'You rage like a madman. Look at João da Nova's beard. You ripped it away in one of your maniacal tirades.'

Fernão could think of no reason he would ever dishonor a man's beard like that. In Portuguese society, as elsewhere, it was a symbol of power and honor. It represented a man's virility and was not to be dishonored.

'I may have lost some control, at times,' Albuquerque admitted.

'And what of the prisoners you took in Qurayat?'

Almeida and Albuquerque stared at one another; the latter clearly angered.

The chamber was tense and silent.

'You cut off all their ears and noses and sent them to Ormuz as a warning,' Almeida said.'

'You know very well the Muslims practice the same based upon the deeds of their prophet,' Albuquerque countered. 'We need to instill into them the same fear, the same terror.'

Fernão knew Almeida could not respond to the military logic, for the Islamic armies only seemed to understand brute force and decisive victory. It was well known that the Turks had impaled countless victims and mutilated many bodies as they forged their empire.

Almeida redirected the conversation. 'Lisuarte, you were present at the battle at Chaul. My son was killed, but was his body retrieved and taken among the prisoners?'

'I saw about 19 prisoners but could not see Dom Lourenço. But we were drifting with the current and lost site of the vessel.'

'Perhaps on this point Albuquerque may be correct. I fear they may have taken my son's body, skinned it, and stuffed it with straw, then paraded before the sultan of Cairo or some other despot. That is what these infidels do!' Almeida paced back and forth with a stirring rage. 'As I said before: He who ate the chick, has to eat the rooster, or pay for it.' Almeida looked his men over. 'I will have my revenge.'

'I can take command of the fleet and hunt down all of them,' Albuquerque said. 'They will dearly pay. I can assure you.'

Almeida stood in front of Albuquerque. 'I am already prepared to lead the fleet. You can wait in Cannanore or stay in Cochin and rest from your labors. I will deliver up the command upon my return according to the king's orders.'

Albuquerque acknowledged his argument. 'Very well. I will stay in Cochin and await your return.'

Almeida set off with his armada for the wealthy Muslim trading port of Dabul intending to wreak havoc in the port. Unfortunately, one of his scout vessels was spotted along the shoreline of Dabul. Without mercy, an enormous Islamic force of 6,000 attacked the lone vessel and slaughtered Captain Paio de Sousa and all his men.

Two days later, Almeida entered the river into Dabul and soon discovered what insolence had been inflicted upon his scouts. He flew into a rage. Almeida convened his captains and commanded them to not only raze the town but to inflict such terror that nobody would ever forget.

The port was protected by a double wooden wall, a ditch in front, and artillery. Four large Gujarati vessels were stationed in the harbor.

At dawn, the Portuguese bombarded the walls and ships with heavy artillery. Armed with chainmail armor and heavy weaponry, three squadrons attacked the three main gates. While they encountered the expected stiff resistance, Almeida dispatched Captain Nuno Vaz Pereira to penetrate the enemy's flank.

Fernão followed his captain into the foray of streaming arrows and artillery. Once they broke through the defensive line, the enemy realized they were outflanked, and fled in all directions. Eventually, the wall collapsed, and the remaining frontal assault troops stormed into the city.

The victory was complete and final—1500 enemy killed. The Portuguese lost 16 and 200 wounded. The viceroy was not content with just a victory, he wanted vengeance. He ordered his men to finish off every living thing. Men, women, children, and animals were slaughtered without mercy. The enemy ships were set on fire and the town ransacked. Finally, the viceroy gave orders to burn everything to the ground. Anyone who managed to survive the inferno was to be immediately killed.

On January 5, 1509, the Portuguese departed the ruins of Dabul and sailed 100 miles toward Chaul where the battle that killed Almeida's son had raged. Almeida knew the city itself was not at fault, only for harboring the guilty. Almeida demanded the city magistrates pay tribute, to which they agreed, given time to come up with it. Almeida was going on toward Mumbai, and demanded it be ready when he returned. The rulers of Chaul agreed to this. Almeida sailed on up the coast.

By this time, the news of the slaughter and razing of Dabul had spread like wildfire across the entire Indian coast. By the time the armada arrived at Mahim, near Mumbai, the town had been completely deserted. The Portuguese soon learned that their reputation had come to equal that of the feared crusaders from centuries earlier, who were regarded under the banner 'Franks' to those whom all western Europeans looked the same. So Fernão was pleased and somewhat flattered the first time he heard the local expression, "May the vengeance of the Franks overtake you as it overtook Dabul."

For Almeida, however, this posed a unique problem. It is hard to destroy an enemy who remains on the run. Almeida knew he would have to provoke them into the open. He called for a scribe to compose a letter, and a courier to carry it to Diu, and set down these words:

> I the viceroy say to you, honored Meliqueaz captain of Diu, that I go with my knights to this city of yours, to take the people who were welcomed there, who in Chaul fought my people and killed a man who was called my son, and I come with hope in God of Heaven to take revenge on them and on those who assist them, and if I don't find them I will take your city, to pay for everything, and you, for the help you have done at Chaul. This I tell you, so that you are aware that I go, as I am now on the island of Bombaim (Mumbai), as he will tell you, the one who carries this letter.

# 4

## *Diu – February, 1509*

At the first light of dawn on February 3, 1509. Fernão was sleeping on the main deck of the *Santo Espirito* when he was awakened by a nudge on his shoulder and Francisco's voice.

'Ready for action, my friend?'

Fernão rubbed his eyes and took in his surroundings in the faint light. The armada of black Portuguese ships had converged along the east coast of Diu. His own ship was stationed for battle near the harbor entrance.

'Indeed,' Fernão said, flashing a grin and rousing himself. He stood up and tested his weight on each leg. 'I suppose I am as ready as I can be. The leg seems to have healed up nicely now.'

'This is a good thing,' Francisco said. 'You will need all your abilities.'

'What is the latest word?' Fernão asked.

'The captain returned last night and informed me of Almeida's plans,' Francisco said. 'You will like this. When the winds pick up and a salvo is sent from the *Flor de la Mar*, the battle commences.' Francisco pointed to an inlet harbor with a fortress island on one side and the mainland on the other. 'We are to take the lead through that channel and take their flagship.'

Fernão put his hands on his hips and studied the approach. 'The bombardment will be intense. But to have the lead, it is fantastic. This will be a time of great glory and honor.'

'Perhaps,' Francisco said. 'But it is more challenging than even that. Their numbers are staggering. The viceroy estimates nearly 200 vessels and possibly 5,000 armed men. Remember, we take them on with 19 vessels and 1,300 men.'

'Yes, but we have superior weapons, tactics and experience,' Fernão replied. 'I always like our odds.'

'I am with you, my friend. But I have more strategic details.'

Fernão turned to Francisco. 'Tell me.'

'You see the Muslims are anchored, much like at Chaul. Two by two chained together along the shore and bows forward. Mirocem's carracks and galleys are first in line, then some Gujarati carracks. Looks like the remainder are staying upstream in reserve.'

Yes. That is the same formation as at Chaul,' Fernão said. 'I am sure the viceroy will not repeat the same mistake.'

'Precisely. The Muslims believe our ambitions of glory to seek prizes will entice us to grapple their vessels and thus fall into their trap. But, instead, we shall bombard their vessels and our best archers will station in the crow's nests. This morning all our men will carry pavises and the ship will be covered with coir netting.

'Ah,' Fernão said. So, that is why we have secured plenty of materials to plug holes and extra casks of water—that is for fires.'

'Precisely,' Francisco said. 'Now listen, this is the best part. The viceroy will remain to command outside the harbor with a skeleton crew of gunners in the *Flor de la Mar* and blockade the port entrance with its large guns. Any attempt to out flank our fleet will be met with intense bombardment.'

'I can see where that would be beneficial,' Fernão said. 'For both the fleet and the viceroy.'

They both chuckled and made ready for the day.

At midmorning, a small caravel was boarding each vessel with a herald to proclaim announcements from the viceroy. Fernão, Captain Pereira, and Francisco stood ready upon the quarterdeck of the oldest ship in the fleet, the *Santo Espirito*. They were in the lead position of the armada and last to hear the viceroy's message. The herald boarded and read from a parchment:

> Dom Francisco d' Almeida, viceroy of India by the most high and excellent King Dom Manuel, my lord. I announce to all who see my letter, that on this hour I am at the bar of Diu, with all my forces that I have, to give battle to a fleet of the Great Turk that he has ordered, which has come from Mecca to fight and damage the faith of Christ and against the kingdom of the king my lord.

The herald paused and looked over the crew of the *Santo Espirito*. All the men were in rapt attention as he continued:

> I promise monetary payments according to rank. Any nobles will achieve higher status, convicts will be forgiven their sentences, and slaves will be freed. I, Dom Francisco d' Almeida, promise all this for victory at Diu.

The herald once again paused until the cheers subdued.

> As you are all aware the Islamic hordes have killed my son at Chaul. If we do not stop these aggressors, the world will be forever lost to the infidels. This will be the decisive battle for

control of India and the Red Sea. The fate of the free world rests upon our deeds today. In the name of Jesus Christ let us achieve nothing less than a decisive victory and holy recompense.

As the edict finished, the crew clanked swords and halberds with shouts of victory and positioned themselves for war.

A short time later, near eleven in the morning, the winds picked up. The *Flor de la Mar* sent one salvo booming across the water to signal the attack. Fernão steered the *Santo Espirito* toward the channel of Diu. Taking the lead, they were the first large ship to confront the enemy, an alliance of Egyptian, Turk, and Kurd warriors, all dressed in red and white cotton. Venetian and Slavic gunners manned their artillery, and reserve naval forces supplied by Gujarat and Calicut remained at the ready.

Almeida had ordered Diogo Pires' galley just in front of the *Santo Espirito* to sound the inner harbor as they pursued the enemy. Muslim artillery stationed on both sides of the entrance to the channel fired a barrage of iron balls at the *Santo Espirito*. Its deck and hull were pummeled, instantly killing 10 men. Fernão and Pereira continued to navigate through the channel under heavy enemy bombardments. Finally, they closed in on their target, Mirocem's flagship. Fernão could see the enemy had also protected their vessels much like their own; shielding with pavises, white castles and decks covered with heavy coir nets, and bags filled with cotton wrapped in wet cow hides for fire protection covered the sides.

Fernão brought the vessel in close and steadied his position for the gunners to take aim on the anchored vessels. A thunderous boom rang out from the *Santo Espirito's* port guns as it fired at the enemy. A carrack near Mirocem's flagship was struck in the bow just at the waterline. Water poured in and it began to list. Fernão watched the crew rush to the other side to compensate. It worked for a few moments but then all the water rushed in and capsized the vessel. Since the events transpired so rapidly, most of the crew could not escape drowning. Cheers erupted from the Portuguese.

It was correctly assumed the oldest vessel in the fleet, the *Santo Espirito*, would take the brunt of artillery fire and may indeed sink.

'We are drawing in too much water,' Captain Nuno Vaz Pereira warned. 'Magalhães, try to bring her next to their flagship.'

'Yes sir.'

The *Santo Espirito* was barely afloat before Fernão managed to steer it near Mirocem's carrack.

'Great work Magalhães,' Pereira said. 'They will think we plan an artillery attack. We wait for them to grapple us . . . but we attack first.'

Almost immediately, Mirocem's crew hauled in their starboard anchor and pulled alongside the *Santo Espirito* to grapple it. Meanwhile, Captain Pereira, Fernão, Francisco, and a contingent of warriors crouched near the edge of the top deck facing the enemy flagship. The enemy threw grappling hooks in great numbers, and several took hold against the ship rigging posts. Once they had pulled on the ropes to bring the vessels close, the Portuguese leaped onto their vessel. Fernão was first to jump. He landed on one foot but performed a tuck and roll to avoid injury and stood face to face with three scimitar wielding Turks. He blocked two strikes but was pinned near the mast. Francisco leaped across and joined the fray. Fernão grinned at his friend's arrival, for now the enemy would face one of Portugal's greatest swordsmen. With rapid strikes and counterstrikes the two pushed the enemy back toward midship.

Meanwhile, Captain Pereira and a contingent had boarded and took the forecastle. Severed limbs and blood covered the deck and the Portuguese were nearing a victory. Captain Pereira watched Francisco and Fernão cutting down the enemy with great speed. He snuck up behind from the enemy flank and put them in a pincer attack. At midship, they had pressed the Muslims together so tight they could not maneuver, and many were slaughtered. Periera grinned as he now faced Fernão and Francisco covered with blood and unharmed. Victory seemed imminent but it was soon interrupted. One of the galleons, to the port side of Mirocem's flagship, had loosed their starboard anchor and maneuvered into position on the opposite side of the *Santo Espirito*. The tide of battle had changed.

'Back to the ship!' Pereira cried out. 'Back to the ship!'

In concern of the enemy outflanking their reduced crew; the men ran across strewn corpses, a slippery blood-soaked deck and leapt back upon the *Santo Espirito*. The enemy galleon grappled from the opposite side and began to board in great numbers.

Meanwhile, the soldiers on the enemy flagship had regrouped and archers sent a hail of arrows upon the Portuguese forces. Fernão took cover for a minute behind a pavise. Through heavy gun smoke, he intermittently observed pitched battles between the Portuguese and Muslim vessels. The sky was black with smoke and the cannons boomed. Almeida positioned the *Flor de la Mar* in front of the channel as a blockade. Countless heavy bombardments from the three-decked flagship pounded the Gujarati carracks in the channel. Fernão could now make out the small oared fustas of Meliqueaz converge to outflank Almeida's flagship. Portuguese and German gunners took aim at the new threat, and with heavy artillery blew apart their vessels. The air was thick with smoke and the heat stifling.

Fernão noticed cannon fire from one of the Turkish ships. He pointed and shouted, 'Take cover!'

A cannon ball slammed into the rails of the top deck. One of the crewmen took the full brunt of the blast, sending him airborne and crashing onto the deck, bloodied and unconscious.

Fernão turned back to notice Captain Pereira struggling to catch his breath in the heat and smoke of battle. Pereira removed his throat guard just above his breastplate and took a deep breath. Just then, enemy archers sent off another barrage of arrows, and one sliced into Pereira's exposed throat. Blood spurted out as he gurgled for air. Fernão went to help but then an arrow slipped through a gap in his armor and pierced his side, just below his ribcage. Fernão fell to his knees and grabbed the blood-soaked arrow but was not able to dislodge it. Captain Pereira raised his right arm in a salute but then collapsed. Sailors carried the captain's body to the lower deck. Francisco discovered Fernão keeled over in a fetal position barely conscious.

'Lets' go my friend, too much enemy fire.' Francisco and another sailor carried him down the stairs to a lower deck then returned to battle stations. After some moments of blackout, Fernão opened his eyes and found himself lying next to the lifeless body of Captain Pereira. With an arrow still lodged in his side, the physical pain now matched the pain in his heart for his deceased noble commander and friend.

The pounding of artillery continued as he drifted off again into unconsciousness.

As dusk arrived, Fernão awoke aboard the viceroy's flagship, the *Flor de la Mar*. Francisco stood nearby moving his sword over a sharpening stone. Fernão groaned and grabbed the arrow stump sticking out of his side.

'Sorry my friend,' Francisco said. 'Surgeons are still too busy. Perhaps tonight one is free enough to extricate the arrowhead.' Francisco continued to move the black sword over the stone. 'I broke it off to give you some mobility but surely it must hurt.'

'What happened?' asked a weary and drained Fernão.

'You mean the battle?' Francisco said, then stared off to the channel. 'It was not long before some of our ships came to our aid and then subdued their flagship. Later, we sank most of their fleet. A large Gujarati vessel would not sink until our entire fleet bombarded it over and over.'

'Mirocem?' Fernão said.

'Mirocem and some of his crews fled ashore and escaped.'

'The fighting is over then?'

'Yes,' Francisco said. 'Most of our ships are anchored offshore now, only a few galleys stationed to keep watch over the vessels we captured.' He looked at Fernão. 'We took a decisive victory over Diu today.'

'Casualties?'

'Hmm. As of now, 32 dead, Captains Pereira and Cão included. About 300 wounded.'

'The enemy?'

'Nearly 800 Muslims killed. Some say over 3,000 dead from all our enemies here.'

'Indeed, a great victory.' Fernão smiled weakly.

It was the next morning before Fernão awoke to some commotion on board the *Flor de la Mar*. Francisco had earlier carried him up to the quarterdeck for fresh air and he was now positioned to simultaneously view the ocean and the main deck below. The men were roused by an approaching small fusta with a white flag raised. A messenger from Meliqueaz offered complete surrender of the city of Diu. Almeida made a precondition before any such arrangements were to be made, they must first-hand over the prisoners from Chaul.

Meliqueaz had calculated well to keep the prisoners safe as bargaining leverage in case of defeat. In prompt diligence, one hour later, he sent the Portuguese prisoners to the *Flor de la Mar*. Trumpets blared and drums beat as the prisoners boarded with tears of joy at meeting their compatriots once again. They were clad in fine clothes of silk, and each carried a bag jingling full of fifty gold xerafins. In addition, the governor of Diu delivered fine gifts of food and promised vassalage to the king of Portugal.

As consistent with Almeida's stratagem; he did not want full control of Diu—only a shipping factory and a peace treaty. The viceroy demanded the Muslim merchants bear the cost of recompense for outfitting the captured enemy fleet. The spoils were to include 3 galleys, 3 carracks, 600 bronze-cannon and 3 royal banners of the Mamluke sultan of Cairo—trophies to be taken back to Portugal. Furthermore, the merchants were to pay recompense of 300,000 gold xerafins—100,000 to be distributed among the troops.

Almeida had one last demand; all the traitors, many of which were Venetian and Slavic gunners, were to be delivered up for punishment. Meliqueaz had no desire to obstruct Almeida's wrath and immediately rounded up the renegades. No mercy was given to the traitors.

Though his vision was blurred by pain and fever, Fernão could still make out grisly images of the punitive sentences carried out with bloody retribution. Some of the fidalgos had forced the renegades into gladiatorial combats to the death. Afterward, Fernão watched a line of terrified prisoners. In front of them was an officer with a xerafin gold coin. One flipside allowed the victim to have a more lenient death by hanging—the other horrific. The officer flipped the coin, and the verdict was carried out. A noose was tied around a prisoner's neck and then duly strung up on the yardarm. A second toss of the coin caused a shudder among the crew and prisoners. A Venetian gunner struggled to break free from two muscular seamen as he was led to a chopping block. First, they secured the feet. Two swift sword blows cleaved off each foot. The seamen tossed the bloodied limbs into a large empty wine cask and landed with a thud. The Venetian screamed in horror as they rushed to secure his hands. Two more swift blows and two hands thumped into the barrel. The line of prisoners gritted their teeth and several urinated upon the deck. This was just the prelude, for they tied the shocked and bloodied renegade gunner to a cannon. A cannon fuse was lit, and an iron ball slammed into the Venetian's chest. Body parts and blood splayed everywhere. Fernão's vision blurred on and off over the next 60 minutes of the affair. Most of the traitors cried out for mercy and when the coin flipped badly, went into a state of shock. Surprisingly, a few prisoners remained stoic and maintained their composure under such duress. However, one prisoner dared to challenge. He vented in rage and spit upon the executioners which only persuaded them to extend the torture, finger by finger, toe by toe, limbs, and inevitably a final execution by cannon.

Later, Fernão discovered how they also punished the traitors on shore in the same manner. Additionally, they burned many alive of those condemned. The viceroy ordered the gates of Diu to be covered in rosaries of dismembered body parts because those Muslims who had killed his son had passed through the very same gates. All the men knew the viceroy would have his vengeance upon the culprits of his beloved son's demise and this was their day of reckoning.

On February 12, 1509, the victorious fleet embarked on their return journey from Diu toward Cochin. Almeida kept prisoners on board as fodder to instill fear upon the enemy. Entering key ports along the way south; heads, feet, and hands were catapulted onto the beaches. In Cannanore, prisoners were strung up and hung from the masts for all to see.

On March 8, they arrived at Cochin. They strung up the remaining traitors until the yardarms strained under the weight just before the fleet entered the port in a triumphal reception and with trumpets blaring. Fernão was assisted by Francisco and another sailor as they disembarked the landing craft near the fortress. The arrow had been retracted but his wounds were nearly fatal. They stepped upon the beach just behind Almeida and his officers. The Captain of Cochin— Jorge Barreto led a procession of clergy and citizens toward the shoreline.

Albuquerque stood among several officers on the beach, but Almeida pretended to not see him. In frustration, he grabbed a tag of Almeida's brocaded uniform and said: 'Ah, sir, here I am. See me!'

The viceroy turned to face Albuquerque and replied: 'Pardon me for not taking notice.' Almeida then rudely brushed past him and followed the procession to the church.

With devotional piety and gratitude for surviving another battle, Fernão, assisted by his comrade Francisco, joined the line of clergy. Master Diogo gave an inspirational sermon and lauded the victorious Almeida for the defeat of the Muslim alliance. Once the service had concluded, Fernão and Francisco dutifully followed the viceroy and officers to the fortress.

At the gate stood Albuquerque, who, once again, beseeched Almeida: 'Sir, seeing that God has given you so complete a victory, and you have avenged the death of your son with so much honor, and there is no more to do in the matter, I beg you of your grace let there be no differences between us, but deliver to me the government of India by these provisions which I here hold from the king, our lord.'

During this conversation Gaspar Pereira approached Viceroy Almeida, whom he had sent for earlier.

Albuquerque's eyes bulged as he addressed Pereira. 'As you are my scrivener, I require you, on the part of the king, our lord, to notify to the lord viceroy and to all the captains, fidalgos, and men here present, these provisions, which here I deliver to you. Our king, our lord, commands the lord viceroy to deliver up to me India, and to set forth on the back of the papers an instrument containing his assent thereto or refusal.'

Viceroy Almeida's face turned red. He turned his back on Albuquerque and before departing replied: 'You have no scrivener dependent on you, where I am.'

Without another word Almeida and his officers entered the fortress, all the while joking and nudging one another in jest at the requisition. Albuquerque stood facing the gate with his hands upon his hips and his long nose flared. Fernão stood inside the fortress gate. He grimaced and reached down to feel his wound. Blood seeped through his garment and stained his hand red.

Albuquerque's eyes narrowed as he took notice of the wound. 'You better get your partner to the hospital.'

Francisco nodded and placed Fernão's arm over his shoulder.

As they turned to depart, loud raucous laughter and jibes could be heard echoing off the fortress walls. At one point, Albuquerque's nemesis, the mutineer—Captain João da Nova, urged the viceroy to send the usurper back to Lisbon in chains, for he was a fool and dangerous to the officers.

As they walked away, Fernão heard Albuquerque muttering, 'Da Nova, you traitorous wretch.'

# 5

## *Cochin – August, 1509*

Once again, Fernão survived a major battle wound. This time he nearly died. Almost five months had elapsed since he had arrived in Cochin and was recently discharged from the hospital, for his recovery was slow.

It was now early August. A pleasant breeze cooled Fernão as he lounged on a hammock strung up between two palm trees, their shade adding to the soothing relief from the summer heat. Fernão's mind raced back over the horrors he endured from the ship surgeons. It had taken several attempts to retract the arrowhead from his vital organs and the pain was immeasurable. Local anesthetic remedies were not enough to curb the sensitivity of the nerve endings. Through the pain, hot climate, and frequent bouts of fever, Fernão's only refuge was in the constant prayers by the ship friar. He turned his head and noticed a figure approaching from a winding path along the hillside. He soon recognized it was Francisco Serrão.

'Magalhães, quit your napping,' Francisco yelled with shortened breath from the climb. 'We need to move.'

'What?'

'Last chance to sign up for the Malacca expedition. An extra supply ship has been requisitioned. They leave next week!'

Fernão, excited, rolled out of the hammock so abruptly that he planted his face into the dirt.

Francisco laughed. 'Nice move Magalhães. I am sure they are looking for a few more *good* men.'

The two hustled toward the fortress.

Fernão stared off toward a well-dressed officer entering the fortress. 'You trust this new fleet commander; Diogo Lopes de Sequeira?'

'Not sure yet.' Francisco reflected a moment. 'He has connections . . . son of a merchant in Lisbon who built a castle for the crown in Lisbon. I heard the king has received Varthema's reports and eager for confirmation. He commissioned Sequeira to spy out the Spice Islands before the Spaniards send their own reconnaissance missions. Intentions are we are to establish a trading port in Malacca. Since April, four vessels have been outfitted, but it appears Almeida is not confident in Sequeira's judgment and has offered a supply ship for support.'

Inside the fortress, a line of Portuguese seamen and soldiers stood before an officer seated behind a teak desk. One by one, they signed a manifest document listing them on the roster for a *taforea*; a supply ship used to transport horses, livestock, and other bulk items. Francisco Serrão and Fernão Magalhães also signed their names and immediately clasped their arms together in celebration for their new quest and their new adventure.

Fernão grinned. 'But, lucky for us we had the chance to join it.'

'Indeed. By the way, during your time in the hospital, intrigues against Albuquerque have escalated. Back in May, Captains Jorge Baretto and João de Nova had recruited other captains to maintain Almeida as viceroy of India. They even went door to door asking for signatures on a document claiming Albuquerque unfit to command as new viceroy of Portuguese India.'

'Interesting development,' Fernão said. 'Shall we try to find our friend Samuel one last time?'

Francisco nodded and they departed.

Downtown Cochin was bustling with merchants plying their wares and services. Fernão and Francisco walked the streets and approached a local eatery. Samuel was seated behind a table with a scroll written in Hebrew. He looked up and saw his old friends approaching. 'Oh my, what a sight. How did you find me?'

'Food of course,' Fernão said. 'You always eat out on Wednesday, just about sunset.'

'Please sit,' Samuel said, then beckoned for a waiter to come. 'I have sampled many foods since you have left. This is one of my favorite establishments. Please, let me order you a fine dish of today's fresh catch. I know you both enjoy the spices.' Samuel spoke in Malabar to the waiter his preferred choice and held up three fingers to emphasize the quantity.

'How many years has it been now?' Francisco asked.

'Hmm . . . almost three years. You two departed Cochin in November of 1506 and now it is August of 1509.'

'So, you should have your freedom soon?' Fernão asked.

'Three months left,' Samuel replied with a sigh. 'I cannot wait. Plan to sail to Lisbon to see my family. Maybe they want to return here with me and join our community. So much I have learned from these exiles of Israel, so much. I wish to continue my studies in Cochin . . . of course my family will have to agree.'

The waiter brought three plates of fresh Indian mackerel accompanied with spiced rice and assorted vegetables. A shared dish of flat bread was served along with a bowl of spice for dipping. Samuel gave a blessing and then all partook, all the while grunting in

65

approval for such a tasty cuisine. As they were engaged in dining and conversation, a loud thunderous boom emanated from a hillside residence near town. Shocked, they all stood up and looked out around the town.

Samuel pointed. 'Albuquerque's house.'

A Portuguese squadron and an elephant were smashing down several houses and pillaging goods from within.

'What the devil,' Francisco said.

'I heard this morning, Albuquerque was placed in irons and sent on Captain Martin Coelho's vessel to Cannannore,' Samuel said, as he leaned in closer to his audience. 'Heard rumors the viceroy had received documents of a conspiracy between Albuquerque and the King of Cochin.'

'Doubtful he was culpable of such an act,' Fernão said. 'Those former mutinous captains of Albuquerque have been conspiring since they arrived in Cochin. Difficult to know who to trust in these affairs.'

'Agreed,' Francisco added. 'We all know Albuquerque can be a stern taskmaster but disloyal to the crown, not a chance.'

'A taskmaster indeed,' Fernão said. 'But forgiving once his temper has subsided. Remember how he despised Captain João de Nova's rebellion and even tore off half his beard in anger?'

'I do,' Francisco said.

'But know this, when João fell ill and died penniless last month, Albuquerque paid for the funeral,' Fernão continued. 'He led the procession with torches in full honor to the burial site. He gave a eulogy honoring how João assisted him in the campaign in Ormuz and was a brave man.'

'He is an honorable man at heart,' Samuel concluded.

All three nodded.

On August 19, the small fleet of 4 vessels of 150 ton and 1 *taforea*, a supply ship—much like a barge, were embarking the last provisions and men, 70 in total. Fernão Magalhães and Francisco Serrão reported on board the *taforea* and took their position on the quarterdeck. Crowds of locals and Portuguese soldiers of Cochin thronged to the shore to see off the fleet. Fernão looked down upon the men on board, taking notice of several officers. 'Not sure why Captain Garcia de Sousa's relationship with Almeida ran sour, but at least he has given us a chance to sail with him.' Fernão continued to scan the vessel.

'I notice some of Albuquerque's officers are on board, the shipping agent—Ruy de Araujo and Captain Nuno Vaz de Castelo-Branco,' Francisco said. 'The viceroy has accused them of conspiring and sent them away on this mission. I expect just another made up charge.'

Along the shore, among the crowd, they noticed Samuel. He was dressed in his prayer garb; the tallit—a fringed white silk garment shawl with special twined and knotted fringes attached to its four corners, and the tefillin—cubic black leather boxes with leather straps worn upon head and arm. After completing his morning prayer ritual, he took notice of his two friends on board the supply vessel.

They waved. Samuel outstretched his arms at 45 degrees, placed thumbs together, then split the left and right pairs of fingers on both hands into a V shape. Samuel had once explained to them that it had originated within the priest class of Jews and represented the Hebrew three-pointed letter, Shin. In this case it meant, Shalom: peace, prosperity, and goodbye. They all nodded in recognition that this may well be a permanent farewell.

The crowds waved and bid farewell with great emotion as the fleet departed the port. Orders were given to sail southeast along the Malabar coast. Fernão aided the pilot and turned the glass ampolleta, then noted it in the ship log. After two days, they sighted Ceylon, and proceeded east to uncharted seas.

Francisco joined the navigators upon the quarterdeck. 'Well, this it Magalhães. We are now sailing waters never navigated by any western vessel.'

'An adventure of a lifetime my friend, praise be to God.' Fernão said while taking in the fresh sea air. 'A blessing indeed.'

After several days they landed on the northern end of Sumatra in a port city called Pedir. The town was surrounded by jungle and swampy marshes with a stifling hot and humid air. A royal messenger delivered a message to Sequeira requesting a meeting to discuss terms of trade. Skeleton crews manned the fleet while scouting teams disembarked to frequent the markets and sample the goods. Fernão Magalhães, Nuno Vaz de Castelo-Branco, Francisco Serrão and a small contingent from their supply vessel landed their longboat and secured it on shore. Fernão had noticed several native fishermen rowing their oars while seated within a giant upturned turtle shell. A Javanese pilot from the flagship was assigned to their crew to assist in translation, for he was familiar with the trade languages used in many ports.

Armed with their black carab swords, they proceeded to the bustling trading hub. Hundreds of money changers lined the streets and conducted transactions. Carts loaded with casks of pepper were transported by slaves from the warehouse to the pier

68

and loaded on large three-masted junks. Francisco halted the men and stared transfixed upon the scene. Fernão stood next to him, both facing the market buzzing with activity.

Francisco smiled and continued to stare at the vendors. 'I thought Varthema was exaggerating.'

'He did say this was a land of pepper and the leading market for it,' Fernão said. 'Up to 20 large junks laden with pepper to China alone, every year.'

They continued through the market. Francisco stooped over a vendor table, held up a hardened piece of gum residue to the light and admired the golden hue. The local vendor gestured for Francisco to hand over the product. He pinched off a few small pieces and placed them on the table. Fernão and the others drew near and formed a perimeter, curious. The vendor lit some hardwood in a small bowl. He waited a few minutes until a hot ember formed and then sprinkled on the pieces of golden residue. A pleasant aroma filled the air. 'Benzoin,' said the Arab merchant through their pilot translator.

The crew looked at one another and shrugged their shoulders.

The Javanese pilot continued to translate for the merchant. 'He says this is what you people call frankincense. Resin from tree bark . . . grown here. Excellent as a perfume, incense, and cure for ailments. He says will give you good price.'

Fernão's mind whirled. He remembered the scriptures, about how the wise men from the east had brought gifts to the baby Jesus, one of which they called frankincense. The product name had been ascribed during the crusades when the Franks brought a special benzoin derived incense from the Middle East back to Europe. He wondered if this was essentially the same product but simply cropped from another variant species of indigenous tree. Fernão leaned over and took in the sweet aroma with its hints of spicy vanilla and balsam, an exquisite and rare commodity. 'I will take one arrátel of it,' Fernão said.

'Four cruzados,' the merchant countered via the pilot translator.

Fernão shook his head and held up one finger.

The merchant responded by holding up three fingers.

Fernão retrieved two cruzados and threw them on the table.

'You bargain well my friend.' He weighed out an arrátel worth of benzoin pieces, poured them into a small pouch and handed it to Fernão. 'Enjoy.'

The crew perused the fine goods as they meandered their way inland. Fine silks of various colors hung from cords and fluttered in the sea breeze. A pleasant morning with aromatic spices filled the air and refreshed the men from their long journey at sea. They pushed past the market and found a great number of elephants wandering in open fields. The local people were yellowish-brown in complexion and of short stature. They had broad noses, flat round eyes, and long flowing hair. The coastal residents lived in large houses of stone, many of which were covered with enormous turtle shells; many sized over 20 feet in length and used as roofs.

Fernão Magalhães, Francisco Serrão, and their Javanese pilot led their crew along the meandering hillside path near the edge of the township. Emerging from a jungle trail, a man approached with a human skull tucked under one arm and a spear in the other. He was naked from the waist up and wore a layered red head scarf. The Portuguese placed their hands upon the hilts of their swords as the wild-eyed native drew near. Encountering the well-armed Portuguese, the native crouched in a defensive posture, raised his spear, and hissed. Francisco stepped forward tapping on his sword hilt and stared him down. Spooked, the wild man screamed then galloped into the tall grass and downhill toward the port.

'What kind of devils have taken that soul?' Fernão asked rhetorically.

'A Batak warrior from the kingdom of Aru,' the Javanese pilot answered. 'They live in the interior, on an island surrounded by a great lake. They are man-eaters.'

'Well, that explains the skull,' Francisco said.

'They are in constant war with their neighbors and take prisoners for ransom. If not paid, they kill them and consume their flesh—cooked or raw. They also eat their own, anyone who has committed high crimes and the old—any too feeble to work.'

'What the . . . Why?' Fernão asked in disbelief.

'Strengthens one's *tendi* or soul powers. The heart, palms and soles of the feet are especially rich in tendi power. They eat all the precious flesh to the marrow.'

'So why keep the skull if the flesh is the source of tendi?' Francisco asked.

'They use them as money, highly prized signs of power. Some traders accept them since they can be used to barter with other Batak.'

'Unbelievable, I thought I had seen everything,' Francisco said.

The men followed a split in the path toward the backside of town and entered the official sector. A crowd had formed in front of a raised platform constructed of bamboo. Two muscular bare-chested men held down the arms of a young Malay. They secured one of his legs inside a wooden block with the ankle gingerly resting upon a sharp curved blade. Fernão and the men joined the crowd. The Malay's eyes dilated in shock as a heavy-set guard slammed a giant mallet down upon the block. The foot thumped on the platform and blood spewed all over. The guard dropped the mallet, picked up the foot and raised it in the air for all the crowd to witness. The two restraining guards shoved a thick bamboo shoot into the open amputated leg cavity and stuffed rags around to stem the blood flow. They carried the delirious prisoner to the open town square and laid him down with a metal pot near his side. Some in the crowd chewed on betel leaves and spit into the pot, a salve for the wounds.

'Almost a daily event,' the Javanese pilot explained to Fernão and Francisco. So many murders and robberies in these parts. Islamic justice requires one amputation for any theft over a tayel in value. A second offense has the penalty of a second limb.' He then pointed to another young Malay prisoner kicking and screaming as he was dragged by several muscled guards to the stage. 'A third offense is grave indeed.'

They strapped him down face first onto a table. Fernão remembered Varthema had described this horrific punishment before; a judicial terror perfected among the Turks and employed across the Islamic empire. A guard held a sturdy eight-foot bamboo shoot with a narrow, sharpened tip. The prisoner pleaded for mercy as the stoic-faced executioner lined up the pointed bamboo tip into his rectum and held it firm. One of the muscled guards then repeatedly hammered a giant mallet into the bamboo pole. The shaft penetrated the Malay's intestines. Agonizing screams echoed across the square, until the bamboo shot out the neck and stifled the horrific sounds into a muddled gurgle. The crowd gasped in horror. Even the hardened Portuguese warriors cringed at the brutality employed. The guards untied the limp body, raised the bamboo pole, and placed the end into a heavy steel bowl with a tripod vice clamps to secure it. Blood drained into the bowl as the Malay's futile muted cries for death went ignored.

'He will expire soon. A fortunate soul,' the Javanese pilot said. 'Some agonize for days until they die.'

The crowd slowly dispersed.

Within days, the Portuguese had secured negotiations with a signed treaty document. They erected padroes—heavy inscribed ballast stones—now employed as evidence of their visit to Pedir in Sumatra. On the shore, near the longboats, Fernão and his crew stared out to sea. Several large junks were anchored in the distance.

'Javanese gypsies . . . sea pirates,' the Javanese pilot said as he pointed to their vessels. 'They live at sea, only come on shore to trade.'

'Interesting life. Why not you? Why not live as a pirate?' Francisco asked.

'Your crown pays better,' he replied with a smirk.

'Well, let us hope you are right. The crown does not pay until cargo is secured.'

The Javanese pilot nodded.

Fernão's crew untied their longboat and rowed back to the ships.

The fleet departed Pedir and soon arrived in the neighboring port city of Pacem (Pasai) where they secured similar business arrangements with the local sultan. Once again, they erected stone padroes before departing Sumatra. The fleet continued their journey southeast and entered a wide strait.

# 6

## Malacca – September 11, 1509

The black hulls of the Portuguese ships anchored off the bustling port of Malacca on the western coast of the Malay Peninsula. The Malacca Strait lay ahead, and beyond and to the west, the island of Sumatra. A palace of Malacca was situated at the foot of a hill. An imposing fortress with palisades and cannon overlooked the port.

Fernão stood on the quarterdeck and assessed the great metropolis. Varthema had told him stories of Malacca, of its immense size and bustling commerce. The city was the central trading hub between the east and west. It linked world trade from China and the Spice Islands of the Pacific to India, the Middle East, and Europe. Now he himself witnessed hundreds of large junks anchored along the shore, some loading cargo and others waiting their turn. Sampans and other oared boats added to the numbers. Fernão estimated Malacca sprawled across ten miles of shoreline. A river split the great commercial city in two; at the mouth where it emptied into the sea, a wide bridge connected the two sides. It was estimated 120,000 residents of many nations took residence here, most in palm-thatched homes.

Francisco Serrão climbed to the quarterdeck. He retrieved a piece of cloth from his trouser pocket and wiped his brow. 'Some stifling humidity here.'

Fernão wiped his forehead with his sleeve. 'I hear you,' he said. 'Another swampland.'

'I am assigned to lead a shore party,' Francisco said. 'We are to scout for trade deals and any useful information. I will let you know if I discover anything good.'

The two stared out to shore. Ripples of heat waves hovered over the city, and the residents sweltered in their daily grind.

'Sorry I cannot join you,' Fernão said. 'I am on duty with the pilot. Say, maybe you can purchase an umbrella to block out the sun.'

'Very funny, my friend.' Francisco turned and left to find his crewmates.

It was not long before the shore party was ready. They rowed into shore and landed their skiff.

Once all had disembarked, Francisco stood before the men.

'Stay tight with me,' he said. 'We have our mission to inventory the trade goods in this port.'

As they perused the markets, they discovered a vast wealth of goods for purchase. Each item the men found was conveyed to Francisco. The fleet clerk used his quill pen and notebook to record the sizeable list: Pepper, cloves, mace, nutmeg, sandalwood, porcelain, musk, pearls, benzoin, colored silks, tin, white damask, brocades, bird plumes from Banda, iron, rhubarb, saltpeter, fine silver, gold, ornate chests, painted fans, toys of all sorts, coral, vermilion, quicksilver, opium, and other various drugs. Many weapons were sold here: lances, daggers, and swords crafted with inlaid metal and quality steel. Local goods were also cultivated on farms in the region, over 1,000 varieties. Francisco stared with delight upon the plethora of exotic women frequenting the markets. The men pointed at some of the most beautiful. Francisco had no interpreter among his men, so he was relieved to discover that many locals were multilingual, for it had been said over 80 languages were spoken in Malacca. He noticed most of the men in the city were brown-skinned and bare-chested. From the waist down they wore short jackets that came half-way down the thigh and were made of silks, scarlet, and cotton. Most wore belts with ornate daggers tucked inside. Francisco fixated upon the exotic daggers and said to himself, 'I wonder where I can find one of those?'

A sailor nearby heard him, smiled, and pointed to a market vendor with a table full of daggers. 'That man has what you seek.'

The men strolled toward the vendor's table. Francisco stared upon the displayed blades.

The merchant looked them over. 'You are Portuguese?' he said in their language, but with an Arabic accent. 'Here are my fine crafted kris. I have many of these daggers to choose from. All of damask steel.'

Francisco admired the workmanship. All were asymmetrical with serpentine double-edged blades, each one at least a foot long, if not more. The dagger's pointed tip gradually widened, until it expanded greatly near the grip. Most of the grips of the kris were curved, with a highly polished reddish-brown wood, and carved with elaborate designs. Francisco's eyes opened wide as he turned the dagger over. An image of an engraved green-hued dragon wound down the length of the blade. He then noticed another identical kris—but with a red-hued dragon image. He held up both, comparing the two nearly identical daggers. 'How much?'

The merchant pointed to the green-hued dragon kris and answered, 'Only 32 piastres.'

'How much in cruzados?'

The merchant moved some hardwood oval beads on a rod in a bamboo abacus to convert the exchange rate. 'Only 24 cruzados.'

Francisco put forward the red-hued dragon kris. 'And this one?'

'Let me check,' he replied and moved some more beads on the abacus. 'Only 200 cruzados.'

Francisco's eyes opened wide, and he whistled in amazement. '*Only* 200. I see no difference. Why?'

'I explain,' the merchant said. 'Before battle, a warrior dips the end with herb poison, and this requires one to always have the poison available.'

Francisco shrugged his shoulders. 'Ok,' he said.

'But the cost is much higher for this one, for it has the poison forged *within* the steel.'

All the Portuguese leaned in with curiosity.

'You see,' the merchant continued. 'It will take a specially trained artisan over a year to forge the blade. He will only strike blows upon it in precisely timed days during each month. It is a ritual steeped from the ancient days. But I assure you, the poison will always work.'

Francisco looked at his men with a frown then turned back to the merchant. 'We do not require poison to kill our enemies. Our blows are precise enough. But I do appreciate the intimidating blades and exquisite engravings.' He grinned at his men. 'Good chance we will find some of these beauties on the battlefield—for free.'

The men bellowed with laughter.

Some merchants who had been observing them whispered among themselves and suddenly departed in haste. Francisco watched them, and his men noticed.

'Should I follow them?' a crewman asked.

'Not now,' Francisco said. 'Maybe they are only jealous of our presence. Let it go for now.' He then took a whiff of his underarm. 'Ay. I stink.' He sniffed the air. 'You all stink too. Maybe we locate a bath house.'

'And maybe some drink?' another crewman said.

Francisco smiled, as if he was considering. 'All right. Let's do it.'

Malacca was the sort of exotic trading center that travelers converged on from all over Europe, the Middle East, India, Southeast Asia, China, and many other nations. Turks were also included in this cosmopolitan mix and their contribution to the city included a marvelous bathhouse along the hillside where many of the upper-class residents lived. After Francisco and the men refreshed themselves with a hot bath, they found a local eatery with a shade canopy and surrounded by palm trees. They seated themselves at a large table and dined with rice, fish, and a strong palm wine. The men were fortunate to find alcohol because Malacca was ruled by a Muslim sultanate. But due to such a variety of cultures visiting the city, prohibition was not imposed as an absolute mandate.

Three young women strolled down the street. They were dressed in colorful silks and short shirts inlaid with gold and jewels. When they took notice of the uniformed Portuguese, they poked one another, and stopped at a local food market across the street from the eatery. As they feigned interest in the merchant's produce, they giggled and toyed with their hair while looking over the Portuguese. The tallest of the three was extremely beautiful and made frequent short glances toward Francisco.

'What are you waiting for Serrão?' chided one of the crew.

'Excuse me gentlemen,' Francisco said. 'I will meet you back at the skiff in a little while.' He took a final sip of his wine, arose, and approached the young woman.

'Are you here for trade?' she asked with a broken Portuguese accent.

Francisco smiled. 'Of course. We hope to establish relations here for long term trading. How do you know Portuguese?'

'My father is Persian and somewhat fluent in your language. My mother is from Java.'

'Does she speak Portuguese also?'

'No. She only knows our native language.'

'What is your name?'

'Amina.'

'A beautiful name.'

'It means truthful and trustworthy.'

'Even more beautiful,' Francisco said, as he continued with small talk behind the restaurant. He gradually gained her trust and enticed her with tales of far-off lands and adventures. But the moment was abruptly interrupted by shouting in the streets, 'Amuko—amuko—amuko.'

Francisco turned and found a bare-chested man with hair formed into the shape of a tiger and slashing his kris blade in a frenzied state. In the street, he cut down men, women, and children. Two men attempted to block his path with their own daggers raised. The wild-eyed assailant moved with great speed and cut them both deep in their arms. Bleeding profusely, they fled the scene in haste.

'Enough of this!' Francisco stomped into the street with his black sword drawn. He twirled it, taunting the crazed lunatic. Unfazed, the amuko bellowed and charged at him. Francisco side-stepped as if eluding a charging bull and then swung his sword across the assailant's neck, cutting his head clean off. Those in the street stood with mouths agape. A few had the temerity to look at Francisco and nod sheepishly.

'What the devil?' Francisco muttered.

Amina ran to embrace Francisco. 'You were fearless. Such a monster you slew.

'What was that?' he asked.

They are called amukos,' Amina said. 'Javanese Moors. They are cunning, treacherous, liars, and skilled in many weapons.'

'But why so crazed?'

'If they fall ill, they consider it a dishonorable death in the eyes of God. Therefore, if one should recover, an amuko will run through the streets like a wild dog, slaying anyone in sight. They will not stop until another one kills him in so-called battle, for only dying in jihad can one immediately enter paradise.'

Francisco stared at the bloodied corpses strewn about the dusty street. 'My Lord, what sorts of people reside in these parts?'

Amina lowered her head against Francisco's chest.

'I must report back to the ship with the men,' he said. 'But I shall return, hopefully tomorrow.' Francisco embraced her and kissed her. Then departed in haste to the pier.

Meanwhile, the merchants of Malacca spread the news of the Portuguese arrival, but not in a celebratory fashion. Many were filled with great consternation at the interlopers venturing into their domain and began to conspire among themselves on how to oust the invaders. The leading factions were comprised of 1,000 wealthy Gujarat merchants along with a contingent of Parsees, Bengalese, and Arabs. These together numbered over 4,000. In addition, powerful Kling traders from India and predominantly

81

Shiite Muslims joined the plot. Patush, their chief spokesman, was a Gujarat trader and had rallied the powerful merchant class with first-hand accounts of how the Portuguese had conquered the coastal province of Gujarat and much of India. He led a procession toward the palace situated at the foot of the hillside. From the gated entrance, guards escorted the entourage inside, through the inner halls, and finally into the royal chamber. Patush and the merchants approached the sultan of Malacca—Mahmud Shah. He was seated upon his ornate throne, all embroidered with silk, jewels, and gold. Patush gestured toward two merchants nearby who held a rolled-up tapestry. They stepped forward and rolled the tapestry across the marble floor. The sultan smiled as he noticed the image of his entire kingdom embroidered into the fabric with vivid colors.

Mahmud Shah had assumed the throne as a teenage boy and was now only in his mid-twenties. He ruled Malacca, capitol of the Malay empire. The sultanate was at the peak of its expansion and prosperity, a golden age. Patush cautiously approached Mahmud Shah, knowing well the sultan was often ill-tempered and ruthless in his actions. But he hoped their bribe of this exquisite gift would sway his favor.

'What is the occasion for such generosity?' Mahmud asked.

'My associates have great concern about the Portuguese who have reached our port and now will surely return here all the time,' Patush said. 'I have seen my own birth city of Diu subjugated by them. They have come to spy out our land and capture Malacca, just the same as India is now in their power.'

'And what do you wish me to do about it?'

'If we kill them now, far away from Portugal, they may never hear of it, and we shall retain our city.'

Sultan Mahmud Shah stared at them, deep in thought. 'I hear your words of caution, but I must, according to our law, consult with the *Bendahara* before I make a final decision.' He then waved his hand for them to leave.

The merchants were well-aware where the sultan's power lie. They doubled their usual bribes to Tuan Mutahir—the Bendahara, for he acted as the royal vizier in matters of state affairs; and was the second ranking official after the sultan. He was a Tamil and already sympathetic to the cause of his Indian brothers. The lavish gifts and the merchant's religious exhortations to rid the infidels in a holy war was sufficient to sway the Bendahara to their side.

Next, the merchants attempted to bribe the Bendahara's brother, Tuan Tahir—the *Tumungo*, chief treasury officer and said to be the wisest man in Malacca. Lastly, they tried to sway the *Laksamana*-admiral of the sea and designated the sultan's chief guard.

Finally, the sultan called a council to decide what to do with the Portuguese. The Bendahara and several royal advisors approached the throne of Sultan Mahmud Shah.

Tuam Mahmud, a chief noble of importance in the community, was designated as spokesman for one faction. He stepped forward. 'The Bendahara, the mandarins, and I, all believe you should kill the invaders immediately.'

'Your opinion is respected and noted,' the sultan said. 'And what is the opinion of the Laksamana and the Tumungo?'

The Laksamana stepped forward. 'We believe the visitors should be well treated and keep their merchandise, since they have come in good faith for trade.'

The sultan's face turned red. 'You do not understand the case of these men. The merchants are right to suspect and act. The Portuguese came to spy out the land so that they can come afterwards with an armada. As I know, and you know, they go about conquering the world and destroying, and blotting out the name of our Holy Prophet. Let them all die! And if any other people come here afterwards, we will destroy them on the sea and on the land. We have more people, junks, and gold in our power than anyone else. Portugal is so far away. Let them all be killed!'

The sultan shook with anger and commanded, 'You will put to sea in your *lancharas* and kill them all. But do not send the Portuguese ships to the bottom. Keep the guns for me and the flagship. The Bendahara will attack those who are weighing goods on land, because we will turn them all out. And you, Laksamana, be careful on the sea, although you alone could take 10 of their ships. I know how you destroyed the Siamese on the open sea, where there were 100 to 1 of ours. And what will you do to such a little force at anchor? Why, those who go to sell them chickens will be a match for them, for they are not fighting men, as I am informed.'

The Laksamana boldly retorted, 'This business is contrary to justice, and I do not want to be in it, and I tell you that I would rather fight against 1,000 men than against these, not because I fear them, but because I am not in agreement with this decision. It will only lead to our destruction.'

The Bendahara's son interjected, 'My lord, I will go if the Laksamana does not want to.'

The sultan nodded and thanked him.

The Laksamana also replied, 'Go, but if your business succeeds, I do not know anything, and all the people of Malacca together are not strong enough to capture these ships, nor is there any reason for it.'

The sultan arose in a rage and gave his final order, 'I should have you killed Laksamana! You are placed under house arrest. Guards, take him!'

A short time later, Francisco and some crewmen returned to the mainland. Amina had been anxiously watching from the beach under a palm tree and ran out to greet her new lover.

'My lovely Amina,' Francisco said, as he wrapped his arm around her shoulder, and gave her a peck on the cheek. 'Perhaps you can show us more of the city.'

'It would be my pleasure,' Amina said. They all followed her through the narrow streets toward the center of the city, passing palm-thatched wood houses and numerous stone mosques with golden crescent moons perched on top gleaming in the sunlight. Entering a city square, they found a crowd gathering and forming a semicircle in front of a rectangular perimeter of bamboo fencing. Guards were stationed in the four corners, all girded with kris daggers tucked in their belts.

'What is this?' Francisco asked as the crew stopped to watch.

A procession entered from a backstreet; native prisoners escorted by an entourage of guards and officials. The prisoners were bound by chains around

85

their necks, arms, and legs. In front, were local native spectators, a mixture of Javanese and Malay.

The prisoners were each placed in front of execution devices. The first man stood in front of a wooden gallows, a second faced a cauldron of boiling water with raging flames burning underneath, and the third stood in front of a shallow pit full of logs and a long oval metal cage above. The cage was connected to a gear system on one end, and then to a long iron bar fastened to a teak covered wheel. An official read the charges in their language.

'Something tells me this may outdo the Sumatrans,' Francisco whispered to one of his comrades nearby. They watched as the first was hanged and his body left to rot in the burning sun. It took three guards to restrain the second prisoner as he tried to escape. Overpowered, the guards threw him into the boiling cauldron. He screamed and writhed in agony as his skin melted off his face and body, soon only the skeletal form remained, and the screams faded away.

'Brutal,' Francisco muttered.

'This is the sultan's idea of justice,' Amina said. 'I can never get used to it.'

Even though the Portuguese were ruthless in their wars, they could only watch in shock as the executioners carried on with their own brutal tactics.

Amina whispered in Francisco's ear. 'The king believes he must instill terror among his people to maintain order. I am so sorry we have come this way. I did not know this was to happen today. We can leave.'

'We shall stay,' he replied. 'I need to know what type of ruler we are dealing with.'

'Very well,' she said. 'The last execution is reserved for the highest offense, usually murder.'

Four guards struggled to restrain the third prisoner. He hurled curses upon the officials and spit at the executioners as he was restrained inside an oval cage. The guards lit the wood in the pit below.

A group of six disheveled natives clad only in loin cloths were led by guards into the execution perimeter. They were all secured with heavy chains. A guard unlocked the arm chains of one of them, shoved him forward, and pointed to the wheel. The native grunted and with a sinister grin began to turn the wheel. The caged man screamed as his flesh slowly roasted like a pig on a spit.

The other chained prisoners nearby salivated and drooled as they watched.

'Who are those beasts?' Francisco asked.

'Prisoners taken from Aru, on the northeast coast of Sumatra,' Amina whispered. 'The sultan always maintains a supply of these man-eaters to increase the fear among the citizens. They have a ferocious appetite for human flesh.' Amina averted her eyes, knowing what was to come next.

Francisco could never erase the grisly scenes he witnessed in the next moments. Once the flesh had been well roasted, the guards threw buckets of water to extinguish the flames. One of the guards used thick gloves to open the oval cage. Pieces of flesh stuck to the door as it creaked open. The chains of the man-eaters were unlocked, and they all rushed ahead to the roasted prisoner, and barring their teeth, devoured the enticing flesh with a maniacal craving.

'What the devil?' Francisco muttered.

Having enough of the sultan's demented and sadistic form of justice the Portuguese turned and walked away.

Francisco turned to Amina. 'I have to return with the men to the ships. I plan to see you again soon.'

'I will wait for you,' Amina said.

After three days in port, the sultan received Sequeira's representatives as envoys of the Portuguese king. Feigning good will and cooperation, the sultan signed a peace treaty document and permission was given for the Portuguese to open a trading factory near the waterfront. The sultan offered to host a magnificent banquet and requested Captain-General Sequeira to bring his officers and men for a celebration. Suspicious, he declined the offer. But, still enamored by the pleasant treatment from the sultan, Sequeira asked to commence trade and load his ships before the approaching end of the monsoon. The sultan offered a great quantity of pepper if they could send all his boats and many men to assist in transporting the goods from their distant warehouse to the pier.

The following morning, all the fleet's longboats and skiffs were loaded with 90 crewmen. Only a single skiff from the *taforea* remained with the fleet. Fernão caught up with Francisco as he was about to climb into the lead skiff. 'Congratulations on commanding the squadron,' Fernão said. 'But stay sharp out there. Captain Sousa thinks something may be amiss.'

'You sure?'

'No, but several Chinese captains had overheard rumors of intrigues and warned the captain-general of impending treachery from the sultan.'

'Right, but I have a nice girl waiting for me in town and a mighty load of pepper for us all. By the way, when are you going to find yourself a young lass?'

'You already know that my lady is the sea,' Fernão replied. 'But who knows, maybe in the future I will meet a lady that understands the life of a sailor.'

'Well, I am off to meet my goddess in the present.' Francisco gave a wink to his friend and jumped into the longboat below.

The crews landed the longboats and proceeded inland to the warehouse. Amina had seen the boats coming in and waited at the port. When Francisco disembarked, she rushed to embrace him. She whispered in his ear, 'You are in danger. The sultan plans to ambush your men.'

'What? How do you know?'

'I hear it in the streets.'

'Maybe just rumors,' Francisco said. He took note of her worried countenance and added, 'I already have the orders to transport the pepper to the pier. But I will keep my eyes open for any danger.' He gave her a kiss. 'Do not worry dear. I will see you soon.'

'Please Francisco, I fear for your life.'

'It will be fine,' he said with a smile and a wink before rushing off to lead his crew to the warehouse.

Offshore, a fleet of sampans surrounded the Portuguese ships. They were two-oared flat-bottomed boats and similar in size to the Portuguese skiffs. The natives smiled, waved, and feigned a desire to trade. On board the supply ship *taforea*, Captain Sousa joined Fernão on the quarterdeck. 'What do you think Magalhães? Let them board for trade negotiations?'

'I expect you will proceed with caution sir. Most of our men are on shore.'

'Then we allow only a few to board, check their motives.' Da Sousa held up three fingers to his crew, a signal to allow embarkation of only three Malay traders.

After some minutes, Captain Garcia de Sousa spotted in the distance a great number of well-armed natives in sampans approaching the captain-general's flagship. 'Treachery!' Sousa yelled. 'Drive out the imposters.'

Immediately, the three Malays were shoved off the *taforea*.

'Magalhaes, take the skiff and go to the flagship. Warn Sequeira.'

'Yes sir,' Fernão replied.

Fernão Magalhães, Nuno Vaz de Castelo-Branco, and Martin Guedes rowed the skiff to the flagship. They came up along the seaward side to avoid being noticed by the natives in their sampans. Once alongside the ship, Fernão quietly climbed on board alone. He found Captain Sequeira in his cabin, stripped to his waist, and hunched over a chess board. The crusader pieces were exquisitely crafted in silver and gold. His opponent was the son of Utimuti Raja, the wealthiest merchant in Malacca. Eight armed Malays stood at attention behind him. The captain tapped his finger on a bishop piece, thoroughly engrossed in thought for his next move. Fernão leaned over and whispered in Sequeira's ear, 'Danger captain, we are being surrounded.' He then quietly exited the cabin.

The captain motioned for a crewman to draw near and whispered, 'Climb the mast and check on the shore party. Give a warning if anything suspicious.'

Sequeira looked up at his Malay opponent while wiping his brow of sweat. 'It is too hot in here. Let us take the game on deck and get some fresh air.'

They carried the board carefully, so as not to disturb the positions of the pieces. On the open deck, the captain and the son of Utimuti Raja sat upon sacks of rice with the chess board resting upon a wood crate and resumed their chess game. One of the Malays behind the captain began to unsheathe his kris. Another Malay facing him shook his head. Meanwhile, Fernão stood near the edge of the vessel. His attention was on the captain but shifted toward the sea and land. He never noticed the Malay's kris unsheathed.

From the upper mast, the captain's scout watched a crowd forming between the shore party and the boats. 'Treachery, treachery!' the watchman yelled.

A puff of white smoke emanated from the Malacca citadel. Sequeira realized it would be the signal for an attack. He jumped from his seat and narrowly dodged a kris strike from the Malay behind him. Fernão and the crew charged the enemy and killed two of them. Outnumbered, the Malays leapt into the sea.

Upon hearing the watchman's warning and the ominous crowd growing, the Portuguese landing party split apart, some rushed toward the warehouse for cover, while others tried to fight their way through the mob toward the beach.

Meanwhile, Magalhães, along with officers Castelo-Branco and Guedes rowed the skiff desperately toward a beachhead.

On shore, the Malays slew many of the Portuguese, for many had been caught off guard and were unarmed. The natives had commandeered all the boats on the beach. But Fernão and his men fought hard to recapture one of the longboats furthest away and brought it out waist high in the bay.

Francisco Serrão and a small squad of ten were able to fight their way toward the beach. A spear struck one of them dead as they pushed onward. Meanwhile, sampans returning from the flagship approached them. Francisco and the men spotted Fernão and his men with the longboat. They splashed into the water and clambered on board. The longboat was now surrounded by hostile natives in their sampans, all armed with spears and scimitars. Hordes of warriors leaped into the waters, and several were able to climb into the longboat. The Portuguese cut them down and threw their bodies back into the water.

Fernão yelled: 'We need to make our escape now! Take the oars!'

The men heaved on the oars and the longboat plowed through two sampans and headed out to sea. The men turned to look one last time. Dead mutilated bodies of the Portuguese were strewn across the beach.

'Just in time my friends, just in time,' Francisco said in gratitude.

Back on board the supply ship, Fernão and Francisco watched events unfold. Apparently, a second longboat had escaped to a small island and a large contingent of large sampan vessels were closing toward the trapped crew of 20 men. On board the flagship, Captain Sequeira slipped his cables and steered toward the enemy. The four other Portuguese vessels followed. Sequeira carefully aimed his cannons at the enemy fleet. They bombarded the sampans relentlessly until most were sunk, crippled or fled. The marooned Portuguese were quickly rescued and returned to their vessels.

Later in the day, Sequeira called his captains and leading officers to a council on board his flagship. Officers from the *taforea*; Da Sousa, Magalhães, Serrão and Castelo-Branco joined the meeting. On the top deck, all the captains and officers stood in a circle.

Sequeira addressed the men, 'As is customary for crucial actions, we have convened here. Sixty men are missing. We estimate at least half killed. How then shall we proceed to retrieve the survivors? Your opinions are all respected.'

'I propose we attempt a rescue and then bombard the city,' Captain Sousa replied.

Many, including all Da Sousa's men, voiced their approval upon this suggestion.

'Perhaps we offer a ransom,' another captain said.

Some agreed with this approach, but most sided with Da Sousa.

Sequeira paced the deck and scratched the back of his neck, then stopped and faced the men. 'Thank you for your thoughts on this matter,' he said. 'Our vessels are undermanned now. We have two logical choices. Shall we attempt a rescue and risk losing more? Or shall we offer ransom and hope for a favorable outcome?' Sequeira placed his hands on his hips. 'I have come to a decision. We shall offer a ransom for our men. Dismissed.'

As they departed, Fernão shook his head in disbelief. He turned toward Francisco. 'A desperate and futile move.'

'Right, a useless gesture,' Francisco replied.

A letter was dispatched via a local messenger with an offer to pay ransom for the release of their men. The fleet waited for two days, but no response. Finally, on the third day, the sultan sent a belligerent gift: a Malagasy crewman, three African slaves, and a small load of spices. The captain-general seethed with anger and delivered his return message. The crew collected the corpses of two Malays slain in the first skirmish on board. They attached a note with arrows protruding from one ear to the other, and reading: *Thus, the King of Portugal avenged the treason of his enemies.*

To catch favorable winds, the fleet left for India. Fernão was standing on the quarterdeck of the *taforea* with officer Nuno Vaz de Castel-Branco.

'I can never forgive the captain for leaving the men without a fight,' Castel-Branco said.

Fernão shook his head. 'I hear you. It is not right, not our way.'

The two nodded.

'So, where is your friend, Francisco?' Castel-Branco asked.

'Captain Godwin's caravel is now short-handed a pilot,' Fernão replied. 'Francisco had orders to assist in navigation.'

The two watched the ship's course from the high position of the quarterdeck.

Shortly after leaving Malacca, the fleet encountered a large Javanese junk. Captain Godwin, on board their caravel, approached Francisco. 'A nice prize, is it not?'

'A shame to return home empty-handed,' Francisco replied. 'But is this an enemy?'

'They are likely in league with the sultan of Malacca, or Javanese pirates,' Godwin said. 'A prize worthy of taking.'

They both grinned in joint approval of their plan. Captain Godwin ordered the crew to give chase. The Portuguese overcame the junk and with grapples pulled the vessels together. A furious fight ensued with stiff resistance from the crewmen of the junk. Unexpectedly, the Javanese turned the tide of battle and began to leap aboard the Portuguese vessel. Francisco was caught in the center of the mayhem.

Watching from the *taforea*, Nuno Vaz de Castel-Branco and Fernão Magalhães took notice of the dire predicament. 'Serrão's in serious trouble,' Castel Branco said.

'Let's go!' Fernão exclaimed.

Once again, they enlisted Martin Guedes and another crewman to accompany them on a rescue mission. The four of them rowed hard and rapidly approached Captain Godwin's beleaguered caravel. Fernão secured their small skiff to the stern, and they clambered aboard to join the melee. Fernão's rescue crew slashed their black swords against Javanese Kris blades and scimitars. Francisco was pinned against the mast with two Javanese pointing their daggers at his throat. Simultaneously, Fernão and Castel-Branco thrust their swords into the backs of the assailants until the tips protruded out their chests. Francisco's eyes opened wide when he discovered the source of his timely salvation. 'Once again, just in time my friends,' he said.

Eventually, they pushed the Javanese crewmen to the edges of the top deck. Suddenly outnumbered, they leapt into the sea. Fernão's crew escorted the men to the flagship and remained on board. Meanwhile, the junk was soon caught up in a powerful current and drifted away from the armada.

With firm resolve to acquire a prize for the crown and punish the sultan's merchants, they once again pursued a junk off the coast of Sumatra. Due to its immense size, it was suspected of carrying a greater prized cargo than the former. The junk was overpowered by a squadron of 28 men under the command of Jeronimo Texeira. They immediately subdued the Malay crew and locked them below deck.

Sequeira's flagship towed the junk. The desperate Malays attempted an escape by cutting holes in the hull, which immediately began to the flood the ship. Meanwhile, Sequeira and several officers, including Magalhães and Castelo-Branco, stood on deck watching an ominous storm front approaching. As the junk took on water it began to list.

'What the devil?' Sequeira exclaimed. The tow rope strained under the heavy load of the flooded junk. 'Cut the line!' he ordered. 'It will take us down if we delay.' Sailors slashed franticly at the rope until it severed.

Texiera's men cried out for help as the currents pulled the junk toward Malacca.

'Castelo-Branco placed his arms on the deck rail and leaned forward. He turned to Sequeira, 'What are you going to do? We should save the crew. They will drift into enemy territory.'

'We lost the prize, and they knew what they signed up for,' Sequeira indignantly replied.

'A disgrace,' Fernão said. 'Never could there be a better prize than to save the lives of our men on that junk!'

Sequeira's face turned red. 'Then go and do it yourself!'

Fernão and Castelo-Branco hurried to the longboat with several assisting crewmates. Franticly rowing, they were able to catch up to the foundering junk and escorted the men on board the rescue boat. Fernão was on the junk assisting the last man on board when he glanced back over his shoulder and heard the Malay crew crying out for help. Fernão looked down at Texeira on board the longboat. 'The key. Throw me the key.'

'You sure?' Texeira asked.

Fernão pleaded his case, 'Please, just do it. They are merchants, not pirates. They only acted in self-defense. They cannot harm us now.'

Texeira fumbled in his pocket, retrieved a square key, and tossed it on deck. Fernão snatched the key and opened the door lock to the lower deck. He ran back across the top deck and leaped back onboard the longboat. As the Portuguese rowed away, the men shouted to Fernão Magalhães words of gratitude for saving their lives. In addition, unspoken silent nods and gestures of respect were given by the crew for his merciful decision to save the foreign merchants from certain drowning.

After the rescue of Texeira's crew, Fernão and Francisco had transferred to the *taforea* to navigate the vessel. Upon the open sea, ominous storm clouds converged closer, as the fleet continued sailing toward India. Stiff winds strained on the sails and waves up to 18 feet high crashed against the decks. Fernão and Francisco struggled at the whipstaff to keep the course, but the sea and the storm were relentless, and the storm seemed to pursue them. After weeks of hammering waves, one of the fleet caravels wrecked on a reef and was unsalvageable. The *taforea's* masts were shattered and it was leaking badly. The crew beached on an island, salvaged all the parts and goods that were useful, then transferred to the remaining three vessels.

The crews continued to endure mighty tempests at sea as they forged ahead. Exhausted, depleted in provisions, and with no prized cargo, the fleet arrived in Travancore. They were now only 200 miles south of Cochin.

As soon as they entered the port, an officer approached Sequiera on the pier and began to brief him. Fernão and Francisco were just disembarking their caravel and watched from afar. After a few moments, Sequira's face turned pale, and his head drooped. The officer soon finished and left.

'I wonder what spooked the captain?' Francisco asked.

'Yeah, I never seen him so solemn,' Fernão replied.

The two drew closer, along with Captain Godwin and Texeira. Sequira tried to compose himself. He turned to the men. 'It appears we have a new governor. Albuquerque has taken command.'

The men looked at one another in surprise.

'I thought he was under house arrest, by Almeida's orders?' Captain Godwin asked.

'He was,' Sequeira answered. 'But one day, a cousin of his arrived in Cannanore in October— Marshal Dom Coutinho. He brought 15 ships and 3,000 men.'

Fernão had heard of the marshal, a member of the royal household and the highest-ranking Portuguese officer to visit India.

Sequira continued, 'The marshal ordered the immediate release of Albuquerque and the two sailed to Cochin to confront Governor Almeida. Realizing the futility of any more delay tactics, Almeida surrendered over his command in early November, then set sail for Lisbon.'

'We will meet him soon then,' Texeira said.

Sequira nervously wiped sweat from his forehead as he contemplated the thought. 'I will proceed directly to Lisbon and report our discovery of Malacca. The other two caravels will proceed to Cochin.'

The men looked at one another in disbelief but dared not question the order.

'Dismissed,' Sequira said.

The officers scattered to their duties to supply the ships for the remaining journey from Travancore to Cochin. Fernão walked up alongside Francisco. 'I know Sequira's real motives to sail direct to Lisbon. He is afraid of Albuquerque. He already crossed him once before.'

'Why should he be afraid? Francisco asked. 'Do not all captains voice their dissent at times?'

'Yes. But he will also have to conceal the event of his indecision and cowardice in Malacca.'

'I see.'

'And he will magnify himself before the king as a great explorer and ignore reporting the unsavory details of his command,' Fernão added.

The two continued onward to the loading of supplies.

# 7

## *Cochin – January, 1510*

While Fernão Magalhães and Francisco Serrão were sailing to Cochin, other events had been transpiring.

Marshal Coutinho was given direct orders by King Manuel to destroy Calicut. Upon hearing the plan, Albuquerque readily agreed, and they had proceeded to inform their ally, the king of Cochin, of their intentions. The king was pleased and provided them assistance. He promised to write his friends, vassals, and lords in the interior mountainous country to commence a war with the Zamorin as a ruse to draw his forces out of Calicut. The king of Cochin offered 20 proa vessels to support the Portuguese soldiers when they disembarked on the shores of Calicut. Additionally, he sent two Brahmin spies to report the condition of the city and size of the army.

Later, during a briefing among Albuquerque and his captains, the king arrived along with his Brahmin spies. They reported that the Zamorin had taken the bait and gone into the interior to fight a war, and few Nair defenders were now left to defend the city of Calicut. The spies informed about how the defenders had constructed a jetty on the beach to which the local Malabaris called, *Cerame*. It was a watchtower constructed with wooden flooring on top of four large tree trunks arranged in a square. A palm-thatched roof was erected above. The Cerame was defended by stockades and six large bombards. They also reported how the Calicut natives had dug many holes on the beach, so that any disembarking soldiers would fall into them and become pierced with sharp sticks. The houses had no armored protection. Albuquerque's captains agreed to attack Calicut while the opportunity appeared in their favor. On the last day of December, they had departed Cochin with 20 warships, besides the *proas* used for disembarking, and 2,000 Portuguese warriors.

On January 3, 1510, the fleet anchored in front of the port of Calicut. The marshal gave instructions to the men that none should lead the charge into the city, but himself. Anyone, including captains, who dared to do so, would lose their head.

The next morning of January 4, the fleet disembarked onto the shores. The currents were flowing with force and the marshal was taken further on down the shoreline. Albuquerque attempted to reign in the men and wait for the marshal. However, the zealous troops had lost patience and proceeded onward to the Cerame. They captured the six bombards and engaged the Moor defenders with lances. The enemy were cut down and the few remaining fled back to the city. Two Portuguese were killed in the opening parley. The men eagerly pried loose the ornate doors of the Cerame and loaded them on a ship. The doors were a well sought-after prize, often discussed about in the court of Lisbon. King Manuel was fond of artistic creations with depictions of animals, birds, and sea life. These doors had what he desired, nature forms engraved upon plates of gold and silver. From the shore, Marshal Coutinho approached. He was morbidly obese, gasping for breath, and sweating profusely. The men had marched far in the sweltering heat and removed their armor.

Albuquerque approached the marshal. 'We waited for two hours,' he said. 'But I could no longer restrain the men. Their enthusiasm was too great.'

'I see you have already taken the doors,' Coutinho said with jealous indignation, for they disobeyed his orders and took the coveted prize before himself. His face contorted and turned red. 'Throw the doors into the sea! I will find greater treasures in the palace.'

'Please, take a rest before marching on.'

Coutinho fumed and replied, 'I know very well you want, that I am not to stir from here; but I mean to go on to the houses of the Zamorin, and destroy Calicut, before I take anything to eat, and let him who will go with me, go; and let him who will not, stay behind.' Enraged, the marshal tore off his helmet and put a red silk cap on. He then picked up his cane and continued toward the city.

Three gunners rolled a mounted field gun—a berço, on its caisson. Alongside, additional soldiers carried the cannonballs and powder in a barrel. A line of 400 men followed in a quest for the spoils of war. Albuquerque came up alongside his nephew D. Antonio de Noronha along with his friend, Rodrigo Rabelo, standing nearby. 'Antonio . . . Rodrigo . . . take 300 men and burn the enemy ships. Then setup a line of defense near the shore. We must be ready. Today we will see what God wills. Many of those you see going won't come back.'

When the marshal neared the city, 30 Nair warriors raised their spears and shields, all the while shouting in their language. Coutinho laughed and remarked to Gaspar Pereira, 'It is almost a shame to fight these little savages who flee like goats. Is this your Calicut, that you terrify us all with in Portugal?'

Pereira replied, 'You will think differently before long. I wager that if we penetrate today, to the houses of the Zamorin, these naked little ones will give us trouble enough.'

'These are not the kind of people who will give me any trouble,' he scoffed. Coutinho then pointed to a great mosque situated in front of the city and yelled, 'Burn it to the ground!'

But, before arriving to the mosque, fatigue dropped the marshal to his knees, and two men had to carry him under their arms. The troops set fire to the mosque and then meandered their way through the narrow city streets, onward toward the palace, and all the while assisting their commander. Meeting with little resistance, the Portuguese burned the palm-thatched houses as they continued further into the city. They entered a square. It was surrounded by houses of the nobility. Here, they encountered a stiff resistance from a body of Nairs. Many of the Portuguese were wounded with arrows, including Lisuarte, the powerful mulatto warrior that Albuquerque so admired. He was the son of the famous explorer, Captain Duarte Pacheco. Lisuarte was clearing the square of the enemy with his two-handed sword when an arrow pierced him in the neck between the corselet and helm. He fell dead. António da Costa also collapsed, decapitated.

Later, the Portuguese approached the palace. It was surrounded by a fortified stockade built of wood palisades. They were met in front of the gates by a force of 200 Nairs. The Portuguese launched an aggressive lance attack, to which 80 Nairs were slain and the remaining scattered into the city streets. The marshal entered the palace gates into an open courtyard and immediately he collapsed upon a platform used for mounting horses. The marshal slept there while his men looted the palace. Elaborately engraved chests inlaid with precious metals were stuffed full of fine silks and jewels. The men were enthralled and stacked their treasures in piles. An ornate door was broken open and the men gasped when they found chests full of gold coins. Inside this royal treasure room, a second door was discovered, full of glistening gold panels. As they tried fruitlessly to pry the door open, 400 Nair fighters infiltrated the courtyard from 2 separate gates. The marshal awoke from his slumber and rallied the men to repel the attackers. Eventually, the enemy retreated into the city streets.

Meanwhile, Albuquerque maintained the rearguard and had stationed his men in a tactical formation at a terrace near the palace gate. A body of Nairs took notice of their position and fired volleys of arrows, wounding many of the men severely. Albuquerque ordered the field gun to fire. Unnerved by the gun, the Nairs fled off into the city with shouts for reinforcements.

Albuquerque sent word to the Marshal twice to retire. But, still angered, he would not listen, and continued to rest in the courtyard while his men pillaged. Albuquerque watched the Nair army increase in numbers. He decided to enter the courtyard alone to try to convince the marshal to retreat. He approached the marshal and asked, 'Sir, how do you wish us to act? For these men require someone to lead the way for them and restrain them from straggling, because the Nairs are many, and the communication with the beach is broken. I fear we shall have a bad account to give of ourselves today if we do not dispose ourselves properly.'

'Very well,' Coutinho finally acquiesced. 'You take the vanguard, and I will remain behind in the rearguard.'

Albuquerque's squad took the flag and departed. From the stockades, crowds hurled stones, hand darts, and arrows. Albuquerque ordered his men not to engage the enemy but to make straightway to the beach.

Meanwhile, the marshal ordered for the palace to be set on fire. Nairs soon infiltrated the palace to extinguish the flames and set upon the Portuguese as they were preparing their retreat. The men were exhausted and no match for the fresh Nair troops. Retreating through the narrow streets, an arrow struck the marshal's foot, sliced the heel off, and caused him to fall. Two men tried to lift him, but due to exhaustion from the fighting and his heavy weight, they could not. Barrages of arrows continued to cut them down as they rushed through the smoke-filled streets. As soon as Albuquerque discovered the marshal's dire situation, he reeled his men around for a rescue attempt. In this maneuver, several of his men were wounded as their small contingent encountered an army of nearly 600 natives. From the top of a palisade, a Nair hurled a short lance and struck Albuquerque through the left shoulder and another penetrated into his shoulder blade, forcing him to the ground. Upon discovery of his uncle's plight, D. Antonio Noronha, and Rodrigo Rabelo brought up a squad of soldiers to the palisade and assisted in the retreat. Albuquerque would have perished, but Diogo Fernandez de Béja and two other men carried him safely to the beach. The men scrambled for the boats and rowed back to the fleet.

The casualties were high for both sides. The Zamorin lost 3,000 warriors. In addition, the merchant fleet and much of Calicut was burnt, including the royal palace.

After a desperate resistance, Marshal Coutinho and 12 of his officers were killed. In total, the Portuguese lost 80 men, many of them captains and fidalgos. Two days later, the fleet sailed to Cochin.

By the second week of January, Francisco and Fernão had arrived in Cochin and were directing native servants to complete the loading of three cargo vessels bound for Lisbon.

'Bring the pepper to that vessel,' Francisco commanded in Malayalam. He pointed to one of the large carracks. One of the locals carrying a heavy sack stopped, turned, and headed in the other direction.

'It is fortunate we were able to sign on for the return fleet,' Fernão said. 'It will be nice to finally bring home a well-deserved bounty.'

'Yeah, five years of service for the crown. A good time to go home.'

'We can regroup and sign on for another mission,' Fernão suggested.

'Maybe,' Francisco replied. 'But you know, after Albuquerque's casualties in the battle of Calicut, he will be wanting to have some retribution. I am not sure that fits into our plans.'

'I understand seeking glory and honor, but his former captains had a point in their complaints. His hard driving pompous nature can make it difficult.'

'I have heard that in his diary entries and correspondences, he titles himself—*The Great Albuquerque*,' Francisco said with a grin.

'I have heard he thinks himself the Caesar of the Indies,' Fernão added with a chuckle. 'I do not expect his defeat at Calicut last week will sit well with him.'

'We just missed the action. If the storms had not delayed our return, we could have joined the battle, and given him a victory.'

'Quite possible my friend,' Fernão replied.

The two continued to steer the goods to the correct vessels.

After they had directed another load of cargo to a large carrack vessel, Fernão ceased his activity. He stared out to sea and then said to Francisco, 'I hear rumors the Spaniards are outfitting exploratory fleets to sail west, perhaps for a new route to Asia. You know, I have seen the maps in the India House depicting a strait, and possibly the path we seek. Behaim knew.'

'I am sorry about your friend. Has it really been two years now since his illness took him?'

Fernão nodded. 'I will honor his work and find the western route to the Spice Islands.'

'You know, we could open our own trading business,' Francisco proposed. 'Create a partnership.'

'That sounds like an excellent concept.'

'Speaking of possible partnerships. Did you find out if Samuel is still in town?'

'I found out that he received his freedom and left for Lisbon,' Fernão replied. 'But maybe he returns to Cochin as he planned.'

'He was an excellent interpreter and a funny man.'

'Indeed. I will miss his wit.'

A loud commotion erupted across the port as servants scattered in panic. The crowd parted and from the center emerged Albuquerque. He was waving a cane like a madman and barking orders. His left shoulder was bandaged, and his left arm supported in a sling.

'Speak of the devil,' Francisco said.

Albuquerque approached Fernão and Francisco. 'Officers,' he said. 'Had enough fight and going home? Are you not going to join my mission to Suez?'

'Sorry sir, but the crown expects these last three cargo vessels,' Francisco replied. 'We are already signed on to navigate.'

'The crown, yes, yes of course. I know our dear king needs his groceries. See to it then.' Albuquerque ambled off to continue preparing his fleet of 23 vessels, bound for the Red Sea.

'Another reason to go home,' Francisco said.

'Definitely,' Fernão added.

Albuquerque disappeared into the crowd.

In mid-January, Fernão Magalhães and Francisco Serrão finally left Cochin with the spice cargo fleet bound for Lisbon. Captain Gomes Freire had left on schedule prior, but the other two vessels commanded by Sebastian de Sousa, and Francisco de Sa were delayed. Fernão stood near the whipstaff assisting the pilot and helmsman on board Captain Sa's vessel. The two lagging vessels sailed together into the night with their charts and experience to guide them. Around midnight, Fernão was off-duty and in a deep slumber on the main deck. A sudden jolt awakened him.

'What the . . .' He jumped and peered over the side in the darkness. The vessel creaked and shuddered as it crashed against a coral reef. Fernão held onto the ship rail. He could see their sister ship listing. They were also in peril.

'We are taking on water,' cried a sailor from below deck. 'We need to plug the holes.' Some crews scrambled to stop the gushing water from the hull while others moved the cargo to the top deck, which took the rest of the predawn hours.

By early morning, both vessels had filled with water, but, fortunately, neither had broken apart. The exhausted crews had salvaged a portion of their prized spice cargo, along with supplies of water and food, and loaded them onto the longboats. They secured a position on a small sandy island nearby.

On the beach, Captain Sebastian de Sousa was staring at a sea chart unfurled upon a fallen palm tree. He turned to both ship pilots. 'What the hell happened?'

'It was dark,' replied one nervous pilot. 'Not sure, maybe missed a turn of the hourglass.'

'Incompetence!' Captain Sousa barked. 'Now we are in dire straits.'

Fernão knew how missing a turn of the clock would result in a miscalculation of their longitude and put the fleet at risk of serious calamity. The captain pointed to his chart. 'We hit Pedro Reef. By my calculation we are 100 miles from Cannanore.'

The seamen murmured to each other. The two captains and high-ranking officers commandeered the longboats and piled in. A panic ran through the crews, all were suddenly aware they were to be marooned. Fernão knew chivalry was commonplace in battle but not yet standard practice in sea rescues.

Fernão looked with concern at his friend standing alone on shore. Francisco was a navigator, but not yet a ranking officer and thus not qualified to join the party. He simply leaned on a palm tree and watched the frantic seamen rush to seize the longboats.

Fernão turned to face the men and said, 'Let the captains and officers go and I will remain with you.' He then turned to those on the boats and implored, 'If they will give us their word of honor that upon arriving to India, they will send us help!'

Captain Sebastian de Sousa stood up in the boat and replied, 'On my honor I will send help as you request.'

The men quieted down and retreated toward the beachhead. Fernão turned to some officers on the longboat to discuss the supply issues and what was needed for their journey. Perceiving Fernão was about to betray them, one of the sailors cried out, 'Oh, Sir Magalhães, did you not promise to stay with us?'

Fernão turned and rushed to the beach and replied, 'I have indeed promised. See me here!' He placed his arm around the sailor's shoulder and then walked with him on the beach to join the other stranded crewmen. The longboats sailed off.

The marooned crews plied their time by fishing with makeshift poles and rigs. In the evening they burned pieces of wood salvaged from the wrecked ships. At first the men were content, but as the days went by, many began to fret over their supplies, for the island was barren except for some scattered coconut palms. If Captain Sousa's longboats were lost at sea or never returned, they would eventually run out of food and water.

Finally, after two weeks, a caravel appeared and approached the island. The crewmen cheered. Fernão slapped Francisco on the shoulder. 'Captain de Sousa is an honorable man. I knew he would send us help.'

'I regret I did not share your enthusiasm,' Francisco said.

Once Captain Antonio Pacheco landed, he invited the crews to fresh food and drink. Once refreshed, the men began to load the prized pepper cargo onto the caravel. Finally, they sailed off for Cannanore.

When Captain Pacheco's rescue caravel reached Cannanore, the first order of business was to unload their cargo. There was no reprieve after this. All the men were immediately assigned to join Albuquerque's attack fleet to the Red Sea.

Albuquerque's armada was comprised of 23 ships, 1,600 Portuguese, 220 Malabarese auxiliaries from Cochin, and 3000 support slaves. The force left on February 10, 1510, on their mission—to seek out and destroy the fleet of the Grand Sultan of Cairo. King Manuel's orders were to halt the Islamic commerce through the Persian Gulf and exact punishment upon the ruler of Ormuz. Albuquerque also had intentions to push further, to invade Mecca, then instigate a war betwen the Sunni Ottoman Turks and the Shiite Persians, thus advancing Portuguese power in the region.

# 8

## Onor – February, 1510

En route to the Red Sea, Albuquerque anchored in the port of Mirjan in Onor (Honavar), India, 100 miles south of Goa.

A *fusta* came up alongside Albuquerque's flagship, the *Flor de la Mar*. It was a light and narrow vessel with a shallow draft. The fustas were like small galleys. Typically, they had 12 to 18 rows of two-men rowing oars on each side, a lateen sail, and at least two cannons. Its design made it fast and maneuverable, perfect for patrolling shallow coasts. On the stern of the approaching fusta, a powerfully built Indian with gold armbands on his biceps stood at watch from the stern of the fusta.

From the quarterdeck of the *Flor de la Mar*, Albuquerque waved at him. He turned to his shipmaster. 'Our contact, Timoja, has arrived.'

'Timoja?' the shipmaster asked with concern. 'Is he not a pirate?'

'He has proven a reliable asset thus far. Let him board.'

'Yes sir.'

Soon, on the main deck, the two commanders met face to face.

'Governor,' Timoja said. 'It is so good to see you have continued your communications with me since Almeida has left.'

'We are always open for negotiations, even from a notorious Hindu corsair,' Albuquerque said with a grin. 'Please join me in my quarters.'

112

The two made their way to the captain's cabin at the stern. The two faced eacher across a wood table. A clerk served glasses of water then departed.

'I see you have a commanding force,' Timoja observed. 'If I may be so bold to speak, where is your mission?'

'I am to seek out the Grand Sultan of Cairo's fleet and defeat it in battle. If I cannot find the fleet, I will go to Suez and burn any ships or galleys we find there.'

'Your plan is good,' Timoja said. 'But, I am concerned.'

'Concerned?'

'You may wish to alter your plans. I have important news. The captain of the Grand Sultan and a force of Turks have escaped from Almeida's conquest at Diu. They have arrived in Goa and have begun to build ships.

'And how certain are you that this is true?' Albuquerque asked.

'I have secret agents and they have informed me of a letter sent by the captain to the Grand Sultan that they should remain in Goa.'

'So, they now have a presence in the city. Should that concern us?'

'Yes. They have skilled carpenters and caulkers building a great fleet of well-constructed battle ships, much like your design.'

'They are building a naval base?' Albuquerque asked with concern.

'Precisely. You see, Goa is an island city, surrounded by two main rivers and a narrow channel on the eastern side full of crocodiles. It is situated five miles up the Mandovi River and well protected from storms. Its perfect natural defense is strengthened even more by strategically placed forts near the passes.'

'Besides its defensive position, what other advantage do they gain by establishing their presence there?'

'Goa has an excellent harbor, a thriving trade in war horses, plenty of timber, fertile plantations, and vast supplies of water. The Moors and Turks plan to establish Goa as a strategic stronghold, to oust the Portuguese from India and once again return the spice routes to Mecca and Cairo. The captain claims the fleet is nearly complete.'

'So, what do you propose?' Albuquerque asked.

'I should inform you of Goa first.' Timoja said. 'You see, I was born in Goa. But I lived in poverty, until I forged my own life at sea. In Goa there is no hope, for long ago, the ruler of Bijapur, Yusuf Adil Shah, had subjugated our city. He is known as the Çabaio and governs our Hindu populace with cruel tyranny and murder. Recently, he robbed 200 merchants and doubled the taxes for all citizens. A Turkish garrison enforces absolute compliance and causes great dissentions among our people.'

'An imposing presence,' Albuquerque said.

'But now there is a way to subdue the city. The Çabaio has died. He was killed in a jihad against the Vijayanagara empire to the south. His son, Ismail Adil Shah, known as—the Hidalcão, has taken power. But he is now at war in the interior country. Goa is not adequately defended and ripe for conquest.'

Albuquerque scratched his beard.

'I can help you,' Timoja said. 'I will align your forces with my people to arrange a swift surrender of the city. They will readily agree, for they despise their Muslim overlords.'

114

'And what do you wish in return for your services?'

'If you give me Goa, I will defend the city for your kingdom against all your enemies. You shall always have a secure trading port in Goa.'

'And what of the king's tribute? You should know that any lands we take are his.'

'I shall promise to pay the annual tribute to your king.'

'Your demands seem adequate,' Albuquerque said. 'Let us proceed to take Goa together.'

'I can provide 2,000 land troops under the command of my cousin.'

'Does he have command experience?' Albuquerque asked.

'Some, but I have Captain Melique Çufecondal. He had fled Goa in fear of the Çabaio and serves me now.'

'He is a Moor. Do you trust this captain?'

'Yes.'

'Very well. Then your forces should march up the coast and destroy any land fortifications while our armada attacks from the sea.'

'I will order it,' Timoja said. He then returned on his fusta to shore.

Once the plan had been relayed to the land troops, the Portuguese fleet and Timoja's fustas sailed north up the coast. Almost midway to Goa, they anchored in front of the fortress of Cintácora. The large fleet of black ships loomed offshore as Timoja's land army approached the fortress. The defenders fled in haste. Finding the fortress deserted, Timoja's men salvaged the artillery, burned the buildings within, then continued their march up the coast.

Albuquerque set sail, and brought the fleet further north and then into the Mendovi Estuary. Fernão and Francisco were assisting the pilot on the quarterdeck of their caravel, the *Cirne*, captained by Albuquerque's nephew, D. Antonio de Noronha.

At the mouth of the estuary, the salt waters funneled into a river inlet. The fortress of Pangim overlooked the entry point. Here the shoreline turned marshy. On February 28, the ships anchored before the sandbar, unable to proceed further.

'I'm starting to think I'm not suited for stifling humidity,' Francisco said, wiping his face and neck with a rag.

'It's so hot here the air is sweating,' Fernão said, smiling at the thought.

Francisco pointed to a crocodile along the banks. 'Look at the size of that beast,' he said. 'This could be an interesting mission.'

'I hope it does not involve too much night work,' Fernão said.

'I hear you,' Francisco added. 'I would not wish to lose an arm or leg. Or worse.'

In the evening, Fernão and Francisco joined the other commanders on board the *Flor de la Mar*. As navigators they were requested to attend.

Albuquerque stood with Timoja and addressed the men. 'I need your opinion on how we should proceed,' he said. 'My nephew and Timoja have recently sounded the bar at two and a half fathoms. But this is only one reading, in one location. I am concerned. We have no pilots familiar with this channel. If we ground, it is unlikely of a timely remedy, leaving us vulnerable. I propose sending some boats to take further soundings and investigate their defenses.'

'Your advice is sound governor,' Garcia de Sousa said.

Fernão gave a nod to his former commander in the Malacca expedition. Garcia nodded in return.

'Any objections?' Albuquerque asked.

Nobody said a word.

'Good,' he said. 'Then Captain Noronha will lead the expeditionary force. We proceed at first light.'

At sunrise, 7 captains with their longboats, 2 galleys, and Timoja with his 13 fustas, all crossed the bar. A few took soundings while the greater force headed toward the fortress of Pangim. The Moor defenders fired their cannons at the boats, but all the shots missed, for they had aimed too high. Noronha signaled for the men to converge to the shore. Artillery continued to shoot just over their heads as they landed their boats. One of the Portuguese stabbed a menacing crocodile in the head with a lance as he disembarked. The men charged the hillside and rapidly scaled the walls. Fernão and Francisco were among the lead climbers and had secured grappling hooks over the fort walls. Just above them, two men were busy reloading artillery. The cannon barrel protruded out a fortress embrasure. There was just enough room to squeeze through an opening on each side of it. Fernão and Francisco slid through with their black swords drawn and immediately cut down the gunners. The remainder of the attack force climbed over the crenellated walls. The Moors counterattacked by cavalry and infantry. But the Portuguese routed them, and any survivors fled to the city. With the Moor fortress deserted, they collected swords, shields, lances and 18 pieces of artillery. Before departing they burned all the buildings within.

Later, Fernão and Francisco accompanied Albuquerque's nephew—Captain Noronha, on board the flagship and reported the events to the governor.

'A great victory!' Albuquerque exclaimed. He then asked, 'And the depth of the harbor is sufficient?'

'We can cross, even with your flagship.' Noronha replied.

'Good news indeed!' Albuquerque exclaimed, then noticed Fernão and Francisco standing behind at attention.

'And these men were at the lead of the attack,' Noronha said. 'Invaluable in our service.'

Albuquerque looked them over.

'Magalhães has the rank of captain and Serrão is an excellent navigator.'

'Indeed,' Albuquerque remarked. 'Well, I need you three to lead another reconnaisance mission. Check Goa's fortress and walls for the best entry point.'

'At your service sir,' Fernão and Francisco said simultaneously.

From the *Flor de la* Mar, Captain Noronha was the first to board the skiff and return to the *Cirne*. On the main deck of the flagship, Francisco turned to Fernão and remarked, 'Great, more adventure.'

'That is why we are here,' Fernão replied.

'Yeah, but just a pain to be noticed sometimes.'

The two lowered themselves from the main deck into the skiff to join Noronha.

On the following morning of March 2, as Captain Noronha was about to depart on his assignment, two leading Moors arrived in a proa with an offer of surrender from all the inhabitants of Goa. Albuquerque told his nephew to proceed with his mission while he would continue to negotiate the terms of surrender.

On March 4, all negotiations had been settled with relative ease, for as Timoja had informed prior, the large Hindu faction of the city desired to rid themselves from the Hidalcão's harsh rule. Outnumbered, the Moor leadership acquiesced to the citizenries demands. Albuquerque proceeded to load the longboats, skiffs, and the proas they had brought from Cannanore, with 1,000 soldiers and 200 of the Malabari fighters. The fleet vessels would remain outside the bar until a more opportune time to bring them into the harbor.

The Portuguese rowed up in front of the city where Captain Norohna, Magalhães, Serrão, and some men were waiting in a longboat anchored. A grand procession was led toward the city by a friar of St. Dominic carrying a large cross. Next, a soldier held the royal flag, made of white satin and the red cross of the Order of Christ embroidered in the center. They entered the gate without any resistance. Albuquerque had expected a stiff resistance at Goa. But with such a quick resolution, he fell to his knees and with tears in his eyes, thanked the Lord for delivering up to them such a fine city without any loss of life. He arose and beheld the leading Moors of the city along with the governors rushing to kneel at the feet of the Portuguese. They surrendered the keys of Goa's fortress to Albuquerque and pleaded for their safety, pledging themselves as loyal vassals to the crown. Entering further into the city, the leading Hindus of the region also pledged their obedience to the Portuguese, for they hated their Islamic taskmasters and negotiated directly with Albuquerque.

Once Albuquerque had surveyed the city, he immediately ordered his men to inspect the fortress.

They found a large arsenal: stockpiles of powder, 40 large bombarderos, 50 falconets, 160 horses, and numerous small hand weapons. All sorts of ropes, cordage and bolt-work were also stored within the fortress. In the port were moored 40 enemy ships of various sizes and 16 fustas. Expecting the imminent return of the Hidalcão, Albuquerque gave orders to reinforce the foundations and walls of the fortress. People throughout the land were employed to assist. Captains and their men were assigned hours of duty to orchestrate the swift reconstruction project. Large storage rooms were also built for corn and rice.

Fernão had reservations about Albuquerque's ill-tempered nature, but over the next seven weeks  in Goa, his respect for the man grew. He admired the prudent move to strengthen the fortress and construct proper storage facilities.

Albuquerque soon discovered the local Hindus practiced the rites of *sati*—the obligation of a wife to burn herself in ritual sacrifice upon the death of her husband. Disgusted by this abhorrent custom, he immediately banned it, to which the native women thanked him very much.

One day, Timoja, along with the principle leaders and nobles from the land, both Moor and Hindu, approached Albuquerque to ascertain what dues were to be paid. They begged him to show them favor since they had suffered greatly under the current regime with a doubled taxation and thus unable to achieve a reasonable living. Albuquerque replied to them that it was not his intention to continue the tyrannies of the Hidalcão, but on the contrary, to show favor, honor and an increased means of living. He then promised to remit the former taxation and they could pay what they were accustomed to pay under the former Hindu lords of Goa, so long as they promised to remain loyal subjects to the Portuguese crown. All were greatly pleased with the new decree.

Later, Albuquerque discovered the citizens were in dire economic circumstances due to a lack of currency. Therefore, to alleviate their situation, he established a Mint to coin gold, silver and copper money. One side of the coin was to be stamped with a cross and on the other, a sphere—King Manuel's signature device. A great festive ceremonial procession with jesters, dancers, and musicians accompanied the Portuguese as they marched throughout the city. They threw coins into the crowds with a decree that it should be the sole currency in Goa and the surrounding territories.

For over a month, Albuquerque's men had engaged in expansive city improvement projects and bolstered the fortress defenses. It was now the beginning of April.

Francisco went to the fortress stables where Fernão was busily grooming a horse mane. 'The governor is sending me on a mission,' Francisco said.

Fernão paused with his brush in mid-air. 'Mission? What kind of mission?'

'He plans to prolong his stay in Goa, and needs me to command a caravel to bring back saddles and provisions from Cochin.'

'You have your first command,' Fernão said with a smile. 'When do you leave, *captain.*'

'Immediately, the monsoons will come soon.'

'I will see you off then.'

The two walked to the harbor. Francisco jumped into a skiff. 'Enjoy the heat of Goa,' he said.

'Enjoy the ocean breezes,' Fernão replied.

Francisco gave a salute then rowed the boat toward his caravel anchored in port.

It was on April 23, when intelligence arrived that two of the Hidalcão's captains were leading an attack upon the island of Goa. They were encamped in the lands of Banda and Condal with a sizeable force. Albuquerque sent Diogo Fernandez to ascertain if this report were true. A contingent of 1,000 Canarese peons accompanied Fernandez and passed over to the mainland in the night. Marching through the tall grass in the dark, they suddenly came upon the Hidalcão's vanguard and were completely routed. Fernandez barely escaped back to Goa with only 500 of their native allies. Albuquerque was greatly alarmed by this news. He made haste to reinforce all the passes and fortify all their towers around the island's 18-mile perimeter with captains, men, and weapons.

Fernão was tending the stables when a large contingent of cavalry and infantry approached. Albuquerque was at the lead and dismounted in haste. He grimaced and clutched his shoulder. The injury from the battle of Calicut had not yet healed. 'Magalhaes,' he said. We need all the remaining horses saddled and requisitioned to our cavalrymen.'

'Yes sir.'

'Can you ride well?'

'I grew up riding.'

'Good. We are short of riders. Come with us.'

The reserve Portuguese forces left Goa and arrived first in the outpost stockade of Benastarim. The fortress was situated on the eastern bank of the Cumbarjua channel. The narrow waterway divided the island from the mainland. Albuquerque placed Garcia de Sousa in charge. As they were selecting men to stay, Sousa noticed Fernão ride up. 'Magalhaes, care to join me?'

'Very much so,' he replied with a smile.

Captain Sousa turned to Albuquerque. 'I could use this officer. He served under my command in the Malacca expedition.'

'Very well Captain Sousa. Since this is a vital stronghold, I will leave you with 100 infantry, 6 cavalry, and four bombards accompanied with gunners. Good luck.'

Albuquerque mounted his horse and galloped off with the remaining forces to reinforce the other crossing points. Each of these passes were easily crossed during low tides. Therefore, many vulnerable points had been fortified with towers built from the days of the Narsinga kings a century before. Albuquerque knew that if they were manned with troops, and plenty of gunpowder and cannon shot, they would be formidable defenses. He also placed squads of infantry in other strategic passes around the island perimeter. Albuquerque then returned to the city.

A few days later, Garcia de Sousa dispatched a messenger to Albuquerque with a warning that the Hidalcão's main army had pitched their camp before Benastarim and were steadily growing in numbers.

The same day, Albuquerque's mounted his horse and galloped out of Goa. He charged across the low tides of the Cumbarjua channel. Several captains rode behind, followed by an infantry squadron. Albuquerque looked out at the grassy field to the east, at the dead bodies strewn about on the approach to the fort. Near a crop of tall reeds, two large crocodiles were tearing apart a corpse. A mosque and some houses were situated upon a hillside. Albuquerque dismounted and climbed the two-level stone fortress of Benastarim. He found Captain Garcia de Sousa commanding gunners to keep loading two-inch diameter stone shot into two large swivel berços. Fernão stood near the captain.

'Captain Sousa,' Albuquerque yelled over the cannon fire.

Sousa turned with a look of surprise. He approached Albuquerque who was at the top of the stairway and away from the cannon noise. 'Governor,' he said. 'I did not expect you so soon.'

'Your reports are concerning,' Albuquerque said. 'In addition to your message, we received intelligence the Hidalcão's forces from Banda, Condral, and other places, have been converging here.'

'It is a sizeable force sir,' he replied.

A gunner fired off another round from one of the swivel guns.

Sousa continued, 'We estimate there are at least 40,000 Persian and Turk fighters. We drove them back behind the hill with our guns. But many have entrenched themselves in that mosque and those houses.'

Albuquerque looked out to the field again. 'Take a squadron and burn those structures. Inflict as much damage as possible and drive them back. This site is a key access point to the city. It cannot fall. You must hold the line.'

'Sousa turned to Fernão. 'Come with me,' he said. 'Let's get this done.'

Fernão nodded.

Sousa's team of six cavalry charged at the mosque and engaged the enemy with swords and lances. Meanwhile, an infantry squad crept through the reeded areas, all the while cautious of the crocodiles. While Hidalcão's forces were distracted by the cavalry, the infantry lit torches and burned the buildings. With smoke billowing out, the enemy retreated behind the hills. The Portuguese returned to the fortress and found Albuquerque climbing onto his horse. 'Good work captain,' he said. 'Keep them at bay. I am going to check the other passes.'

Albuquerque and his contingent galloped away.

On May 1, the Hidalcão sent two Moor converts—a Portuguese and a Venetian, to Albuquerque expecting a favorable response due to the formidable army he had raised. A Portuguese spy, João Machado, asked to see Albuquerque in private. Machado confided that he was a convict left on the Swahili coast and was later taken as a slave and forced into service to the Hidalcão. Machado insisted he was a loyalist to the crown and promised to continue delivering intelligence in the future. But for now, he would relay the message given to him.

The Hidalco wished to establish an alliance on account of the great name Albuquerque had acquired among the Moors, and that he was not surprised at the fall of Goa because he knew for certain that Timoja had intrigued with the Hindus of the land to deliver up the city to the Portuguese. The Hidalcão now begged him earnestly to surrender the island and the lands of Goa, and in exchange he would give him another place of his own on the seacoast, whichever he selected, wherein to erect a fortress. But if he, Afonso, were unwilling to carry out this that was asked of him, he was to know for a surety that the Hidalcão would on no consideration quit his military position until he had cast him out of the city, for the whole future of the state depended on this issue.

Albuquerque pondered a moment the consequences of his response. He told the messenger—João Machado, to let the Hidalcão know how much obliged he was for the good will he had shown, and the advice he had given, and that he hoped

125

it would please God to give him such knowledge of the truth that he might ultimately obtain true salvation.

Albuquerque then asked him to deliver in person this message:

I, Afonso Albuquerque, had not taken Goa merely to lose it again, for Goa could only belong to him who had also the dominion of the sea, namely, the King D. Manuel, his Lord; but he would be very glad to come to terms of peace with him, seeing that hereby not only would the Hidalcão increase the stability of his own position, but he would infuse great terror among the neighboring states, and this advice he gave as a man of 60 years of age and well experienced in arms, to him who was but a young man and badly advised. Furthermore, if the Hidalcão placed any reliance on his hopes of succor from the Grand Sultan, he had greatly erred, for the rout that D. Francisco Almeida had inflicted upon the Rûmes had been so thorough, that they could not be able to rally to his assistance at that juncture; but he begged the Hidalcão to be sensible enough to raise the siege and take himself off, and surrender Dabul, wherein he, Afonso, might erect a fortress, and on these conditions peace should be made, but if the Hidalcão did not choose to carry out all that had been laid down, it was no use talking any more in concert, for this would always be the ultimate answer that he would give him.

Later, the Hidalcão sent back the messengers again, but this time it was the Venetian, Baldrez, who spoke directly with Albuquerque. The Hidalcão was greatly surprised at the rejection of terms, but he

126

would promise him, before many days were passed, that he would be sorry for the message that he had sent.

Baldrez continued to relay the circumstances. The Hidalcão had amassed numerous infantry and cavalry with plans to pass over to the island by rafts. He mentioned also how the Turks among the forces had no intention of any terms, for they would again be lords of Goa or die in battle—even by the hundreds of thousands if required to attain their goal. Albuquerque was unphased by these threats and simply crossed his arms and stared out to the fields of battle.

A few days later, Fernão and Sousa were on lookout in the fortress of Benastarim. They spotted a long line of combat porters moving down a dirt path. Drawing closer, they could see they carried timber beams, ropes, two berços, and several smaller guns. One of the Portuguese soldiers climbed the fort and presented Sousa with a sealed letter. The captain opened it and read. He scratched his beard and then turned to Fernão. 'It appears we are to build a stockade along our western wall, to face Goa, and urgently.'

'Facing the city?' Fernão asked.

'A Portuguese spy named João Machado has informed the governor, that the Moors in the city are in direct communication with the Hidalcão. Albuquerque fears they may revolt at any time and try to take control of this fortress. We are to prevent this from happening at all costs.'

'How may I assist sir?'

'For now, I need you to continue the watch. I will appoint my brother Duarte as commander for the new stockade section. We will place the two new berços facing Goa.'

Captain Sousa's men erected the fortress with great speed. During the construction, the eastern front swelled with new enemy recruits every day, all carrying fresh supplies and armaments. Sousa had enough and handed a letter to a soldier. 'Take this to the governor,' he said. 'And make haste.'

'Yes sir,' the soldier replied, then hustled off.

The next day, Fernão and Sousa were on the second level of the fortress, when they heard Duarte de Sousa yell out from the new stockade, 'We have company brother!'

'Who is it?' Garcia de Sousa asked.

'Come here and see!'

Fernão and Sousa climbed over to the new stockade. They joined Duarte and observed a squad of Portuguese combat porters and soldiers rolling an immense cannon with a nine-inch diameter barrel.

'I see the governor takes our position seriously,' Garcia de Sousa said. 'They sent us a *camelo*!

'I expect we can deliver more damage with this marvelous piece of iron,' Duarte de Sousa replied with a grin. 'Thirty-two pounders of misery.'

'Indeed,' Fernão smiled.

All three men laughed.

Over the next days, the big gun was lifted into position on the old fortress, facing the hills to the east. When its power was finally unleashed, it wreaked havoc upon the Hidalcão's army and held them in check.

# 9

## *Goa – May 17, 1510*

With the monsoon rains pouring down and the tide out, 700 Turks crossed the pass of Agasim on rafts. As dawn broke, they were discovered, and Dom Antonio de Noronha aimed precise artillery shots, smashing the rafts into pieces. The Portuguese put all of them to the sword, save three who escaped. Simultaneously, another contingent of 2,000 Turks crossed on the other side through the lagoon. Menaique, Timoja's captain, was stationed at the remains of the older section of Goa and spotted them. He leapt upon his horse and led 200 natives to attack. Most had already crossed, but nearly 40 were hiding motionless in the mud. As they attempted to escape, Menaique put them all to the sword.

The Turks retaliated with a vengeance. They pushed onward to the fortress of Benastarim. Fernão and Captain Sousa were in their usual station on the tower and watching the eastern front. Suddenly, splashing could be heard from the west. Then, Duarte Sousa yelled, 'Fire the guns!'

Two berços fired off.

Back on the tower, Captain Sousa exclaimed, 'We have company on our western flank. We need to help my brother in the stockade.'

'Let's go,' Fernão said.

Two gunners and an infantryman followed them down the stairs. They crept undercover along a perimeter of reeds as they moved west toward the stockade. They gaped as they watched the hordes storming toward the stockade and lining up with their bows. Duarte's gunners sent off another round. The

Turks launched a barrage of flaming arrows at the stockade, setting fire to the timbers. Several of the small squad were hit with arrows. Smoke and flames engulfed the fort. Vast numbers of Turks continued to cross the waters and joined the battle. Another barrage of flaming arrows slammed into the stockade. The Turks launched spears in great numbers. One gunner was hit and fell off the wall. With the smoke and flame unbearable, Duarte and the remaining men leapt off the wall into the throngs of raging Turks. They were immediately cut down with scimitars. Captain Sousa watched his brother decapitated. With rage, he lurched forward, but Fernão held him back. 'Captain,' he said. 'You cannot. They are too many.' Fernão said with reluctance, for he never shirked from battle. 'I will join you in revenge for your brother, but this would be suicide.'

Captain Sousa turned to face Fernão and said with gritted teeth, 'We shall indeed have our vengeance.'

'How do we get back to the city?'

'Come.'

All the men quietly slipped through the reeds along the riverbank which widened as they pushed south. After ten minutes, the captain lifted some palm thatches off a proa.

'Very clever captain,' Fernão said.

The men climbed on board and silently rowed toward Goa.


Later, Fernão and Soussa entered the city and reported to Albuquerque. 'Sir,' Captain Sousa said. 'Benastarim has fallen.'

'How?' Albuquerque asked.

'Nearly 2,000 Turks stormed the fortress. They burned the new stockade.'

'What about your brother?'

Sousa lowered his head, speechless.

'They decapitated Duarte,' Fernão said.

'They will pay for this!' Albuquerque responded, seething with anger.

Suddenly, a large uproar could be heard throughout the city. A soldier came running up to them and spoke while trying to catch his breath, 'Sir, the Turks have broken into the city. The Moors are celebrating their arrival in the market square.'

'All of you, follow me,' Albuquerque said.

They gathered a total of 50 armed men and entered the market square. Upon their arrival, the emboldened Moors dared to attack. Furious upon such insolence, Albuquerque ordered his men, 'Split up and burn the city and put to the sword any Moor you find.'

Fernão and Sousa followed Albuquerque. Rounding a street corner they found Timoja hard pressed in close quarters fending off a squad of Turks. They charged at them with such force that they fled. Timoja and those with him were spared certain death in that moment.

As the battles raged around the island, the Portuguese were pushed back into the city. After tense fighting, 30 Portuguese were killed and many were wounded. About 2,000 enemy insurgents lay dead throughout the streets. The Hidalcão's army was so numerous that is was impossible to defend the city and Albuquerque ordered all his captains and men to retreat to the city fortress. He ordered the captains to take positions upon the stockades for a strategic defense. Albuquerque believed the fortress and their arms would be able to withstand the enemy onslaught until they could receive reinforcements from Cochin. All the captains felt quite the opposite and insisted they should immediately retreat to the ships. They believed the fleet should not be put in risk since it guaranteed the safety of all their Indian possessions. Only his nephew D. Antonio de Noronha and Gaspar de Paiva—the chief alcaide of the fortress, sided with Albuquerque. It was not long until he reluctantly acquiesced to the captains pleas to retreat.

'However, we will not do so in vain,' Albuquerque said. 'Remove all the guns, hamstring the horses in the stables, then cut off the head of the governor and all the spies of the Hidalcão.'

The captains obeyed. They killed 150 of the leading Moor's of the city and proceeded to burn anything useful to the enemy. They also laid out pepper and copper bars to slow their pursuit as the enemy collected the highly-valued items.

Finally, on May 20, Albuquerque was the last to leave and embarked his vessel. He ordered the fleet to sail and they anchored in the middle of the harbor, a strategic position due to its great width and distance from shore. When the Hidalcão was informed of their retreat he sent 400 Turks and 2,000 native warriors, along with artillery, to the fortress of Pangim with orders to harass the Portuguese fleet.

As more Islamic armies approached Goa, the captains anxiously desired to set sail. Fernão had accompanied Captain Noronha on board the flagship for a status report. He walked into a maelstrom of arguments between the pilots and captains on board the *Flor de la Mar*. The pilots argued it was too dangerous to cross the bar in this monsoon season. But the captains would not relent. After incessant bickering, Albuquerque appeased the captains by sending one vessel, the *St. John* for a supply run to Andejiva. They were escorted by Timoja and two of his fustas.

Fernão stood on the main deck, along with Noronha, Albuquerque, and the captains. They watched the ships approaching the bar. Timoja yelled and waved to the captain of the *St. John*, warning that conditions were not acceptable to cross. The captain would not listen and pressed forward. The tide was low, and with hardly any wind to carry them over the bar, the *St. John* grounded and broke into pieces.

Albuquerque addressed the captains, 'We will have to maintain our position here before the bar, until the seasonal weather changes. But we will be exposed to enemy attack.' He turned to Fernão. 'Where the devil is your friend, Serrão! He left in early April for supplies and reinforcements.'

'I do not know sir,' Fernão replied. 'It is unlike him to be late.'

Albuquerque's face reddened. 'I assure you. He will pay dearly for this insubordinate delay.' He then turned and walked away.

Fernão was back on the *Cirne*. His heart raced and a cold sweat ran down his back as the re-armed fortress of Pangim resumed another daily bombardment of artillery upon the fleet. Cannon balls of stone screeched through the air and smashed into the Portuguese vessels. By evening, Fernão had counted 50 large cannon balls pummeling the ships. With the escalation in artillery fire, even the most battle-hardened of the Portuguese could not endure this continued onslaught for much longer.

As the days went by, strict rations were ordered to only four small biscuits per day. The men soon became sick as starvation set in. Fernão watched desperate men catching stray rats and boiling leather skins from their personal chests. They found whatever they could to survive. Fernão poked at his ribs protruding under his skin. He wondered why Francisco had not yet returned from his supply mission which should have arrived by now. Timoja had men on shore as spies, and sent them on errands for fresh water and food, but many were intercepted by the enemy and killed. Two soldiers were so dejected they fled to the Moors and reported the desperate conditions of the crews.

One day, the Hidalcão sent a messenger to verify the account. Fresh provisions from shore including chickens and sheep were sent as gifts to the Portuguese. Perceiving the Hidalcão's intentions to spy out any weakness in their ranks, Albuquerque shrewdly flipped the situation in his favor. He ordered the master of the ship to retrieve some of the supplies that had been reserved for the sick. They cut open a barrel and filled one half with wine. Next they wrapped all the remaining biscuits into a piece of sail and set it next to the wine.

Albuquerque then ordered the crew to escort the Moor on board. The ambassador relayed the Hidalcão's message as followed: The Hidalcão did not wish to fight a dishonorable war against a starving enemy but with sword in hand.

Albuquerque responded that he was not accustomed to accept gifts from enemies in time of war. Furthermore, these gifts of wine and biscuit which I offer the Hidalcão are mere tokens of what we have in our stores which are so plentiful that we do not have enough men on our ships to consume it all. With this stinging rebuttal the messenger was sent off. Word of this clever maneuver spread throughout the ships and the men would never forget it.

With continued artillery bombardments from the fortress of Pangim upon the fleet, Albuquerque's patience wore thin. He called for a meeting of all his captains and proposed an assault upon the fortress at once. Dissentions among the captains arose since many held various opinions contrary to one another. Albuquerque declared that he himself would go fight and if any should wish to join the mission, they would be much welcomed, but those who remained were not obliged to do so. Acknowledging the governor's determination, the captains pledged to unite their forces to oust the enemy.

In the evening, a young sailor fled to join the enemy. Albuquerque assumed the deserter would inform the Hidalcão of their plans and would order reinforcements to the fortress to thwart any attack. Nevertheless, Albuquerque did not waver.

Just before daybreak, on June 14, they launched a multi-pronged raid. The Portuguese caught their enemies asleep and unable to respond in time. The enemy evacuated the fortress—4,000 Turks and Moors. Near the gate, a heavy engagement ensued; 150 Turks, 100 Hindu natives and 3 captains of the Hidalcão were killed. The Portuguese lost a number of fidalgos and leading men in the fleet. They fought valiantly and were subsequently honored by all the men. The goal of disarming the fortress was achieved. They collected all the cannon and munitions, and then carried it off to the ships.

Soon afterward, one of Timoja's men arrived with news from the city. The Hidalcão had built a fleet of 25 vessels. They were an assortment of proas, fustas, and watch-boats, all armed with artillery and many men. Their intention was to burn the Portuguese fleet. Albuquerque sent out a reconnaissance mission of the port, comprised of three galleys under the command of Diogo Fernandez de Béja, to verify if the news of a new fleet was true.

On board the *Cirne*, Captain Antonio de Noronha approached Fernão on the main deck. 'Magalhães,' he said. 'Ready the longboat with a crew of armed men. The governor has ordered all the captains to be ready to assist the galleys.'

'Yes sir,' Fernão said, then departed to his task.

The bend in the river made it impossible for the Portuguese to monitor the advance of their own galleys nor any advances of the enemy fleet. Therefore, Albuquerque ordered a watch-boat positioned midway between. Captain Noronha and Fernão were in their longboat waiting. All the captains had a boat in the water at the ready and tied off to their ships. The watch-boat signaled to Noronha that the Turks were launching their fleet. Noronha yelled to his crew and to all the other boats at the ready, 'Row! Row!'

The men rowed with all their strength. As the tide was full, they soon caught up to the galleys. Now, in sight of the oncoming Turkish fleet, Noronha yelled, 'Attack their watch-boats!'

The galleys rowed hard. Once in range, they fired their artillery at the watch-boats. A large cannon on the prow of Fernandez' galley fired a 32-pound stone ball. It struck both watch-boats with one blow and shattered them. All the Turks were killed, either by the blast or drowning.

Fernão saw the blast from afar, but as they drew near the galleys, he witnessed first-hand the carnage inflicted upon the enemy lead boats. All had been blown to pieces. The remainder of the Turk's fleet retreated to the port and prepared for a defense. The Portuguese boats approached the port and the galleys fired heavy ordnance, killing many and forcing them further back. Noronha's boat rowed close to a *galeota* tied to the dock. It appeared to be in the final construction phase, but still navigable.

'Magalhães,' Noronha said. 'Nobody is on board that ship. Let us take it as a prize for my uncle.'

Noronha's boat came alongside the *galeota* and the crew boarded. They began preparing to take it out into the harbor. The Turks spotted their activity and noticed the other Portuguese vessels were some distance offshore. They rushed toward the *galeota*.

'We have company sir,' Fernão said.

'Let them come,' Noronha replied. 'We shall have this prize.'

The Turks surrounded the *galeota* and fired off barrages of arrows. Noronha was struck in the knee by an arrow. Soon, Fernão and all the crew were fighting in close quarters, their black swords stabbing and cutting, and clanking against scimitars and daggers. It was a lengthy engagement. In the end, three captains of the Hidalcão were killed. The Portuguese suffered many wounded. The Turks sent for reinforcements. The Portuguese struggled in vain to free the *galeota*, but too many of them were wounded making the task impossible. Noronha could not stand on his leg. The arrow was lodged in a way that caused him much pain.

'Sir,' Fernão said. 'We should leave. The Turks will return shortly in greater numbers. We are in no condition to man this vessel.'

Noronha winced in pain as he stared off toward the city. The Turks were returning in massive numbers. 'It is a shame we had no support from our own. They should have come to our aid.'

'I agree sir, but we should depart while we can.'

Noronha nodded. Fernão took his commander's arm around his shoulder to walk him to the ship rails.

They clambered onto their boat and joined the others as they rowed back to the fleet.

'Shall we come alongside the governor's ship?' Fernão asked.

'No,' Noronha said, as he writhed in pain. 'Bring me to mine.'

Fernão understood that he did not wish to be seen by his uncle in such a feeble state.

Upon hearing of the news of his nephew, Albuquerque took off on a skiff and then boarded the *Cirne*. In the captain's cabin, he found Fernão and a doctor watching over Noronha. The governor knelt and placed his hand upon his nephew's sweaty forehead. Noronha was conscious but groaning. Albuquerque arose and turned to the ship surgeon and asked, 'What can be done?'

'I recommend amputation of the leg,' he replied.

'Never, never,' Noronha said in a weakened voice. 'It is not that serious a matter to need such a drastic procedure. It will heal in time.'

The surgeon shook his head in disagreement.

Fernão remembered his own leg injury and it had healed. Perhaps Noronha was right.

For eight days, Albuquerque's nephew suffered a spreading infection and inflammation. At last, his body gave out, and the young Captain Antonio de Noronha succumbed to his wounds. He was only 24 years of age. Fernão and the doctor were near the body in the captain's cabin when the governor entered. Albuquerque knelt before his nephew and wept.

Fernão and all the men respected Albuquerque's nephew as a hero. They were aware the governor would dearly miss his most trusted confident, advisor, and loyal commander of men and vessels. Antonio de Noronha was recognized as a noble warrior who feared God, as did his uncle. Later, Albuquerque gave orders to bury his nephew ashore at the foot of a large tree.

After the fortress of Pangim was overthrown, the Hidalcão continued his appeals to make peace. But, Albuquerque had become disgusted by the constant lies and harassments from the Hidalcão's agents, for among the messengers were Portuguese traitors who had deserted the fleet and converted to Islam. They were dressed in fine clothes and would prance across the shoreline upon their horses while yelling rude and disparging accusations against the commanders, and all the while seducing the crews with beguiling words to desert. They promised excellent wages, liberation from their squalid conditions of hunger and a blissful content life—but only for those who joined the Islamic confederation.

One day, the Hidalcão sent two Turk messengers along with a Portuguese traitor named, João Deíras, originally a Gallician and one of their former ship surgeons. Albuquerque had enough of these brazen taunts and enticements, always with intentions to ensnare his weary men. He gave orders for Pero Dalpoem to bring his expert marksman on shore. They were to shoot any traitorous fool who dared to approach them.

Fernão observed what had become a customary ritual from the main deck rails on board the *Cirne*. João Deíras rode his finely caparisoned horse toward the shoreline. His servants accompanied him. The scene was orchestrated to demonstrate his high-ranking status. The former Portuguese ship surgeon bellowed out disrespectful and haughty words against the governor while seducing men to desert, all the while prancing his horse to and fro across the shore. Meanwhile, Officer Pero Dalpoem had landed their skiff on the beach and observed.

After witnessing the rude taunts, Dalpoem had enough. He ordered João Dílhanes, his bombardier, to shoot Deíras and promised that he would not be held responsible. The marksman dropped to one knee behind the skiff, raised his arquebus, sighted upon the mutinous traitor, and fired off a round. The precise shot struck João Deíras in the chest. He fell off his horse and landed on the ground with a thud. The Turks rushed over to check the body of Deíras and confirmed that he was dead. They were aghast at such an affront. But Pero Dalpoem assured them he was condemned as a deserter by the king of Portugal and sentenced to death. Furthermore, he warned to never bring forward any more men like this, for they would also be executed as they have just witnessed. The Turks feigned an apology, unwilling to suffer the same demise as their messenger. Pero Dalpoem replied there would be no more of these worthless visits and then departed in their skiff to report back to Albuquerque.

In the meantime, the Hidalcão continued his attacks by land and sea while the Portuguese ran out of supplies and had to enforce even stricter rationing. Men deserted and captains bickered to the point of mutiny. Sensing a moment of weakness and subsequent capitulation, the Hidalcão once more offered terms of peace. Knowing Albuquerque was reluctant to entertain anymore entreaties, the Hidalcão decided to send one of his chief captains— Mostafação, for negotiations. After the usual offers in the presence of the Portuguese command, the captain whispered in Albuquerque's ear a proposal that the Turks would surrender Goa if he would give up Timoja to the Hidalcão.

Albuquerque fumed with rage upon such a blatant assumption that he would betray the long-time ally of Portugal. He said to Mostafação that Goa was a possession of King Dom Manuel and promised he would return soon to take his seat in the palace of Goa. Furthermore, he planned to make Timoja a great lord in the kingdom of the Deccan. Albuquerque then sent the captain on his way with his final answer.

The Portuguese continued to endure starvation and sickness. They sent a few covert scouting missions on shore and were able to attain enough to survive until the weather changed.

On August 16, a heavy rain poured down upon the Portuguese fleet as they finally crossed the bar out of the harbor of Goa. After a grueling six-month long war campaign, the gaunt and feeble crews manned the sails as best they could. Fernão stared blankly out to sea as he stood upon the quarterdeck feeling empty and alone, reflecting on what had transpired and wondering what may lie ahead.

# 10

## *Cochin – October 10, 1510*

Fernão entered the gate of Fort Manuel and presented a guard with a document. The guard looked it over then pointed toward a path running along the perimeter wall. Fernão nodded and proceeded along the path until he reached a dark stairway. He climbed down three levels. A guard stood in front of a dark corridor. Fernão once again presented his document. The guard read it over, grabbed a torch from the wall, and signaled for Fernão to follow. Rats scurried about the shadows.

'The governor was quite displeased with this prisoner,' the guard said. 'He ordered us to work him over good.'

They passed several prison cells and arrived in front of one marked number five.

The guard turned and grinned, revealing his set of rotten teeth and gums. 'No matter how much pain we inflicted, the prisoner insisted he was innocent.' The guard chuckled. 'But don't they all?' He fumbled through his set of keys until he retrieved one marked five and inserted it into the steel keyhole. The door creaked as the guard shoved it open.

In the shadows, on the dingy floor and with his back against the wall sat Francisco, disheveled and thin. He squinted his eyes and noticed Fernão and the guard enter. As Fernão drew closer, a putrid stench made him almost vomit. He covered his mouth and nose with one arm. 'You smell foul. Smells like piss, or something worse.'

'I will bet I feel worse than I smell,' Francisco replied with a raspy voice. Here to rescue me once again, I see.' He rose to one knee but was too feeble to stand. Fernão assisted him to his feet.

Francisco held up his two iron-bound arms and grinned at the guard. 'Mind opening these?' The guard retrieved another key and opened the irons. Francisco rubbed his wrists covered with purple-colored bruise marks. 'Damn Albuquerque!' He kicked a dish of mushy soup into the wall which sent several cockroaches into the shadows.

'What happened?' Fernão asked, wishing to hear Francisco's account.

'As you know, Albuquerque sent me from Goa to fetch supplies in Cochin, way back in April. But when we arrived here, the old vessel was unseaworthy. By the time it was refurbished, the monsoons set in, and the weather had turned too foul to sail.'

'How long have you been here?'

'Well, once the governor arrived with the fleet to Cannanore, a month ago, he sent a messenger to Cochin with orders for my arrest. Albuquerque did not even wait to hear my own account. I am innocent of the charges of insubordination.'

The guard rolled his eyes and muttered, 'Whatever.'

They exited the cell, turned down the corridor, and up the stairs.

'So, how is it that I am released?' Francisco asked as he climbed the last step which emerged back onto the path along the fortress wall.

'Your brother,' Fernão replied.

'My brother?'

'Yes. João's ship arrived with some others in Cannanore and accompanied us to Cochin. Once he was informed of your situation, he immediately questioned the shipbuilders to verify your claims of innocence. It turns out, your brother pestered

143

Albuquerque until he acquiesced, and agreed to listen to the testimonies of the workers repairing the vessel. You were vindicated and Albuquerque apologized to your brother for the error.'

'You think he will apologize to me with full pomp and ceremony?' Francisco said sarcastically.

'So, your first captaincy was a success.' Fernão chuckled.

'Very funny.'

'As you know, Albuquerque may be quick to punish, but he often forgives. I expect you will soon have another chance to captain a vessel.'

'We shall see about that, shall we?'

Fernão signed for the release of Francisco and the two exited the fort.

'I am supposed to attend a council,' Fernão said. 'Albuquerque summoned a meeting of our naval and merchant captains along with the leading officials of Cochin.'

'You expect he wants to persuade the merchant captains to join another assault on Goa?'

'Not a good time for that,' Fernão replied. 'The monsoon headwinds will not give us enough time to take Goa, much less prepare the cargo vessels bound for Lisbon.'

The two walked to the barracks. Francisco stared at his bed. 'I have thought every night about sleeping in a real bed.' He rubbed his belly. 'And some food.' He sniffed his arm. 'And a bath.'

'I will catch up to you later,' Francisco said. 'I expect Albuquerque still may be sore that he had to admit his error in judgment on my case and may not wish my presence today.'

'Yes. Maybe best to avoid him for now.'

'Give greetings to my brother. I will meet him after the meeting.'

Fernão stood at the gate and nodded to the captains and officials of Cochin as they entered the fortress. He grinned as Captain João Serrão ambled up the hillside toward the gate. 'Fernão Magalhaes,' Serrão said. 'It has been many years has it not?'

'Four and a half, sir,' Fernão replied.

'That is right, Cannanore. I remember you took a hit from the enemy . . . did not look well. Francisco told me you also took a serious wound in the battle of Diu, almost died.' Captain Serrão put his arm on Fernão's shoulder as they walked into the fortress. 'The devil seeks to destroy, but the Lord heals.'

'You know, I have always had divine grace in my life,' Fernão confided. 'I have never been sick with anything other than a slight cold and always blessed with recuperative powers, even from the most grievous of injuries.'

Serrão nodded and then the two filed into a chamber with the captains, leading merchants, and officials of Cochin. All gathered around the chamber in a semicircle, two rows deep. In front of them stood Albuquerque—governor, viceroy and captain-general of the Indies. Fernão and Serrão stood in the front row, on the far left.

Albuquerque cleared his throat. 'Gentlemen, I have convened this council for your opinion concerning a second raid on Goa. It is not my intention to act rashly or seek retribution based on our last endeavor, but only in concern for the service of our king. As you are all aware, Goa is a strategic harbor and once we take it, we control all trade in the entire region of the Deccan. I am certain that the region will crumble after we subjugate Goa, for the land has many provinces under many captains—

mostly Turks and Persians who are in constant war with one another.'

Albuquerque paced back and forth as he continued. 'We must take Goa, for if the enemy takes control, they will harass our vessels when they stop to port for supplies in nearby Anjediva. The alliance between the Hidalcão, kings of Cambay and the Zamorin of Calicut will only strengthen if they are able to summon assistance from the Grand Sultan of Cairo. This cannot occur, for it will endanger our entire Indian enterprise.' Albuquerque then halted his pacing and spoke again from center stage. 'Opinions? Suggestions?'

'And what if we proceed with our entire fleet, so distant from our base?' A captain in the back row asked. 'Will it not endanger our possessions here? Will not the Zamorin take advantage and seize Cochin?'

'I hear your words,' Albuquerque said. 'We shall leave an adequate garrison for defense. And I do not plan a lengthy stay this time.' He paced the floor and then clenched his fists. 'In this moment, we have a powerful and mighty fleet, all gathered in one place. Now is the time to strike!'

Captain Sequeira looked around the room and nodded at some other captains. Sensing their backing, he put forward his proposal: 'We hear your words, but many of the merchant fleet have been preparing to return with our cargo to Lisbon. Would it not be reasonable to allow those dedicated vessels to continue their mission? For that is why they have come to India.'

Many captains voiced their favor of this suggestion. One captain bellowed out, 'The season is too short to allow the merchant fleet to join.'

Captain Sequeira nodded in agreement, and further incited the merchant captains and businessmen of the city to oppose the proposed measure, causing dissentions to echo across the chamber.

João Serrão turned his head to Fernão and winked. He addressed the men, 'Perhaps we should hear the opinion from Fernão Magalhães, one of our best navigators?' Serrão lightly elbowed Fernão in the side.

Albuquerque nodded his assent.

Fernão took one step forward and turned to face everyone. 'It is a noble proposal to take Goa,' he said. 'But our merchant fleet should continue with their plans. The monsoon headwinds will not allow our cargo vessels to arrive to Goa before early November. Any such delay will not allow our vessels to make repairs, complete transactions, load cargo and sail this year to Lisbon.'

The council spokesmen and merchant captains immediately seized this advice and clamored for Albuquerque to permit the cargo fleets to proceed to Lisbon.

Although, flustered by their stubborn objections, Albuquerque responded calmly. 'I will not force any to accompany the mission against their will. That will be all.' He waved his arm at them.

As they departed, Fernão suddenly felt uncomfortable. When he looked back at the room, Albuquerque was staring at him. He appeared angry.

Fernão recovered from his ordeal, and soon he and Francisco were again at the dockyard, loading supplies as the war fleet bound for Goa set sail. The war fleet consisted of 28 ships, and 1,700 Portuguese soldiers accompanied by 300 Malabar fighters. Fernão expected he would soon hear of the armada's heroic exploits. He was content to remain in Cochin as a reservist, to defend the outpost, and to secure the rewards for his five years of service to the crown.

Meanwhile, mariners struggled to hoist an elephant onto one of the cargo vessels bound for Lisbon. 'More gifts to the king I see,' Francisco said.

'Third one today,' Fernão replied. 'Hopefully, the cargo sails for home on time.'

'You secure your contract with Abraldez?' Francisco asked.

'Yes. A nice arrangement. I loaned him 100 cruzados to purchase pepper with 10 percent yearly interest.'

'Sounds good.'

'Well, that is not all. We also bypassed the 10 percent usury law.'

'What is that?' Francisco asked. 'On top of the initial deal?'

'A 140 percent profit plus 500 percent gains when the pepper sells,' Fernão replied.

'Well done my friend,' Francisco said. 'I also need to secure some trades before departure.'

The war fleet anchored in Onor (Honavar) to take on fresh supplies and water. Timoja was in the city for his wedding to the king of Garsopa's daughter. With news of the fleet's arrival, Timoja and the king hurried to the port to speak with Albuquerque. They informed him that Goa's defense was minimal; 3 captains commanded 4,000 troops—Turks, Rûmes, Coraçones and a contingent of native archers. The Hidalcão was engaged in a war far into the interior and would not be able to arrive in time to reinforce Goa. They pressed him to act with haste on such a timely opportunity and pledged their assistance. Albuquerque proceeded with caution, always skeptical of any alliance with privateers, or unproven foreign alliances. But Timoja had proven reliable in the past which made him more willing to proceed with their plan.

On November 25, 1510, the allied fleet anchored in the harbor of Goa. The Portuguese stormed the city and attacked, pushing the enemy back to the fortress gates. But there, the defenders rallied, and an intense battle ebbed back and forth. Finally, the Portuguese pushed through the gates. An infantry officer, Manuel de Lacerda, was hit in the face by an arrow, but continued to fight on. Upon entering the gate, a mounted Turk charged at him, but Lacerda slipped the blow and struck him dead. He then mounted the horse and charged ahead, breaking off the arrow shaft. Blood streamed from his face and stained his armor red.

The Turks rallied with a squad of 500, and of these 100 were cavalry. The Portuguese were hard-pressed, until Albuquerque led his men in a furious charge against the enemy with their lances, wreaking havoc on horses and men alike. Two of the three captains of the Hidalcão were killed, and the remaining Turks cut down or routed. Manuel de Lacerda rode up toward Albuquerque, dismounted the finely caparisoned Turkish horse and presented it to him.

Taking notice of the arrow stub lodged in his face and his blood-stained armor, Albuquerque embraced him and remarked: 'Manuel de Lacerdo, I declare to you that I am greatly envious of you, and so would Alexander the Great have been, had he been here, for you look more gallant for an evening's rendezvous than the Emperor Aurelian.' Albuquerque mounted the horse he was given by Lacerdo and ordered the troops to likewise commandeer the horses left behind by the fleeing Turks. He told them to press ahead with their victory. In the end, the Portuguese suffered 40 dead and 150 wounded.

Once the city had been subdued and fortified, Albuquerque wrote to the king on December 22, 1510:

> The letter I wrote to your Majesty about the capture of Goa was dispatched the same afternoon, as I determined to send a ship to Cannanore to overtake the vessels of which were loading there; and instruct them to call here on their way in order to show the natives how great was the power of your Majesty's fleet. In the capture of Goa, the Turks lost over 300 men, and the road between Banastery Gomdaly was covered with the bodies of those who were wounded and died in their attempt to escape. Many were also drowned while crossing the river. I afterwards burnt the city in which for four days the carnage was fearful, as no quarter was to be given to anyone. The agricultural laborers and the Brahmins were spared, but of the Moors killed the number was at least 6,000. It was indeed a great deed, and well carried out. Some of the principle natives, from whom the Turks had taken their territories, becoming aware that Goa had been captured, came to my assistance, and by taking possession of all the roads leading from the city, cut off all escape for the enemy, and put them all to the sword, giving no quarter. My determination now is to prevent any Moor entering or leaving Goa, to leave an adequate force of men and ships in the place, then with another fleet visit the Red Sea and Ormuz. The ships which the Moors were building are being

completed and launched. I have plenty of iron and nails, and a great number of carpenters, artisans, and laborers, so that any number of vessels your Majesty may desire can be built here. We captured several Moorish women, whom I have married to several men who are desirous of settling here . . . the capture of Goa alone worked more to the credit of your Majesty than 15 years-worth of armadas that were sent out to India.

Fernão was surprised when Albuquerque returned with his fleet to Cochin, since they were supposed to continue onward and initiate operations in the Red Sea. Albuquerque immediately summoned all his fleet captains to a meeting. He also requested that any mariner who served in the previous expedition to Malacca to make an appearance. Francisco and Fernão were on that mission and so made their way to the fortress. Once all had gathered in the inner chamber, Albuquerque heard the testimonies of those who had been to Malacca and discussed strategy with the officers.

On the following morning, in an open courtyard, Albuquerque stood on a wood platform and addressed the entire fleet, 'For those of you who have not heard of the events which transpired in our last mission, I will briefly recount. We conquered Goa and thus have won a strategic stronghold for the crown. Once our adversaries received news of our victory, they sent their ambassadors. The kings of Cambay and Narsinga, even the Zamorin, have all pledged to pursue new alliances and peace. Furthermore, Miroçem, captain of the fleet for the Grand Sultan has suspended operations against us. We have achieved a worthy goal.'

The men cheered and clanked their weapons together.

Francisco leaned toward Fernão's ear and said, 'A great victory. But will he admit the cargo fleets would never have made it to Lisbon, if instead they had accompanied him?'

'I doubt that very much,' Fernão replied with a grin.

Albuquerque continued, 'After Goa was fortified, we proceeded toward Aden, upon the king's desire to establish a fortress there. Unfortunately, heavy weather at the shoals of Padua forced us to turn back and remain in Goa.'

Fernão said to Francisco, 'We all know about the shoals of Padua.' The two chuckled.

Albuquerque turned his head down in a moment of brevity. He then raised his head again and continued, 'I have disclosed the following only to a few select captains. As you know, the king of Malacca and his Bendahara have betrayed our good will when they ambushed our expedition under Captain Sequeira. They took 19 prisoners including Ruy de Araujo. In Goa, I received a letter from Ruy, which was smuggled aboard a trading junk from Malacca. He informs us all 19 are alive. But they have been under confinement under the greatest abuse, unspeakable tortures, with intent to break their faith and become Moors. The king is a tyrant. He robs and harasses many of the merchants who dare port in his city. It has been said this king has a great army and fleet, a formidable force.'

Albuquerque looked over his men until the story sunk in and the rage built behind their eyes. 'Gentlemen, I have set my mind to sail to Malacca and demand our men be freed and paid in high recompense for our cargos stolen. If they shall not

152

comply, a righteous and holy retribution shall be unleashed! I, Albuquerque vow to make them pay, in submission or in blood!' Are you with me?'

The men cheered in support. Fernão turned to Francisco. 'Ready for some payback?'

'Absolutely,' Francisco replied. 'This is one mission I will not pass up.'

The fleet set out for Malacca with 18 ships, 3 of which were galleys. The armada sailed east, carrying 700 Portuguese and 300 Malabar fighters. Passing Ceylon, a storm arose, and one of the galleys was lost. Captain Simão Martinz had not been informed of the heavy load of copper aboard his vessel and the power of the storm caused a leak to spring at the prow, causing the vessel to founder and sink. Fortunately, the entire crew were rescued by Duarte da Silva's galley. Anchoring in Pedir, Sumatra the fleet found João Viegas and eight of those who had been imprisoned with Ruy de Araujo. All the 19 prisoners had attempted to escape but only these 9 were able to evade capture. Viegas informed them how the king of Malacca had tortured them so they would renounce their faith. Several of their company had their hands and feet bound and without any anesthetics, were forcibly circumcised. One died from severe blood loss.

João further relayed that the King of Pacem was harboring a certain leading Moor from the city of Malacca, named Naodabegea, who had been the chief instigator in the ambush of Captain Sequeira's fleet. Albuquerque let all this information circulate among the crews, knowing the news would embolden his men.

The armada anchored in the nearby port of Pacem (Pasai), Sumatra. Albuquerque requested the king deliver to him the Moor who had been implicated in the murder of their Portuguese comrades. The king said he had heard of such a man in his city but was unaware of his whereabouts. He promised to make a search. After some time, the king announced the Moor must have fled. Albuquerque sensed the king was not forthright and most likely in league with the scoundrel, and so left Pacem in haste.

It was not long before they caught sight of a *pangajaoa*, a long oar-driven vessel capable of good speed. Captain Aires Pereira was in the *taforea* and closest to the vessel. Albuquerque ordered them to give chase. Captain Pereira and his men launched their longboat. They rowed hard until they drew near their target and came alongside. The Moors took up their arms and would not allow the Portuguese to board their boat. In the fighting, Captain Aires Pereira and several men received wounds, but gave as good as they got. Pereira leaped into the Portuguese boat and fought with fury. The Moor captain was gashed with many deep cuts but continued to trade blows with Captain Pereira. Eventually, the Moor captain was overpowered and knocked unconscious.

The Portuguese leaped into the pangajaoa and anyone else who dared resist was quickly put to the sword. Eight Moor prisoners were tied up. When they returned to their longboat, they found the Moor captain slumped over, nearly dead. Captain Pereira ordered the men throw him into the sea even though he was still alive. But as the men took notice of his fine clothing, they decided first to strip him down. An ornate bracelet of bone set in gold was found on his wrist. When they took it off, blood poured from his wounds, and he died. Pereira was astonished by this and took the bracelet along with the captive Moors to Albuquerque. The governor asked the Moors who this captain was, and what use was this bracelet to him. They replied this was Naodabegea, a leading Moor from Malacca. He was on his way to warn the king of Malacca of the Portuguese fleet. The bracelet was made from the bones from animals called *cabals*. They live in the mountain ranges of Siam. It was said that those who wear the bracelet tight to the flesh shall never lose any blood no matter how many wounds they may receive. But if the bone material is removed from the flesh, the blood will once again flow out. Albuquerque was so impressed by this unique object that he kept it as a gift for King Manuel.

# 11

## *Malacca – June 1, 1511*

Toward evening, Albuquerque's fleet of 17 black-pitched Portuguese ships entered the harbor with flags raised. Before anchoring, they sounded the trumpets and fired off a salute of artillery. Fernao and Francisco watched from the deck of Captain Abreau's carrack, where they were stationed as navigational officers. Little did they know their upcoming actions would reverberate down the annals of history for all time.

'I expect we will have to wait on the ship awhile,' Fernão said. 'Albuquerque will try to persuade the sultan to acquiesce and release our men without any bloodshed.'

'Albuquerque will play nice at first,' Francisco added. 'But once our men are back in our fleet, well, I would not want to be the king.'

As the days unfolded, Captain Abreau briefed his leading officers, including Magalhães and Serrão, on the status of each message sent between Albuquerque and the Sultan of Malacca—Mahmud Shah. The first message from the sultan was to make peace. He also claimed that the Bendahara had been put to death for inciting the ambush and murder of the Portuguese soldiers under Captain Sequeira's prior visit. The sultan insisted it was not his own fault concerning these events. Albuquerque feigned belief in the crafty sultan's apology. He calmly demanded the release of the prisoners and recompense to be paid from the Bendahara's estate for the seized cargo. The sultan replied they must make peace before any such

156

bargains could be made. He then delayed any efforts to release the prisoners.

Albuquerque had initially distrusted Ruy de Araujo regarding the conspiracies surrounding his transition to power as the governor and viceroy of the Indies. However, he now had come to the realization the Portuguese agent was indeed a loyal officer and must be rescued at all costs along with his men. Even while imprisoned in Malacca, Ruy de Araujo continued his covert work by relaying smuggled messages. He informed the governor with intelligence that the sultan was constructing new stockades of formidable strength along the seaboard.

Receiving this news, Albuquerque sent a message to the sultan stating that it did not look like any sort of friendship was intended, for no prisoners were returned, and stockades were erected as if they were to commence a war.

The sultan continued to refuse any prisoners until a peace arrangement was sealed. Albuquerque finally had enough, and sent out four armed boats to reconnoiter and test the enemy responses. As soon as the patrol boats left, the ships of the Moors responded by sending out a fleet of 20 *pangajaoas* past the river's mouth to meet them. Albuquerque sent another four boats to support the others, from which the Moors retreated. The sultan again sent his customary response. Albuquerque received the message but knew it was full of lies and deceit.

Ruy de Araujo sent another message to Albuquerque stating how the sultan was nearing completion of his defenses and ready for war. In addition, the Turks, Rûmes, Gujaratis, and Coraçones were offering bribes to the sultan and governors in order to halt any formal deals allowing access to their trade markets. Even the Islamic priests were employed to preach lengthy diatribes against the Portuguese. The leader of the Gujaratis—Xabandar, stressed the importance to stall until the monsoon season arrived, for the Portuguese would of necessity have to depart. The sultan heeded the advice and made haste to complete the remaining fortifications.

Albuquerque's patience had been longsuffering, but now it wore out. He sent another message informing the sultan that he had news of what really had transpired. The Bendahara was sentenced to death for plotting an uprising and not for anything to do with the Portuguese. Furthermore, the sultan had ordered the Christians tortured in order to force them to renounce their faith. Some had been abused so bad they capitulated and feigned conversion. He had put up with such talk, and delays, in hope that a peace and friendship could still occur. But, since no serious attempt to complete a truce was put forth, he would have him know that none of his men would remain, day by day, in this port without having wreaked vengeance for the treason inflicted upon the captain and soldiers of the king of Portugal, all ordered by the Sultan of Malacca.

Albuquerque then convened a meeting with his captains and desired their opinions. They all thought it was not right for him to have such patience toward the Sultan of Malacca, for since their arrival no intentions of goodwill had been indicated. Furthermore, all the delays were simply ruses to fortify and prepare for war. With all in agreement, the captains and Albuquerque prepared a final signed document to be delivered with the following message:

> King D. Manuel, his lord, had sent to the port of Malacca a captain, with certain ships, which came bearing more of merchandise than of our

men, out of a desire which he had of establishing peace and friendship with him; but, in violation of the safeguard which both the sultan and his Bendahara had granted to this captain, they had notwithstanding stolen all the property and murdered or imprisoned the Portuguese—as had already been the subject of complaint—and labored as much as they possibly could to seize his ships, but miraculously our Lord had delivered them from their hands. The Sultan of Malacca should therefore know for certain that unless orders were issued for the immediate release of the Christians and restitution of the property which had been captured in the ships, that he (Afonso Albuquerque) would certainly destroy him, and take his city away from him, and he held God to be the judge between them and he and his governors were the cause of their own destruction; for, by following the advice of the Gujaratis—deadly enemies to the Portuguese—he (the Sultan of Malacca) would not take any steps towards concluding terms of peace with him. As for the present fleet which he had now with him, it had no thoughts about the monsoon—as the Gujaratis had pretended to the sultan—neither was it losing any season of voyage; nor was it searching for a cargo; for the ships of which it was composed belonged to the fleet which the King of Portugal employed for the government of India, and it was of no consequences to them whether they remained one year or ten in that harbor; and the Sultan of Malacca should rest quite sure that unless he gave up all thoughts of prosecuting a war which he wished to make upon the captains and men of the

King of Portugal; he would very soon lose his estate.

In the presence of the sultan's messenger, Albuquerque signed the document. With disregard to the governor's message, the sultan continued for six days with stall tactics and false pledges. Albuquerque was incensed and sent ten boats to burn several buildings along the waterfront and all the Gujarati ships they could find. Realizing Albuquerque would not be deterred, and running out of options to stall, the sultan released all the prisoners and asked the Portuguese for a list of any complaints to be written down. Albuquerque countered. He upped the ante by demanding a site within the city to erect a fortress, as well as a steep recompense for the goods stolen from Sequeira's expedition. The sultan fell back to his delay tactics, sending out spies and raising flags of war upon the stockades.

Meanwhile, the captains from five Chinese junks in port visited Albuquerque to offer their support in waging a war against the sultan; for their vessels had been held captive for days and were to be incorporated into the Malaccan fleet in a war against the kingdom of Aru. The Chinese merchants were indignant that the sultan had confiscated all their merchandise and acted as a ruthless tyrant. Albuquerque thanked them very much for their offer and only agreed to accept the *barcas* of their junks to be used to disembark their soldiers. The Chinese asked that if their services were not required they could be allowed to depart to their lands. They promised that any Portuguese vessels encountered in the future would be remembered with respect for the kindness shown to them, and if Malacca should fall into his power they would send 100 junks per year full of merchandise to trade. Before departing, they warned Albuquerque that the city had over 20,000 soldiers—Javanese, Persians, and Coraçones, all with great martial skills. The sultan had additional reserves of native warriors, 20 armored war elephants and massive stores of artillery. The Chinese doubted any army could conquer this city and feared for the outcome.

Albuquerque again thanked them for their concern but said he was already determined to undertake the mission, and the size of Malacca's army was inconsequential, for God's power was greater than man's. He suggested they stay and behold the mighty display of the Portuguese fighting spirit and tactics of war, then report to the king of China all that occured. They accepted his offer to watch the battle from one of the Portuguese galleys he would station for them near the disembarkation point.

As soon as the Chinese left, Albuquerque called all the captains, fidalgos, and leading officers to a meeting. He set forth the arguments for establishing a fortress since Malacca was one of the greatest trade ports in all the world, a link between the far east and India. In addition, the Malays would always harass and capture Portuguese vessels, unless they were sailing in a large fleet armed with numerous men and heavy artillery. They debated among themselves until they reached a conclusion; they agreed that establishing a fort would further the crown's interests, and waging a war upon the city must require a severe punishment upon the sultan for his tyranny and stamp out his haughty pride.

But over the following days, the captains began to differ on the strategy of attack, thus forcing Albuquerque to make the decision. Ruy de Araujo was consulted for his opinion since he had some knowledge of the land. He proposed they attack the bridge first and thus would divide the city in two. The sultan could not easily reinforce the other side if they held the bridge with a well-armed squadron. Albuquerque agreed, and ordered the attack to commence two hours before dawn, in the early morning of Santiago Day. The forces would be split into two battallions. The first unit was to take the mosque and palace on the west side. The second unit, led by Albuquerque, would take the city on the east side.

Before dawn on the morning of the attack, Fernão stood on deck watching the moon over the city. A man of middle height, shoulder length blonde hair, blue eyes, and an aquiline nose drew near—Captain Abreau.

'I expect the trumpets will sound any minute,' Abreau said. 'As part of Albuquerque's squadron, our plan is to overpower the stockades from the city side. Ready for victory, Magalhães?'

'Always ready for victory sir,' Fernão responded with a grin.

'That's the right answer.' Abreau smiled.

'If I may ask, why did Albuquerque wait to attack on the Day of Santiago?'

Abreau looked at him. 'He is a knight of the order and very devoted to this saint. You served under him in Goa, did you not?'

'I fought in the first raid.'

'I see,' Abreau said, looking out over the water. 'Perhaps you never heard what occured in the second raid, the conquest of Goa.'

Fernão shrugged his shoulders. 'Not sure what you mean.'

162

'Well, Albuquerque ordered a demolition project on some old walls. The stones were to be used for reconstruction of the defenses. Behind one of the walls a cross was discovered, all made of copper. News of this spread all over the city. When Albuquerque was informed, he summoned all the priests and those with him to see for themselves. They carried the cross with great devotion and shed tears as they made a procession to the church. After many inquiries of the citizens nobody could remember any Christians to have ever visited this city.'

'A miraculous sign!' Fernão said.

'Indeed. After that, Albuquerque and all those with him believed with all their hearts they would overcome, regardless if they faced an enemy countless in number and armed with heavy artillery. Once Goa was conquered, the mosques would be turned into houses of prayer and dedicated unto the Lord.' Abreau clasped his hands together behind his back and smiled. 'You know, many believed it was Santiago who came to their aid. After Goa was taken a number of Moors inquired who was the captain with shining armor and a red cross. They wanted to know who marched with the Christians, striking down the Moors, for he alone had taken their city from them.'

Fernão turned toward Abreau with eyes wide open. 'Incredible! Then we fight on a good day. The Day of Santiago.'

'Yes we do. Let us persevere until victory is complete.'

'Aye,' Fernão said.

Suddenly, the trumpets blared from the ships to wake the crews. Francisco approached Fernão on deck while rubbing his eyes. 'The one day I would like to sleep a little longer.'

'Yes, but duty never sleeps in, my friend,' Fernão chuckled.

'To the boats men!' Captain Abreau yelled, 'To the boats!'

Crews scrambled to fetch their personal gear and weapons and then climbed down the ropes to the boats waiting below. Both the Portuguese longboats and the borrowed Chinese barcas were boarded in disciplined order. The armada of landing craft untied from the Portuguese ships and the merchant junks, then all tied up to Albuquerque's flagship, the *Flor de la Mar*. Once a general confession was made on board, the boats proceeded toward shore en masse, all converging toward the bridge at the mouth of the river.

At sunrise, they disembarked their craft. Men flung down planks over the sandy beach to protect themselves from the hidden traps of sharp four-pointed steel caltops and gunpowder mines. The Moors unleashed their cannons from the stockades. The artillery was aimed too high and sent screeching iron balls over the Portuguese as they gathered on shore. Marksmen from the enemy stockades fired their matchlocks and wounded several men. Once the volley of artillery was spent, Albuquerque ordered the trumpets sounded and with a war cry of 'Santiago,' they charged the bridge stockades, each squadron to their assigned side. Moors rushed forward to defend with their lancemen and archers. Captain Abreau led his contingent in a spirited charge; Fernão and Francisco guarded his flank side. All were clad with breastplates and steel helmets. The Moors unleashed a barrage of arrows from the stockades while others rushed forward with long lances and shields. The battle raged hard with both sides taking losses.

Meanwhile, the squadron which disembarked on the mosque side of the bridge forged their way into the stockades and routed the Moors. Moments later, the sultan showed up upon his war elephant and his son upon another. The sultan's brigade of 20 elephants were equipped with wooden castles and accompanied by a large body of warriors. The sultan compelled the Moors who fled to return to their stations in the stockades. When D. João de Lima, Fernão Perez Dandrade, and those in their squadron saw the sultan, their rage erupted.

'Remember what they did to Ruy and the others,' Lima said.

'They will pay in blood,' Dandrande replied.

Demonstrating no fear of the war elephants, the squadron forcefully crushed the Moor advance party and took control of the mosque.

A large contingent of the sultan's forces had converged to reinforce the city side of the bridge. Inspired by the squadron taking the mosque and bridgehead, Albuquerque and his captains rallied and stormed the stockades. Archers and blow guns shot poisoned arrows, wounding many Portuguese. Fernão dodged several arrows as he climbed the stockade wall. Francisco snatched the coat of a Moor and flung him off the bridge. With a spirited assault they forced entry into the stockade and cut down a great number of Moors, which in turn, caused others to flee. Below the stockade walls, several Portuguese were slumped over, having succumbed to the poisoned arrows.

From one of the bridge stockades, the sultan's captain—Tuão Bandão, was so alarmed upon the rout of the Moors that he ventured out with 700 Javanese fighters and 2 other captains to reinforce the city-side of the bridge with intentions to attack the Portuguese forces from the rear.

Albuquerque noticed them approaching from one of the city streets. He pointed to the encroaching army. 'Sousa . . . Abreau . . . Pereira . . . finish them off!'

The three captains led their men into a frontal assault. Fernão retrieved a long pike from one of their fallen comrades and joined the line. He had trained in the new weapons regiment as a pikeman while in Cochin. As the Moors rushed ahead, he crouched and girded the pike. Several others joined him with pikes and lances. The Moors had never seen such intimidating weaponry, and were no match for the disciplined maneuvers. In the first wave of the Portuguese attack, the Moors were skewered by the long pikes, and the survivors fled in fear toward the bridge.

Captain Lima's squadron was now stationed at the mosque. From a distance, they spotted the fleeing Moors and immediately rushed to cut them off in front of the bridge. They slew many. Those remaining trapped between the two squadrons frantically jumped into the sea to escape. But the Portuguese mariners in the patrol boats were strategically positioned and finished them off.

Once Captain Lima returned to the stockade, he discovered the sultan retreating up a hill, and immediately ordered an attack. In pursuit of the sultan, they fought the enemy through the streets. The sultan and his son were both mounted on the lead elephants and when they discovered the Portuguese in pursuit, they steered their elephant brigade and army of 2,000 Moors back to the fight. The Portuguese awaited their approach at the head of a city street. The imposing elephants forged ahead. Their tusks, girded with sharp blades, swung dangerously back and forth. Mounted archers fired off poisoned arrows. The sultan's elephant led the way and faced off against the Portuguese. But, without fear, Captain Gomez de Lemos squared off directly in front of the charging elephants. Another pikeman came alongside to help confront the menacing beasts. From the elephant carriages, archers sent off a barrage of arrows at the Portuguese front line. Lemos was struck under his right arm but disregarded the wound. Lemos and the other pikeman stabbed at the sultan's elephant, one poked at the eye and another into the belly. The elephant bucked and reared in agony. It then turned and charged the Moors, crushing any in its way and causing a great stampede of the others. The sultan's elephant halted a moment. It seized the driver with its trunk, slammed him to the ground and dashed his body into bloody pieces. The sultan, his hand already wounded in the battle, lept out of the elephant castle. He grabbed his son and they both slipped away in the confusion.

Near the bridge Albuquerque had forced entry into the stockades and routed the Moors. They continued to pursue them through the city streets. Abreau's men were in the forefront and slashed their way ahead in close combat. Francisco cornered two Moors in an alley. They each unsheathed their kris blades, each of their dragon engravings glistening in the light. But, with a few swift maneuvers of his sword, Francisco disemboweled one and soon decapitated the other. He bent over the bodies and retrieved their kris blades from their limp bloodied hands. He tucked them in his belt and joined his group.

The Moors were converging in great numbers and the fight grew tense. Albuquerque realized they were hard-pressed and ordered a retreat. Arriving to the bridge they began to erect palisades facing the city and another toward the mosque. The fortifications were constructed of mast poles secured in barrels and sails hoisted in between, all designed to deflect poisoned projectiles. They also setup artillery facing the city.

Francisco and Fernão were tying up a sail to one of the poles when they overheard Albuquerque barking orders, 'Captain Paiva, take 100 men and set fires to the city.' He looked around. 'Captain Martinz, take 100 men and burn the sultan's houses near the mosque.'

Francisco retrieved the kris daggers he had confiscated and held them out before Fernão. 'Pick one.'

Fernão scratched his beard as he looked over the two well-crafted blades. He reached for one with a black dragon engraved along the side.

'Nice choice. A souvenir. Might as well keep something useful on this trip.'

'Thanks. You know, I have wanted one of these for a long time.'

'Better to get one in battle than from a vendor, no?'

'Yes,' Fernão replied. He secured his sheathed blade into his belt. 'And a perfect blade for cutting another notch in the victory belt, is it not?'

'This battle may deserve an extra large notch,' Francisco replied with a grin. 'We have our work cut out for us here.'


As the day waned, the suffering from the intense heat and grinding work forced the men to plead for a withdrawal. Twice they approached the governor with their complaints. Acknowledging the circumstances in regards to the stifling heat and the 70 wounded,

Albuquerque capitulated to their demands. He ordered they confiscate the 50 large cannons in the stockade and fall back to the ships. Fernão and Francisco heaved one of the cannons down the stockade platform toward the beach, all while dodging poisoned blow darts, arrows, and lead balls from matchlocks. Finally, arriving at their vessel they were able to take a well deserved rest.

In the haste of retreat, Captain Gomez de Lemos, the hero facing off against the elephant brigade, had been taken to their vessel. On the quarterdeck, Fernão watched the surgical operation on the main deck below. The captain was held down by two crewmen as another approached wielding a hot iron rod and stared over a bloody hole in the leg.

The captain gritted his teeth, 'Get to it man!' The hot iron sizzled as it was applied forcefully to the wound. He merely grunted and then took a sip of water from a canteen by his side. Fernão was informed later that Captain Lemos remained the sole survivor of all those struck by poisoned arrows or darts.

# 12

## *Malacca – August, 1511*

Once the Portuguese had returned to their fleet, the Sultan of Malacca began to strengthen the stockades, and doubled the bridge artillery. The Moors built more palisades in the city, added artillery near the mosque, and on the beach they stacked prickly brushwood—all soaked in poison.

Albuquerque ordered Captain Abreau and his crew to prepare one of the four-masted junks for battle to take the bridge. In proper position, this massive vessel could overlook the stockades and allow his men to overpower the enemy forces within. Fernão and Francisco prepared shelters on board the junk for protecting the soldiers and provisions from the heat and rains. Artillery and munitions were stationed in strategic points on the principle decks. When all had been readied, a caravel and a galley escorted the junk as it passed over the sand bar before the bridge. Fernão felt a thud as the junk suddenly grounded. Its hull was deep and could not pass during the neap tide. Albuquerque ordered another junk with less draught to make an attempt but it also could not pass over.

Watching the helpless grounded junks, the sultan loaded barges full of firewood, pitch and oil. At high tide, the inflammables were set on fire and the barges sent down the flowing river toward the junks. Perceiving the sultan's intentions, Albuquerque ordered his men to station their boats in position to harpoon the flaming barges and drag them off with their iron chains. For nine consecutive nights they fended off the the incendiary barges.

During this time the Portuguese repaired their weapons and built a magazine for the crossbows. The agent of the fleet readied barrels, picks, hoes, hatchets and all materials required to construct stockades and mantlets upon the bridge once they commandeered it.

On August 9, Albuquerque convened a council of all his captains and principle officers on board his flag vessel, the *Flor de la Mar*. Captain Abreau thought it useful to allow Fernão and Francisco to attend, for they both had captained vessels and were war veterans of many campaigns. On deck, Albuquerque addressed the men with intention to resolve the recent disputes among some as to whether it was beneficial to the crown in taking the city and building a fortress within.

Albuquerque clasped his hands behind his back and presented his case: 'Sirs, you will have no difficulty in remembering that when we decided upon attacking this city, it was with the determination of building a fortress within it, for so it appeared to all to be necessary, and after having captured it I was unwilling to let slip, the possession of it, yet, because you all advised me to do so, I left it, and withdrew; but being ready, as you see, to put my hands upon it again once more, I learned that you had already changed your opinion: now this cannot be because the Moors have destroyed the best part of us.'

Albuquerque paused a moment. 'Gentlemen, in such an important matter to the crown, I request you put your answers down in writing, for I will not bear the responsibility alone.'

He unclasped his hands and placed them forward with palms facing upward in an earnest plea to reconsider. 'There are many reasons which I could allege in favor of our taking this city and building a fortress therein to maintain possession of it. I will

171

point out two reasons only why you should not turn back from what you have agreed upon.'

Albuquerque clenched his right fist and continued his harangue. 'The *first* is the great service which we shall perform to our Lord in casting the Moors out of this country, and quenching the fire of this sect of Muhammad so that it may never burst out again. Never again!'

Fernão looked about the room and could see captains and officers begin to nod in agreement, for all despised any Islamic strongholds in the world.

Albuquerque continued, 'I am so sanguine as to hope for this from our undertaking, that if we can only achieve the task before us, it will result in the Moors resigning India altogether to our rule, for the greater part of them—or perhaps all of them—live upon the trade of this country and are become great and rich, and lords of extensive treasures. It is also well worthy of belief, that as the Sultan of Malacca, who has already once been discomforted and had proof of our strength, with no hope of obtaining any relief from any other quarter—16 days having already elapsed since this took place—makes no endeavor to negotiate with us for the security of his estate, for our Lord is blinding his judgment and hardening his heart, and desires the completion of this affair in Malacca.'

Fernão remembered the biblical story of the Exodus, how the Lord hardened the heart of pharaoh in order to display His glory and power. The governor's rhetoric echoed in his heart.

Albuquerque continued. 'The *second* reason is the additional service which we shall render to King D. Manuel in taking this city, because it is the headquarters of all the spiceries and drugs which the Moors carry every year hence to the Straits, and without our being able to prevent them from so doing;

but if we deprive them of this, their ancient market there, there does not remain for them a single port, nor a single situation, so commodius in the whole of these parts, where they can carry on their trade in these things.' The governor made some final comments then the commanders voted their opinions. After such a persuasive speech the majority now favored taking the city and building a fortress. Thereafter, orders were given for a fully united assault on the bridge, early the next morning.

Fernão Magalhães and Francisco Serrão were on the quarterdeck assisting Captain Abreau navigate the massive junk towards the bridge. Closing to within a crossbow's distance, the Moors opened fire upon them from several different directions. Large matchlocks sent steel bullets whizzing past their heads. Fernão snatched up a pavise to deflect an incoming barrage of poisoned darts and arrows. Bombards shot heavy lead and stone balls across the decks from one end to the other, smashing the planking and masts.

Fearlessly, Captain Abreau continued to bark out orders from the exposed quarterdeck. Unfortunately, he was the first hit. A bullet from a matchlock smashed into his jaw, knocking out half his teeth and much of his tongue.

Albuquerque was sailing next to the junk and saw Abreau's mouth full of blood and yelled out: 'Captain, come on board my vessel. You must be attended to.'

'I—can—still—command!' Abreau gurgled. His words could barely be understood as part of his tongue was hanging down and his was mouth was full of blood.

'Take him aboard my vessel,' Albuquerque demanded the crew of the junk. 'Captain Dalpoem will take over command until further notice. Abreau was brought across the gunwhale and Fernão and Francisco assisted the captain across the deck as artillery fire whistled past.

The junk overshadowed the bridge with its lofty height. From the mainmast castle, Portuguese gunners fired their matchlocks and crossbowmen shot bolts repeatedly. Francisco and several men along the rails of the junk lit dangling fuses that were inserted into large tin cans of gunpowder, all packed with metal shards. They heaved them onto the bridge below with devastating explosions and flesh-penetrating shrapnel. Overpowered, the Moors fled the bridge and retreated to the stockades on the sides of the bridge. Watching the Moor forces in disarray, Albuquerque ordered a full assault of boats to make a landing.

Fernão and Francisco joined the invasion force. Planks were again used to avoid the landmines and poisoned bushes. They forced their way to the stockades and fought the enemy vigorously until the Moors were finally routed. Once the bridge was secured, they raised the flag of Portugal high. In this early strike, the Portuguese had lost three men with many wounded, but the Moors suffered a considerable number of casualties.

Albuquerque immediately ordered a company to take out the mosque, and another company to destroy the palisades erected by the Moors in the city street facing the bridge. When the captains arrived at the city palisades they met a nominal force and were able to quickly take possesion.

However, those raiding the mosque side met with a formidable resistance by the sultan's elephant brigade and an army of 3,000 warriors. Keeping watch from the bridge, Albuquerque took notice and sent up a large body of men to reinforce his troops near the mosque, and this made the difference. Once the sultan had been routed with his army, Albuquerque stationed some captains at the mosque, then fell back to secure the bridge.

At the bridge, the munitions of tools and supplies from the junk were offloaded and two strong palisades erected with heavy guns for defense. Remembering his last mistake of fighting in the intense heat, Albuquerque ordered the junk and bridge to be covered with palm leaves to protect the men from the sun.

A flare up of Malaccan warriors began to pound the captain's squadrons stationed at the city palisades.

Albuquerque realized he needed to respond quickly and called to his leading men. 'Captains— Lima, Pereira, Martinz, Afonso, and Simão Dandrade.' He pointed toward the city. 'Take that street. Give no quarter to anyone!' He looked over the remaining captains. 'Paiva, Dalpoem, and Fernão Dendrade. You need to reinforce those under seige over there.' He pointed in another section of the city.

Captain Abreau entered the palisade with a bandaged jaw. Albuquerque smiled. 'Fit for action?'

Abreau responded with a resolute nod.

'We need your spirit and your company of good men,' the governor continued. 'Please join Paiva and the others.'

Albuquerque faced the men. 'I will follow up with the remaining forces once we establish the bridge. Gentlemen, let us take Malacca today!'

The men rallied and stamped their weaponry on the bridge planking with a thunderous crescendo.

Storming off into the streets they cried, 'Santiago!' Regardless of the vastly outnumbered forces, the Portuguese squadrons unleashed a furious assault against the Moors.

Captain Abreau led his men through the city streets until they encountered an onslaught of arrows and bullets from fighters covered by the surrounding buildings. Abreau pointed to a high tower where a Moor had fired off his matchlock.

Fernão nodded and pursued his target.

Abreau then pointed to a crossbowman just visible on a building rooftop.

Francisco took off in the indicated direction.

In front of the Portuguese, an enormous horde of Moors charged forward in the street. Abreau signaled for the pikemen to engage. They stepped in unison with shields in tight formation and raised their long pikes in horizontal combat position. The Moors halted, faces twisted in fear, as the first two victims were stabbed. The blades exited past their spines, and then retracted forcefully. The Moor's innards were ripped through and splayed all over the street in bloody pieces.

Fernão raced up a series of stairs then stepped onto a narrow ledge to make his way toward the marksman. Salty sweat poured down his brow and stung his eyes. He unsheathed his new dagger and peeked around the corner. The marksman shot a round into the city street below. Fernão reached around the corner and shoved his razor-sharp kris deep into the Moor's side. The wavy contour of the blade allowed it to easily penetrate between the ribs. Fernão twisted the blade upward, then sideways. The Moor stared at him in shock as he withdrew the bloodied dagger. Fernão kicked him off the tower, then picked up the matchlock and fired upon the encroaching Moors in the street below.

Meanwhile, Francisco forced his way through a street-level wooden door. He climbed through a labyrinth of passageways and stairs until he finally made the rooftop. The Moor heard the rooftop door bang open, turned, raised his crossbow, and fired. Francisco barely dodged the bolt, and it slammed into the doorway. The Moor hesitated between reloading the crossbow and drawing the dagger from his belt. The delay was more than enough for Francisco to close the distance. He rushed forward, his own *kris* cradled in his hand. He brought the dagger up under the Moor's jaw, forcing the blade upward, lifting the man up and dropping him like a sack of flour when he yanked the blade out. The Moor dropped the crossbow and staggered forward, clutching at his throat as his own blood covered his hands. He dropped to his knees, then collapsed. Francisco snatched up the crossbow and the arrows from the dead man's quiver. He took a position on the roof edge, loaded a bolt, then fired off a round into the back of an axe-wielding combatant about to ambush Captain Abreau from a looming terrace. The axe-man fell forward and landed with a thud. Abreau looked up and saw Francisco giving him a salute.

On the street below, the Portuguese regiments held their line with great discipline and continually thrust their long pikes at the stunned natives. The Moors were unaccustomed to such weaponry and tactics. Portuguese with crossbows and matchlock marksmen aimed every shot with precision. With the relentless energy and passion of the Portuguese, the Moors were soon routed. Any who fled to the sea were put to the sword by the patroling Portuguese mariners.

As the sun set, the last of the troops entered the heavily fortified bridge palisades. Albuquerque ordered the patrol boats in the river to fire constant artillery bombardments on the city. For ten days and nights they pounded the city until it was engulfed in flames. Any Moor who dared to forage food from the city risked death. Merchants began to plead for surrender and allegiance to the Portuguese. Albuquerque agreed to allow the friendly Chinese, Hindi and Burmese merchants to hoist flags over their residences so they would not suffer destruction or plunder when the Portuguese entered the city as victors.

Albuquerque arranged for an orderly plunder of the city in timed shifts for three full days and nights. The treasure was bountiful. An incredible cache of 3,000 artillery were taken, 2,000 of these were of bronze. One particular bombard of considerable size had been a gift from the Zamorin of Calicut to the Sultan of Malacca. These artillery pieces were complemented with finely-crafted carriages, unmatched even in Lisbon. The Malays were renowned for their skill as gunsmiths and their work was comparable to the highly regarded Germans. The Portuguese confiscated 3,000 matchlocks and numerous other weaponry. The crown received 200,000 cruzados in coin and a stool encrusted with jewels estimated to be worth 60,000 cruzados. In addition, four golden lions, pearls and jewelry valued at 400,000 cruzados were also reserved for the crown. The queen would receive the prettiest of the slave girls for her entourage, and many were highly-skilled in embroidery.

In addition to personal artifacts gathered in their raids, the common soldiers received 4,000 cruzados worth of gold each and the captains 30,000. These were highly lucrative rewards, for a noble in Lisbon could live well for an entire year on 1,000 cruzados.

After a grueling six week siege on Malacca, the captains wished to return to Portugal with their wealth, but Albuquerque insisted they honor their commitment to build a fortress and establish a stable government before they left. The locals were to be given much of the responsibility to govern their affairs with minimal control by the Portuguese. The Sultan of Malacca had fled the country and no longer remained an immediate threat.

As word spread about the stunning victory of the Portuguese, many nations in the region sent ambassadors to forge alliances and trade negotiations. All those present in the conquest came to conclude it was thus far their greatest victory. No Portuguese armada had yet encountered such an intense struggle, against such numbers of artillery and fortifications.

# 13

## *Malacca – November, 1511*

Construction on the new fortress had begun in mid-August. As the weeks stretched on, however, the crew's desires to return home only intensified. Work continued, under pressure from Albuquerque to complete it before the coming monsoon season. They pushed themselves to finish the task at hand as quickly as possible by working both day and night shifts. In one month, they had constructed a wood planked fortress with sturdy timber fastened to its perimeter. But the work along the marshy river had begun to grind to a slow pace, for many suffered from the intense heat and infirmities set upon them. Local citizens had to be conscripted to assist, for most of the men were now malnourished from strict rice diets and suffering malarial fevers. For one period of three days, the dead had to be stacked in the captain's barracks, for there was nobody well enough to bury them. Still, the work continued.

Once the wood-based fort was completed, they began to fortify it. Since most of the city was made of wood, stones were collected from surrounding regions and shipped to the harbor. They also demolished the tombs of the kings and the mosques, then transported the stones to the construction site. The fortress was named, *a famosa,* which was translated as 'the famous.' It included an imposing 36 foot tall gatehouse that towered above the city. The Portuguese were so weakened from sickness they had to conscript 1,500 of the former sultan's slaves to complete the stone work. Albuquerque insisted the slaves were to be paid for every day worked.

Fernão Magalhães and Francisco Serrão were near the bridge ordering the conscripted slaves to load some carts with stone blocks for final work on the gatehouse. Francisco wiped his face with his shirtsleeve, 'This heat is crazy,' he said. 'But at least we have evaded the fevers.'

'I am lucky in that regard,' Fernão said. 'Blessed with a good constitution. I had a bad cold once as a boy. But once I recovered, never a sniffle since.'

'But you make up for it with your propensity for injury in battle,' Francisco quipped.

'Point well made, my friend, but even then, I have recovered every time, thanks be to God.' Fernão glanced at the sky, then the sea.

Out to the harbor, small transport vessels were being loaded along the river near the bridge. They would then row further out to deliver the cargos to the Portuguese fleet vessels.

Francisco pointed to Albuquerque's flagship, the *Flor de la Mar*. 'Loaded with the greatest treasures ever to have been captured by our nation. And a nice and beautiful part of it—some of that is ours.'

'Yes, but you think it will make it to Lisbon?' Fernão asked. 'The 400-ton flagship was the finest and largest ever built of the Portuguese fleet. But that was nine years ago. Since then, it has been plagued by intermittent leaks, and I do not believe the latest refitting has been done properly.'

'I know that Albuquerque wants to leave before the season changes,' Francisco said. 'I think this is perhaps too hasty. I only hope it arrives. All our fortunes rest on a safe return of that vessel.'

'Well, Albuquerque's entire personal wealth is on that ship. I'm sure he will take every precaution.'

'Tell that to the weather,' Francisco said, smiling.

The longboats in the bay were now shuttling cargo to three war vessels and a junk.

'Hard to believe this is where we part company,' Fernão said.

'I have been thinking about this also, after everything we have been through,' Francisco said. 'Who will I find trouble with now?' He smiled and winked.

'I'm sure you will manage.' Fernão laughed.

A longboat, empty, pushed off from the junk. The next boat approached, and a crewman threw a rope to a deckhand on board the junk.

'Looks like your fleet to the Moluccas may be ready soon,' Fernão said.

'Indeed, the source of the finest spices; cloves, nutmeg, and mace,' Francisco replied with excitement. 'Worth a fortune. Forget the pepper and cinnamon. Cloves, that is our destiny my friend. Finally, we can setup our own business enterprise with the gold we acquired here.'

Fernão smiled and nodded.

I wanted to tell you that when the cargo arrives to customs in Lisbon take my share and purchase enough goods for trading,' Francisco said. 'I will arrange the spice deliveries from the Moluccas.' He noticed his friend was not quite as enthused. 'I am sorry to learn you must remain here with the patrol fleet. I really wish you were coming along.'

'Do not concern yourself,' Fernão said. 'You earned it. It was good that Albuquerque at least honored Captain Abreau's courage in taking Malacca and rewarded him with the command of your expedition to the Spice Islands.'

'Well, Abreau wanted both of us to captain the other two fleet vessels, but Albuquerque was not in agreement.'

'I know. He must still hold a grudge from my embarrassing him in the council meeting in Cochin. So now I get to stay here, captain a small patrol, and wait.'

'It has been a long time my friend,' Francisco said. 'Over six years since we first—.'

A teenage boy was leading two oxen, both were secured by a harness and attached to a bullock cart loaded full of heavy stones. The cart's wheel dipped into a rut and shattered into pieces. The heavy stones rolled out the back and thumped on the ground. A muscled Portuguese sailor raged, 'You fool! The cart is overloaded!'

'I was told to load it full at the mosque,' the boy said in nearly perfect Portuguese.

Fernão and Francisco looked at one another, then strode off to investigate.

'You lie,' the sailor yelled at the boy. 'Our men would never order this.'

'I do not lie. They told me to load it full.'

'Why you dirty slave. I will—.' The sailor raised his hand to strike the boy.

Coming up from behind, Fernão grabbed the sailor's arm. The sailor turned, sneering. 'What the—.' The sailor's face went slack, and turned red.

'That will be enough,' Fernão said. 'I'm sure it must have been a mistake.'

Francisco stepped forward next to Fernão. The sailor recognized the two new captains. 'Yes, perhaps a mistake,' he replied sheepishly, then backed away and left.

Fernão looked over the boy. 'How do you speak our language so perfectly.'

The boy raised his head slowly and replied, 'I clean fish in the market. I often speak with merchants from India. Some know your language and one taught me in exchange for fish.'

'And how did you acquire fish?' Francisco asked.

'I catch fish from shore, along the beaches and reefs. The fishermen do allow me to fish with them in the deep sea. But I am a good fisherman and someday I will fish in the deep.'

'How old are you?' Fernão asked.

'Eighteen.'

'What's your name?

'Alam. It means, "the whole world."'

'Where are you from? Fernão asked. 'How did you become a slave?'

'The Sultan of Malacca was searching for more slaves and had raided my village in Sumatra,' he replied. 'My father and mother were killed defending our home. I was taken as a slave.'

'How many other languages do you speak?' Francisco asked.

'Many,' he answered. 'I know 9 very well, 12 others in part.'

Fernão glanced at Francisco, who nodded in return.

'Come with us.'

'Where do we go?'

Fernão smiled. 'To visit the commander. Do not worry. You will be fine.'


At the fortress, *a famosa*, they found Captain Abreau in an officer's quarters. He was leaning over a table looking at a navigational chart, which another officer was carefully copying. 'Ah Serrão and Magalhães,' Abreau said. 'What brings you here?'

Alam stood between Fernão and Francisco. Fernão put his hand on the boy's shoulder. 'Well, sir,' he said. 'I was hoping to requisition this slave. I need him to assist me in my patrols.'

'Any reason for this particular slave?'

'He is fluent in many languages. And would be a strong asset in dealing with the islanders.'

Captain Abreau scratched his chin as he looked at the teenager. 'Very well. Sign the papers with the agent.'

'Thank you, sir,' Fernão said as he tried to view the map being sketched.

'Oh, by the way,' Abreau said. 'This is one of our finest pilots, and a skilled map-maker, Francisco Rodriguez. Albuquerque assigned him to join our expedition.'

The men nodded to one another.

Abreau continued, 'Our forces confiscated a sea chart from a Javanese pilot. It contains fantastic details on their trade routes. It will be useful on our expedition to the Moluccas. Albuquerque is quite excited about the chart. He plans to bring it on the *Flor de la Mar* and deliver it to King Manuel. We are making a copy.'

'May I have a look?' Fernaõ asked.

Abreau nodded.

Fernão and Francisco scanned over the chart. The script was Javanese, and it depicted the extensive trade routes between Java and Brazil, the Cape of Good Hope, the Red Sea, Persian Sea, India, Malacca, Clove Islands, China, and even to remote Formosa. The compass bearings and many remote kingdoms were mapped in detail. Fernão memorized as much as possible.

'Captain Serrão, we leave in three days,' Abreau said. 'I have assigned you as deputy commander of our fleet.'

'Yes sir,' Francisco said. 'I appreciate your confidence in me and won't disappoint your trust.'

'Now, if you will excuse me,' Abreau said. 'There is quite a lot still to be done before we depart.'

The three took their leave and went off to find the agent.

It was late November, when the small fleet of three Portuguese warships and a junk, were ready for departure to the Spice Islands. Two carracks were to sail; Abreau was to captain one—the *Santa Catarina* and Serrão the other, named—*Sabaia*. The third ship, a caravel, was to be captained by Simão Afonso Bisagudo, and a trusted merchant named Nehodá Ismael was to sail the junk, loaded with merchandise for trade. Each ship had a Javanese pilot to assist, mainly due to their familiarity in the trade routes. The fleet also carried 120 Portuguese sailors, and 20 slaves from Malacca to work the pumps. Albuquerque had given specific orders not to take any prizes or harass any merchant vessels. They were to render assistance to any vessels in distress. Also, they were to offer gifts to any kings or lords they met and observe all the local customs, all intended to create good will. This was to be a mission of peace and exploration to establish new trading partnerships.

Fernão was walking alongside his translator, Alam. They met Francisco near the bridge.

'A fine day for sailing,' Francisco said. 'Wish you could join us.'

'Indeed,' Fernão replied. 'I expect you will have an epic journey.'

Francisco looked at Alam. 'Please take good care of my friend while I am gone.'

'I will try,' Alam said.

Francisco turned to Fernão. 'If I plan to send you a letter when I arrive to paradise, where would I send it?'

Fernão paused a moment. 'I think best you send any correspondence to the India House in Lisbon. I plan to return home as soon as they send reinforcements here. Good chance I may sail by early May, then use our funds to setup the enterprise.'

Francisco nodded. 'Very good then.' He gave Fernão a big hug and then they shook hands. Fernão and Alam saluted Francisco as he walked off to the longboats.

During the month of December, Fernão captained a small caravel patrolling the coastlines of Malay and the nearby islands. He took careful notes and made detailed charts. Alam assisted in translation when they frequented the ports to acquire intelligence. They sought out information regarding foreign defensive positions and cultural knowledge, both deemed important to the crown. Fernão gave daily lessons to Alam in reading and writing upper-level Portuguese. On some days he would bring Alam to the priest for private instruction in the faith. Both relished their time deep-sea fishing and cooking fine meals on their boat. The time passed quickly.

One day, during their patrol off the coast of Sumatra, they stopped in the port of Pacem and went for a meal in the local market. Alam overheard a Sumatran merchant conversing with another about searching for the shipwrecked, *Flor de la Mar*.

Alam tapped Fernão on the arm. 'Sir, Magalhães. These men speak of the governor's flagship. They say it has sunk and are planning to dive for it. They hear rumors that it was loaded with treasure.'

'What?' Fernão asked. 'Where? When?' He looked at Alam, then at the merchants. 'Come, time to earn your keep again.'

He approached the men and spoke in Portuguese, while Alam rendered the translation into the local Sumatran dialect. 'You speak of our vessel, the *Flor de la Mar*.' He folded his arms, stood imperious, and mustered all his authority. 'Tell me more.'

Taken by surprise, and fearful, one of the merchants stuttered, 'Please . . . sir . . . please . . . we were only thinking of the safety of the vessel. And its cargo. We are only curious. Really.'

'Tell me of the wreck. How did it happen, and where? Are there any survivors? Was anything salvaged?'

The other merchant replied more calmly. 'Please, let me recount what we have heard from one of your sailors.'

'Tell me everything you know.'

'Yes. It was not too long ago, maybe three weeks ago, when four Portuguese survivors landed here in a small *almadia*. I was one of those they first met and was given their account in detail. Later, they were brought to our governor who treated them well, and then they embarked on a Portuguese vessel bound for India.'

'Any names?'

'No, I am sorry.'

'Any other survivors?'

'Yes! A crew of Javanese landed here in the barge from the junk. They reported the junk was lost.'

'How did the wreck occur?'

'They say there were two sailing pairs; Albuquerque's *Flor de la Mar* was escorted by the *Trinidad* and a junk was flanked by the *Enxobregas*. They were sailing at night and had just passed Powder

188

Island when a tempest arose. At the north end of the Straits of Sumatra, the sea shallowed, and the *Flor de la Mar* hit the reef. The flagship broke into two pieces and massive waves crashed across the decks. Some of the crewmen were washed into the sea. The *Trinidad* dropped anchor near the *Flor de la Mar* and weathered the gales all night.

They say Albuquerque ordered his crew to cut the mast into pieces and strap it together along with a board on top. They tied themselves to the raft and used a piece of wood to row toward the *Trinidad*. With great difficulty they neared the vessel. Ropes with buckets attached were tossed to them and they were finally pulled on board. Meanwhile, the remaining crew were desperately building rafts. In a rescue attempt, the junk tacked near the *Flor de la Mar* but soon it reversed course leaving the crew to their fate. The Javanese crew on the junk had no desire to risk their lives, so they mutinied and killed all the Portuguese on board, except the four surviving mariners who slipped away in the confusion on their small craft, who we assisted here.'

'What treachery!' Fernão said, then swallowed his anger. Calmly, he asked, 'What of the cargo. Was anything recovered?'

'They said it sank,' the merchant nervously replied. 'They never mentioned if anything was saved.'

Fernão leaned on his fists upon the table and stared into the merchant's eyes. 'Tell me the truth. Did they salvage anything?'

'I swear. The survivors claimed it sank. They had nothing . . . nothing was saved.'

Fernão exploded with rage. He slammed his fist into the table and yelled, 'Albuquerque you fool. You lost it all!'

Outside the market, his rage turned to a sullen depression. The greatest cargo of gold, jewels, and valued artifacts ever transported on a single vessel— all lost. Fernão contemplated his 4,000 cruzados. All his grandiose dreams to enter the lucrative spice trade dashed to pieces and sunk to the bottom of the sea.

'You think it can be found?' Alam asked cautiously as they walked away.

'In the dangerous reefs, doubt it. I'm afraid it is lost for all time.'

In the months that followed, Fernão tried to forget about his crushing financial loss from the sinking of the *Flor de la Mar*. Instead, he renewed his quest to spread the faith. He reclined on a hammock strung up between two palm trees at his temporary residence near the beach. It was a wood house with a palm-thatched roof. Alam was cooking some rice in a pot over some embers in the sand. 'Alam, are ready for your baptism today?' Fernão asked. 'It is good you do so before we depart for Lisbon. The seas can be dangerous, and one must be certain of salvation to ride out the storms with steadfast faith.'

'I am ready, sir Magalhães. I know the Lord Jesus paid for our sins by dying on the cross and then rose from the dead. His resurrection is our hope and salvation.'

'Yes, you are indeed a believer. Have you decided upon a Christian name?'

'I would like the name of Enrique. He sponsored great expeditions to explore the world. He was a godly prince of your kingdom.'

Fernão smiled. 'I see you have remembered some of my stories.

'I would be honored to bear his name,' Alam said with conviction.

190

After breakfast, Fernão and Alam stood at the entrance of the newly constructed church, *Our Lady of the Annunciation*. They watched the priest approach. He wore a white surplice and a purple stole.

'Are you ready?' the priest asked.

Alam nodded and they all entered the church and walked to the entrance of the nave. The priest went through a litany of ceremonial rites. Finally, they moved in front of an eight-sided stone baptismal font. The priest knelt and asked God's help. He then rose, signed himself with the cross, and said to Alam, 'God, come to my rescue.'

'Lord, make haste to help me,' Alam replied.

'Glory be to the Father,' the priest said.

'As it was in the beginning,' Alam said.

'Enrique, formerly Alam of Sumatra.'

'Present.'

'Do you believe in God the Father almighty, Creator of heaven and earth?'

'I do believe.'

'Do you believe in Jesus Christ, His only Son, our Lord, who was born into this world and suffered for us?

'I do believe.'

'And do you believe in the Holy Spirit, the holy Catholic Church, the communion of saints, the forgiveness of sin, the resurrection of the body, and the life everlasting?'

'I do.'

Fernão, acting as godfather, took Enrique by the shoulder and had him bend down over the baptismal font. The priest took a ladle and filled it with water. He said, 'I baptize you in the name of the Father.' The priest poured some water from the ladle over Enrique's head. 'And of the Son.' He poured more water on his head. 'And of the Holy Spirit.' A third time, the priest poured water.

Fernão retrieved a candle set in a silver holder. He lit it and handed it to Enrique.

The priest then said, 'Take this burning candle as a reminder to keep your baptism innocence. Obey God's commandments, so that when our Lord comes for the joyous wedding feast you may go forth to meet him with all the saints in the halls of heaven and be happy with Him forevermore. Go in peace, and may the Lord be with you.'

'Enrique and Fernão both said, 'Amen.

# 14

## *Lisbon – July 14, 1512*

Fernão left Malacca in the late spring on the next cargo ship bound for Lisbon. He had completed seven years of service to the crown and was relieved to go home. Enrique remained the servant of Fernão and accompanied him on the lengthy journey.

Upon his arrival to Lisbon in June, Fernão Magalhaes signed for his allotted stipend as a servant of the king's household. It was called a *moradia*, a paltry sum. But it also included an *alqueire* or measure of 30 pounds of daily barley.

However, today, July 14, was an eventful day. Fernão was promoted to the rank of a *fidalgo escudeiro*—the second rank of the first order of Portuguese nobility—for his outstanding service to the crown. He was now entitled to own a coat of arms and his pension was increased to 850 *reis*, a considerable sum. Enrique accompanied him to the Royal Treasury to collect the first disbursement. Fernão then signed for his pay from a clerk and departed with a smile.

'Sir, you are happy today,' Enrique said.

'I suppose I am grateful, promoted from fourth level of nobility to second, and with enough pension to live on for a while. Good for both of us, is it not?' Fernão smiled. 'But most important, the increase in pension will raise my position in court.'

'I am happy for you, sir,' Enrique replied with a smile.

The following day Fernão and Enrique walked down along the bustling dockyards to pay a visit to the customs house. 'Are you doing business today?' Enrique asked.

'I hope so,' Fernão said. 'I am planning to collect all my investment funds from the Indies plus interest and a bonus. I had an arrangement with a merchant named Albraldez.'

'Will you buy a house?'

'Perhaps, but rent for now. I promised Francisco we would enter the private spice trade. As you know, we lost our start-up funds when Albuquerque's flagship sank. But my other investment may at least give us a slim chance, if I can leverage the funds. I need to find an interested merchant willing to take a risk on the enterprise. Fernão opened the door to the customs house and approached a uniformed officer. 'Good afternoon.'

'Can I help you?' the officer said flatly.

'Can you check if Dom Abraldez has processed his shipment?'

The officer sighed and thumbed through a stack of stamped documents, stopping to read one. 'Yes. Looks like it was processed.'

'Does it have an address for his residence?'

He looked at Fernão, weighing his appearance against his own ability to be bothered, then scribbled a note and handed it to Fernão.

'Thanks,' Fernão said, snatching the note from the officer's fingertips.

They left the customs house and meandered through the hilly streets of town, through the bustling commercial sector, into the residential district, and finally arrived at a quaint two-level estate overlooking the Rio Tejo. Fernão was momentarily shocked at the sight of numerous servants moving elaborate furniture pieces out of the house and into a line of horse drawn carts. He nervously approached a well-dressed man who appeared to be in charge and was recording all the goods as they were loaded.

'Pardon my asking, but is this the residence of Abraldez?'

The man glanced up from his notepad and raised an eyebrow. 'And you are?'

'Fernão Magalhães. I am looking for Abraldez. We have business to discuss.'

'I bet,' said the man with a big grin. 'He is dead. Let me guess, he owes you money?'

'Yes, quite a lot.'

'Well, many creditors have paid their visits, but no luck for any of you. Coincidentally, Abraldez's father has disappeared. Some believe he fled to Galicia to avoid his son's creditors. I am sorry.'

Fernão's heart sank. Yet another blow to his fortunes. He walked away with his head lowered. Enrique followed him. Fernão brooded as they walked. Soon they arrived at their two-bedroom rental house located only a few blocks distance from the India House. Fernão retired early to his bedroom and spent the night punctuated in fitful sleep and wakeful moments of self-pity.

The next morning, on the balcony, Enrique prepared a breakfast of eggs and toasted bread with a sweet jelly. He squeezed fresh oranges into two large glasses. Orange groves had been in fashion in Lisbon ever since the voyagers discovered the precious commodity, a rich delicacy enjoyed by everyone. Fernão arose and rubbed his eyes and slipped on some loose trousers. He exited the bedroom and found Enrique seated on the balcony sipping a glass of orange juice. 'Sorry sir, I was thirsty. I expected you would awake soon.'

Fernão looked over the fine breakfast platter and fresh juice. The sunny morning and fresh breeze lightened his dour mood. 'Do not worry, Enrique. You are family here.'

'Thank you, sir.'

'And you do not have to call me *sir*, unless among other fidalgos.'

Thank you, sir—uh . . . I mean, thanks.'

Fernão smiled, and picked up the other glass of juice, and semi-raised it to Enrique, as if he was making a toast. 'Well. Maybe this day will turn out better. I was thinking all night if there were any other way to get my funds. You know, I can never give up . . . never will. It goes against my nature, against my honor.'

Enrique listened attentively. 'What is your plan?'

'It begins at the royal treasury,' Fernão said, sipping at his orange juice.

Later that day, Fernão discovered the crown had never paid for a consignment of pepper purchased from Abraldez. He sent formal requests to King Manuel for the treasury to pay the funds owed to him from the Abraldez estate, plus interest and legal fees. However, the king was known to be a miser, irrespective of anyone's rank. He had even railed against Vasco da Gama when the latter requested funds to double his men's pay as reward for the victory against Calicut. So, it was no surprise to Fernão when his petition was met with an apathetic response and subsequently ignored.

Snubbed again by the crown, Fernão needed respite and decided to finally pay a visit to his brother and sister. He taught Enrique basic horsemanship as they journeyed to Sabrosa in the Traz-os-Montes of Northern Portugal.

Approaching the family estate, memories of Fernão's childhood flooded his mind. Upon the death of their parents, the Magalhães brothers were sent to the royal court as pages. Their younger sister remained under the care of the family relatives who helped maintain the farm as best they could, but it began to deteriorate. Diogo's chief desire was to return home and manage its affairs, but he needed funds to restore its condition. Once Diogo secured his share of pay for service to the crown in India, he had returned on the first cargo fleet back to Portugal.

Fernão and Enrique rode up a dirt path leading to a timber farmhouse. Nearby was an outdoor stable. Three horses were penned in with wood fencing. As they drew near, Diogo rushed out of the front door of the farmhouse. 'Brother!' he yelled. 'You have come home.'

'Good to be home brother,' Fernão replied.

A woman in her late 20's turned a corner from behind the house and walked toward the stable with a bucket of water. She glanced to her side and saw the visitors. She set the bucket down and asked. 'Fernão? Is that you?' She rushed over to the group.

'Yes, Isabel,' Fernão replied with a big smile.

'You are so grown up,' Isabel said. 'I barely recognized you with your thick beard.'

'And you have grown into a beautiful young woman,' Fernão added, then dismounted and hugged his sister.

'Who is your friend?'

'This is Enrique. We met in Malacca.'

'Malacca?'

'I have many stories to tell.'

'I expect you do,' Diogo interjected. 'Let us go inside and have some lunch.'

It was a refreshing time in his old home. Over every meal, Fernão recounted tales of harrowing

197

events and exotic peculiarities in the lands he visited. Diogo and their sister Isabela were riveted upon every word. The Magalhães brothers taught Enrique how to hunt wild boar and deer in the rugged mountains. An avid angler, Enrique particularly enjoyed fishing in the plentiful rivers.

Toward the end of their mountain trek, Enrique was cooking a fresh catch of fish over a campfire, when Diogo pondered their future. 'It is good of you to visit us. Will you stay?'

'I would like to, but need to get back to the India House, make some plans.'

'After you lost everything, are you sure it is a good idea to continue?' Diogo asked.

'I promised Francisco to partner with him. You are welcome to join us.'

'I miss the adventure, but I am content here managing the estate. But, who knows, perhaps one day we will have another mission.'

After supper, they retired to their blankets under the star lit sky. But Fernão's mind was already plotting a course into the future.

After returning to Lisbon, Fernão busied himself for nearly a year in the India House. He pored over the latest sea chart revisions and newest navigational instruments along with many of the most esteemed pilots and captains. Enrique was also kept quite busy. Upon completion of his daily tasks, he would visit the markets and the bustling wharf to acquire greater proficiency in the western languages—English, French, German, Dutch, Portuguese, and Spanish.

One day, a letter arrived at the India House. Fernão stared at the seal with its foreign script and curvy lines. He took a seat and anxiously cut the end of the envelope with his kris blade and read its contents:

Greetings Fernão. I hope you are faring well my friend. I wish to relate my travel routes and experiences since we left Malacca in November of 1511 to which you may consider useful. But first, do you remember Amina, that girl I met on my shore patrol, during our first tour to Malacca? She was part Javanese and quite beautiful. I tried to find her after the siege on Malacca, but she was nowhere to be found and this devastated me. Well, my life forever changed when I found her during our first stop for provisions in the trade port of Gresee, Java.

Apparently, she had fled with her father and mother during the siege and went back to their homeland. Was this a divine providence? I do not know for sure but am disposed to believe in the affirmative. I decided to marry her that very day and took her with me on the voyage. I guess it was an act of faith. As deputy commander of the fleet, I had some extra privileges and given permission to take her on the voyage. You know, my friend, I may one day have your level of belief.

Now concerning our journey. Our native pilots informed us of the geographical names as we sailed east. So, after departing Java, we passed a few small islands. Near Sapudi Island, incessant leaks began to plague my unseaworthy old vessel. Remember? It was the Cambay vessel our men acquired in the Goa campaign, the *Sabaia*. We burned it and then distributed our crews among the remaining two fleet vessels. The supply junk continued to sail as it was. Watching the islands of Bali and Sumbawa on our starboard side, we soon approached a peculiar island called Gunong Api. It had a cone-shaped mountain that spit rivers of fire which flowed down to the sea. It was an incredible sight and wish you could have witnessed it. We then continued past the islands of Buru, Amboina, and Ceram. We anchored in a haven called Guli Guli. The weather turned foul as winter set in, and we could not reach the Moluccas in these conditions. Therefore, we proceeded to Banda and wintered there for three months. I acquired a junk here to replace the *Sabaia*, and we loaded our vessels with cloves, nutmeg, and mace. With our fleet fully loaded, we set course to return to Malacca. Unfortunately, soon after departure, we encountered a great storm, and my junk was separated from the other vessels. We shipwrecked on the shoals of Lucipara in the Turtle Islands.

We all survived. I ordered my crew of nine Portuguese mariners to salvage the skiff and any provisions from the wreck. We rotated daily watches. One day, a junk approached, and we hid in some bushes near the beach. While the sea pirates searched our wreck, we quietly rowed our skiff out to their junk and ambushed the few crewmen on board. They begged us not to maroon them on this desolate island. Having been marooned ourselves, we were sympathetic to their pleas and promised not to do so if they brought us to Amboina. Upon arrival, some merchants from Batochina urged us to aid the sultan there who was at war with a rival. With nothing of value in our persons we decided to see what fate would deliver us and agreed to their request. Although we were few, our fighting

200

skills joined with the sultan's army were no match for his rival. It was not long before word spread throughout the islands of our presence and our services were in demand once again.

The King of Ternate, Abdul Hassan Al Buleis, "Boleyse," summoned our aid in a dispute with his father-in-law, Al Mansur, King of Tidore. It was only a simple matter of displaying our martial skills, along with a touch of diplomacy, and we resolved the quarrel. King Boleyse appointed me his grand vizier and my men were enlisted as his personal guard. We also confirmed that we were the first Portuguese to ever visit the Moluccas. You know, these islands are so far east that Spain may one day claim them as their own.

It really is a paradise here, like I believed it would be. The weather is warm but pleasant due to the ocean breezes. I must describe the bountiful spices in all five of these islands. The clove trees are high quality and quite amazing. They only grow in the mountains of the five Molucca Islands. Every day clouds descend upon the mountains and perfect the cloves. The cloves are harvested six times per year. The trees average about 30 feet in height and are wide as a man. The leaves are like that of a laurel and the bark a brownish-tan color. On the tips of the branches the cloves are clustered in 10 to 20 clove heads, much like myrtle berries. When the cloves sprout, they are a pale white that gradually turns green, when ripe—red, and when dried—black. I know you have seen the dried cloves during shipments to India. Sampling the local cuisines with cloves has been an exquisite delight. You know I love the spices. Oh yes, nutmeg and mace are in abundance as well. The crop is much like our walnuts. Once the fruit is opened it reveals the seed—nutmeg which is wrapped in orange-red blades—mace. These spices are exceptional additions to many dishes. The spices are so bountiful here and the opportunity for great wealth is ours for the taking. I wish you were here to witness for yourself. I hope this letter has arrived to you and I look forward to any return correspondence. All merchants frequenting the Moluccas know the King of Ternate and can find me in his company. Your friend, Francisco Serrão.

Fernão smiled with the good news. His best friend had not only achieved the goal of reaching the Spice Islands but was on the verge of a spiritual awakening. Fernão slipped the letter into his shirt pocket and returned home to find Enrique busily mopping the floor. 'Hurry and finish that,' Fernão said beaming. 'Tonight, we shall find ourselves a fine restaurant and celebrate!'

'What is the occasion?'

'Francisco has reached the Moluccas and the reports of abundant spices are true. I will show you the letter over dinner.' The two departed for a night out on the town.

It was August 13, 1513, when all Fernão's planning and vision, finally began to come to fruition. Fernão stood next to his brother, Diogo, and Enrique on a war galley specially designed for cavalry transport. They were anchored off Belem, along the waterfront of Lisbon.

'I heard Gil Vicente's play *Exhortation to War* had a spectacular standing ovation in the royal palace,' Diogo said.

'I hear it was a tragicomedy and quite clever,' Fernão agreed with his brother's assessment.

'Seems hard to believe we are embarking on another mission,' Diogo pondered. 'I really was fine on the estate. But when the king requests one's service—'

'So here we are,' Fernão said, finishing his thought. 'Assigned to Captain Aires Telles' cavalry regiment.'

'Manuel must really want to send a message to Muley Zayam for not paying the tribute owed,' Diogo added. 'I guess King Manuel took it as a personal affront to his rule and wants to make a statement.'

Enrique held his hand above his eyes to block the sun as he scanned over the countless ships in the Tejo. 'How many in our fleet?' he asked.

'We have 400 ships, 18,000 men of war, and over 2,000 cavalry troops,' Fernão replied. 'King Manuel's nephew, Jaime—the Duke of Braganza, will command our armada with João de Lisboa as chief pilot.'

'By far the most powerful armada to ever have left the shores of our home,' Diogo remarked, his chest swelling at the thought of it.

# 15

## *Azamor, Morocco – August 28, 1513*

The foreboding gathering of dark Portuguese ships amassed off the coast of Morocco and hoisted their red-crossed flags. When the tide rose, the shallow draft galleys fitted for horse transports were the first to enter the mouth of the Oum Er-Rbia river, all flowing toward the imposing walled city of Azamor. An immense army of Moors had stood up along the walls of the city. Diogo pointed toward movement in the wild brush along the riverbanks.

'You see that?' Diogo said.

'Yeah,' Fernão replied. 'Ready for battle?'

'Ready to serve the king,' Diogo replied.

The two brothers unfastened their steeds from the transport slings and led them toward the ramps. They tightened their saddles and inspected the stirrups.

The captain of their transport galley ordered, 'Lower the ramps!'

Fernão and Diogo finished securing their armor and strapped on their helmets for battle.

'Time for glory brother,' Fernão said with a grin.

The Magalhães brothers took the lead and charged down the ramp. Their horses splashed into the river and quickly scrambled onto shore. Archers fired arrows and darts from the city walls. As the Portuguese cavalry pushed forward, Moors hidden in the bushes charged from their flanks with lances.

'Watch out!' Diogo yelled at Fernão, just as a Moor shoved a lance into his brother's horse. The loss of momentum thrust Fernão over his steed, and he landed in a mud pit. Fernão rose to one knee, and barely had time to draw his sword before two Moors were upon him.

Diogo whirled his steed around and charged at them from their rear flank. He cut them both down. Fernão saluted his brother. He then turned and looked at his horse lying dead upon the ground. Fernão kneeled and stroked its side.

'Sorry about your horse brother,' Diogo said.

Fernão nodded and arose. He leaped on Diogo's horse and the two rode to join the frontline attack.

Meanwhile, the Portuguese continued to storm the city, and the Moors continued to resist with a determined defense. For three days, the enemy continued to fight. Finally, a lucky shot by a Portuguese gunner had splattered their general into pieces. With the supreme commander obliterated before all to see, the demoralized Moors either fled or surrendered. The city swiftly capitulated.

Although the Moors had given over the city, they had regrouped with their reserve warriors in the desert and embarked on daily harassment raids. The Magalhães brothers were in the stable preparing their horses for another daily patrol to engage the enemy marauders and drive them away.

'Did you ever get paid for your horse,' Diogo asked.

'Not exactly,' Fernão replied. 'The quartermaster only paid me 3,700 reis.'

'Really? Officer's rate should be near 13,000.'

'That is what I thought. Preposterous. I wrote the king to adjust the pay accordingly, since my horse was in honorable service to the crown.'

'You think he will honor your request?'

'He should. But, of course, knowing his demeanor and his court sycophants, likely not. Nevertheless, I must request on principle.'

The Magalhães brothers accompanied a small squadron into the desert. But this day, they encountered a superior force of Moor cavalry and were quickly surrounded. Upon his steed, Fernão charged ahead to engage the enemy. In the melee, he was struck in the left knee by a lance. The pain was intense as the imbedded shaft bobbed up and down with the movement of his horse. Taking notice, Diogo rode up and grabbed the reins to steer them into a retreat while their comrades continued to fight. Once they were a safe distance away, Diogo dismounted and then carefully removed the lance from his brother's knee. It was a bloody mess and Fernão grimaced in pain. Diogo quickly wrapped the wound, and they rode back to Azamor.

On the following day, Diogo entered a temporary officer's quarters and found his brother lying on a cot. 'So, what is the news?' he asked Fernão.

'Ship surgeon says the lance split the tendon.'

'But you are not a cripple.'

'No, but he was certain that I will always have a limp.'

'Nothing he can do for that?'

'Nothing. Lifelong he says.'

'Well, at least you will be able to walk.'

Fernão nodded and looked away.

'The duke's fleet is returning home,' Diogo said.

Fernão turned his face back to Diogo. 'And you are going with him?'

Diogo's countenance turned serious. 'I did my duty and answered the call to arms by the king. You realize Isabel is managing the farm alone?' Diogo grinned. 'Brother, I left you back in India when you were wounded. I will not do that again. I am here to finish this mission with you to the end.'

Fernão smiled, then shifted the conversation. 'So, who will take the duke's command?'

'A war veteran, João Soares—Count de Meneses,' Diogo replied. 'I hear a capable leader, respects the men under him.'

'Yes, I know him. All these things are true.' Fernão grimaced as he raised himself up to a seated position with his back against the wall. He saluted his brother. 'I am glad you are staying.'

Diogo returned a salute and walked away.

Three months later, Fernão limped into the new commander's quarters steadied by a walking stick. João Soares sat behind a rustic desk browsing over some documents. He glanced up at the figure limping into his office doorway. 'Ah, Fernão Magalhães. I met your brother this morning. He mentioned your unfortunate encounter with a Moor lance.'

'Yes, it is true I'm afraid.' Fernão said. 'It's just a scratch. I am ready to return to duty.'

'Diogo also mentioned you had fought in many battles in the east, seriously wounded in two.' He lifted his shirt revealing a long scar along the rib cage. 'Took a lance myself, quite painful. Nearly killed me.'

'I do not doubt it. You are fortunate,' Fernão said. 'And blessed.'

Soares smiled. 'I hear you have been riding out daily, not many take such initiative.' He rose from his desk, walked to the window, and stared out to the courtyard full of cavalry preparing to ride out. 'I need men like you in my command, a war veteran.'

'How may I serve?' Fernão said.

The commander moved back to the desk and unfurled a chart and traced his finger across several points on the perimeter of Azamor. 'We need to end these incursions. We need to reach an agreement with some of the desert tribes. They would pose a formidable alliance against the enemy. They know the trails and the enemy tactics. But how do we contact them?'

'If I may suggest sir. I have a trusted servant, skilled in many languages, including Arabic. With your permission we can ride out today and request their aid.'

'You are resourceful Magalhães. Permission granted and good luck. Report to me as soon as you have any information.'

'Yes sir,' Fernão said. 'If that is all, then—'

'One more thing,' Soares said. 'You and Captain Álvaro Monteiro will serve as my quartermaster-majors, in charge of the war booty. I do not trust the senior officers, too close to the duke and the court.'

Yes sir,' Fernão replied. 'It is understood.'

'Good. Take care of yourself. You are valuable to me.'

Fernão saluted him and limped away.

Over the next few months, and with some frustration, alliances were gradually formed with the desert Bedouin, and the Moor incursions gradually faded away. The senior officers occupied their time by continuing to make complaints about Fernão's appointment as a mere junior officer to the highly coveted position of Quartermaster-Major.

Near the end of March 1514, news arrived of a Moor army amassing in great numbers. It was comprised of troops from Fez and Mequinez who intended to oust the Portuguese from Azamor. Commander Soares led his troops out to engage, and on April 12, they met in battle. The Moors lost 2,000 warriors and the Portuguese endured their own wounded and dead, albeit in much lesser numbers. But the Portuguese realized quickly they were outclassed in manpower. The Moor army continued to push forward, throwing warriors at the Portuguese in overwhelming numbers. In desperation, Fernão and Enrique rode out to enlist the aid of the desert nomads. Meanwhile, the Portuguese cavalry began making staged retreats with an objective to slow the Moor encroachment. But the sheer size of the invading army was impossible to halt.

Finally, one day, Fernão appeared in the distance over a sand dune with a massive alliance of tribal warriors. The Portuguese cavalry turned and gawked in surprise.

Diogo was near Captain Álvaro Monteiro. He grinned and said, 'My brother has arrived.'

Captain Monteiro yelled, 'Magalhães! About time!'

Fernão raised his black sword and charged down the dune with the allied warriors swarming behind. They crashed into the Moor lines with raw violence. The Moors clashed right back. Bodies fell and blood flowed. During the encounter, João Soares was hit in the leg with a rusted lance and Fernão stood over him, fighting off attackers, until others could drag him safely back. Fernão, always efficient with his blade, pushed forward with the others. Eventually, the Moors were routed. The end of the battle was a respite for most, but a headache for others.

As quartermaster-majors, Magalhães and Monteiro were obligated to inventory the entire herd of animals left behind by the fleeing Moors, and then distribute the spoils among the men. Even with enlisted help from the squadron it was not until evening when the count was complete. There were 200,000 goats, along with 3,000 horses and camels.

Considering the difficulty to drive the entire herd back to Azamor, the two quartermasters decided to lighten the load and reward the allies with 400 goats.

Over the weeks, rumors began circulating that the quartermaster-majors had misappropriated the crown's assets by selling a portion of the booty for personal profit. Furthermore, by this transaction, they were accused of giving aid to the enemy. Magalhães and Monteiro insisted they were blameless and only had given a small recompense to their allies and promptly dismissed any further accusations as hearsay. Matters seemed in check until their commander's sudden and unexpected death in early May. Apparently, the rusted lance point had caused an infection that spread until he succumbed to it. A new commander, Pedro de Sousa, was placed in charge, for he was the next highest-ranking officer. With João Soares now disposed, the officers pressed ahead with their complaints and rumors.

One day, Fernão went looking for Monteiro, and found him in the courtyard. 'You want to join me?' Fernão asked.

'Pardon?' Monteiro squinted his eyes in the sun.

'I am off to Lisbon today, to seek my increase in my royalty allowance.'

'Isn't that a risky venture my friend? Leaving without permission? And with accusations pending against us?'

'Only rumors and false claims. You know that. But if they pursue this, then the only way to clear our names is to petition the king himself. The new commander does not know us and will eventually give in to the senior officer's demands.'

Monteiro scratched his beard. 'You may be right. Worth a chance. But I will remain for now. Someone must answer our accusers. May God bless your venture.'

Fernão smiled and saluted, then went toward the port where Diogo was waiting for him.

'I know you have to appeal the honor of our name,' Diogo said. 'I will do what I can here. Safe journey.'

'See you soon,' Fernão said. He then boarded a caravel bound for Lisbon.

As a legitimate member of the royal household, Fernão had the right to petition the king for an audience, but he had to wait his turn due to Manuel's busy schedule. Fernão bided his time between the India House and the dockyards. Speaking with the captains in the India House, he had learned of an extraordinary event that occurred during his absence from Lisbon. In February, an emissary had arrived from Ethiopia representing the long sought-after Christian potentate of the east, Prester John. An Armenian, 50 years old, named Mateus, was the ambassador representing Eleni, Regent Queen of Ethiopia. She had sent with him a letter, on behalf of her twelve-year-old step-grandson, the future King Dawit II, who was in attendance with the envoy. She claimed he was descended from both the legendary Prester John and King Solomon. The letter opened with: *In the name of the Father, Son and Holy Spirit, Three Persons and One God.* The letter mentioned a Portuguese visitor named Pêro da Cavilhã who had settled in their realm and was considered an ally. Fernão surmised this must have been one of the two spies dispatched by King João II to locate the fabled Prester John. Apparently, their mission succeeded.

Queen Eleni warned how the Lord of Cairo was building many ships and galleys to war against the

Portuguese fleets. She proposed an alliance stating they could assist them against the Muslims in the Red Sea and Cairo. Although, they were not a maritime power, nor had enough wood to construct fleets, they could supply enough provisions for 1,000 ships. The queen promised in the letter:

> We shall give you many men in the Straits of Mecca and Bar-el-Mandab, or else India or Tor, to sweep the Moors from the face of the earth, for we are powerful on land.
>
> With this ambassador we send a cross of the wood on which Our Lord Jesus was crucified at Jerusalem, and which was brought to me from there, and of which I have made two crosses, one to remain with me and we send you the other with our emissary. We could have sent you much gold, but we feared the Moors through whose lands our envoy must pass would take it from him.

The captains also informed Fernão of Manuel's response. The king was so overwhelmed with joy that he sent a copy of the letter to the pope informing him of the momentous event—an envoy received from the fabled kingdom of Prester John. Manuel gave orders to prepare a return embassy with a staff of skilled musicians and artisans. In addition, chests full of treasure were to be sent as gifts to the regent queen. After he left their company and was wandering home, Fernão's thoughts raced with the possibility of a burgeoning alliance with the legendary Christian empire of Prester John. He wondered if this was indeed the kingdom. Was the empire still mighty as reported in the historical accounts, or only a mere vestigial remnant of the glorious past? He hoped it was all true.

Fernão eventually received notification that his request for an audience with the king had been granted. His recent entry into the nobility filled him with optimism and confidence as he stood in the center of the Palace Square. The scene before him had changed since his initial departure to India in the spring of 1505. Manuel had tired of the original royal palace on the hill. It was too cramped for the ambitious builder, and too far away for him to properly supervise the incoming treasures frequently arriving to port. The new royal edifice was named the Ribiera Palace due to its proximity on the waterfront.

Fernão admired the entire royal complex from his vantage point in the center of the Palace Square. He faced westward. To his left stood the Ribiera Palace with its primary facade facing the Tejo River. The ground floor was dedicated as a warehouse, to store cargos of spices and treasures from the returning armadas. It also served as the royal armory. The upper floors contained a royal library, chapel, and grand hall. An imposing crenellated terrace with a fortified bastion was equipped with heavy artillery, and a beautiful hanging garden on a veranda projected outward over the water.

The main palace tower on the far left was connected to the royal residences on the far right by a long multi-storied section in the center. The ground floor of this central structure was an extension of the royal warehouse. The upper floors were long arched loggias with their columns and open views of the Palace Square. Fernão conjectured they ought to be identified as verandas since they were open on both sides. To Fernão's right was the India House on the ground level with three internal courtyards in the rear. The top floors comprised the royal residence quarters which all faced inward to the courtyards. Fernão had at times observed the king looking out his window at the bustling dockyards receiving new cargos and the loading of provisions on new outbound ships.

He walked toward a doorway located on the south end of the India House. A guard examined his appointment document and sent him along with an escort. They climbed a stairway—Fernão with some difficulty—to the second level and walked south toward the palace. He admired the galleries of specimens from Africa, India, and the Far East. Fernão leaned on a railing as they climbed another stairway. Its walls were tiled, and most designed with armillary spheres or nature themes. They entered the Grand Hall, principally used for receiving dignitaries and crown appointments. Tapestries hung from the walls, many of which depicted famous events and battles of the Portuguese enterprise. At the far end of the hall was the king, seated upon a golden throne with purple cushions atop a two-stepped dais. He was waving his extraordinarily long arms to conduct an orchestra of musicians. A gathering of courtiers clapped in overtures of feigned applause.

As Fernão approached, limping, all heads turned and the music subsided. He became aware that his darker swarthy features and short stature contrasted with the tall light-skinned court sycophants.

'Ah Fernão Magalhães,' King Manuel said. 'I have been expecting you. It has been quite a long time. What can I do for you today?'

Fernão bowed and maintained his distance. 'I do not wish to take much of your time, but only wish to remind your highness of my status as a noble, and of my service to you and the kingdom.'

Manuel tapped his fingers on the throne's arm rest, already impatient. Fernão, thrown off guard, continued.

'Perhaps you have not been informed of my time abroad. I have fought in numerous battles and endured serious wounds in three of them.' He limped one step forward. 'This injury is from a lance in Morocco.'

The courtiers murmured and jested among themselves. One near the king, whispered in his ear. 'I hear he fakes the limp.'

Manuel frowned.

Fernão cleared his throat and took a breath. 'I wish to have my allotted increase in *moradia*.'

The king's face reddened. 'My . . . oh my. I was expecting you would address the accusations from your actions in Azamor.' The king whispered to a servant, 'Bring the letter.' Then to Fernão, 'You wish to defend yourself?'

Fernão remained stoic.

The servant returned with the letter. The king waved it in the air. 'You have been charged with leaving your post without permission. Furthermore, you have grave charges held against you and have gone unanswered.'

'Baseless charges and unworthy of response,' Fernão fumed with indignation. 'I am innocent.'

'The moradia is denied,' said the king. 'You will return to Azamor to face the charges held against you.'

Fernão bowed and slowly turned. The courtiers chuckled as he limped away.

Humiliated, Fernão returned to Azamor to face the charges. But after an inquiry found nothing of substance, the charges were dismissed. In the end, nobody dared to put their name in writing against a veteran of countless wars for the crown, and especially without adequate proof of wrongdoing. With his letter of acquittal, he departed for Lisbon, along with his brother, who had finished his term of service. When they arrived in Lisbon, Diogo departed north to manage the farm while Fernão remained in the city.

King Manuel was in no hurry to entertain another meeting with Fernão. The months passed with no response. Fernão patiently bided his time frequenting the India House and the dockyards, always searching for new innovations in navigational instruments and maritime discoveries. As he plied his time diligently to his work, he discovered many of those who served with him in Azamor had already been promoted by the king through crafty intrigues and court favors.

On Trinity Sunday, June 3, 1515, King Manuel held an exhibition and invited the city. Fernão and Enrique left their rental flat and meandered their way through the city streets toward the dockyards. The contrast between rich and poor was never so evident as it was now. Nobles, courtiers, and wealthy merchants, dressed in velvet and fine silks, frequented the finest restaurants, and flaunted their wealth without compunction. The vast treasures of the east continued to flow into Lisbon—the new center of trade and emporium of the west. It was only in the previous year that the record shipment of treasure arrived from Calicut. With Albuquerque controlling large swaths of territory, the Zamorin sued for peace and cemented his entreaties to the crown with vast treasures, such as a necklace valued at 10,000 cruzados, and the Zamorin's personal exquisitely embroidered draperies. From Vijayanagar, rich jewelry, pearls, and a dagger of gold inlaid with precious stones were presented to the king.

Strolling the city streets, Fernão and Enrique marveled at the opulent wealth. They watched the affluent nobles whisked away to their various residences in ornate gilded carriages and sedan chairs. Yet, in contrast, the down-trodden and destitute begged in front of the numerous gates and churches.

'How come there are so many beggars?' Enrique asked.

'Some of these are able seamen that simply squandered their gains,' Fernão replied. 'But many are veterans of the war campaigns fallen on hard times. Maybe they were denied their basic pay, or perhaps shipwreck survivors and lost everything. You see all these magnificent churches and fine buildings? All were built upon the backs of these men, all willing to risk their lives in service to the crown.'

'With all this wealth, could not the king help?'

'Good luck with the grocer king,' Fernão laughed, knowing that Manuel's obsession with all the transaction of goods had given him the reputation of a grocery clerk. He turned serious. 'You know, even his top commanders have often been denied their due recompense. The king chooses to keep the profits for the royal treasury and personal projects. Our veterans are left on their own.'

The two entered the Royal Square on the wharf. Along the perimeter, wooden grandstands had been setup, and were filled to maximum capacity. Timber barriers sectioned off the main square. Crowds filed in along the perimeter and remained standing near the buildings. Fernão and Enrique found an open vantage point near the water's edge.

King Manuel and his royal entourage stood on the veranda overlooking the cheering and waving citizens. He raised his long arms in a gesture of good will to his subjects then nodded for the event to commence.

From the eastern side of the square, and near the Estaus Palace, an elephant was guided toward the crowd. Many had never seen such a mighty beast and cheered wildly at the wonder. Meanwhile, a giant door to the warehouse under the Ribiera Palace was unbolted. A menacing creature of great girth appeared. It had skin resembling armor and a large intimidating tusk protruding from its snout. The crowds gasped in awe.

'Have you ever seen one of those?' Enrique asked.

'I had heard stories of such creatures during my tour in Africa,' Fernão replied. 'But I have never seen one.'

A merchant next to them leaned in and said, 'It was a gift from the King of Cambay. I heard the king wants to test a theory, based on the testimony of Pliny the Elder, that the rhinoceros and the elephant are the most bitter of enemies. All are curious to which creature will attack first. Will the rhinoceros' horn first gut the elephant's underbelly, or will the elephant first gore the rhinoceros with its tusks?'

As the elephant neared, one could see it was young, and the tusks were not fully developed. The rhinoceros trotted toward it. The elephant, already rattled by the crowd noise, was unnerved by the approaching rhinoceros. It whirled about and charged through an iron gate, and into the city streets. Citizens leaped out of the way as the elephant headed straight back to its stable in the Estaus Palace. The event was short-lived but exciting.

Not long after this, Fernão received another letter from Serrão. He read it over several times on the balcony in their rental home. 'Is that from your friend?' Enrique asked as he brought in a jug of water.

'Yes. An interesting letter. He reiterates his belief that the Moluccas are much further to the east than many believe.'

'Why is this important?'

'Unfortunately, it could mean the islands are located within Spanish domain.'

Enrique stared blankly. 'I do not understand.'

'I can give you a brief explanation,' Fernão said and gestured for Enrique to take a seat next to him on the balcony. 'You see, with both Portugal and Spain exploring and claiming new lands, disputes eventually arose. Therefore, in 1494 a treaty was agreed upon by the two nations in Tordesillas, Spain. A line of demarcation between the two poles was established 370 degrees west of the Cape Verde Islands. All discoveries to the east side of this line belonged to Portugal and to the west side belonged to Spain. The line runs through the bulge of the southern continent. Thus, Cabral's discovery of Brazil was in our legitimate jurisdiction.'

Fernão sensed confusion in the young lad. He retrieved an orange, then with a quill pen made rough outlines of all the known major continents. He drew a line from the top to the bottom. The line cut through the bulge of Brazil. 'So here we have the treaty line. But one may ask, what about the other side of the globe? How do we know who has the rights to the lands discovered there?' Fernão drew a line from the other side of the orange, top to bottom, then set it upon a small table. 'This is the theoretical antemeridian line. No treaty yet exists for this demarcation since few have explored this far, and the science of longitude has not been perfected yet. Now the question is this. Did Francisco discover the Moluccas on Portugal's side of the antemeridian, or Spain's?'

Enrique picked up the orange and observed the lines. 'He seems certain it is far to the east. Spanish territory?'

'Quite possible if his estimation is correct. With the spice trade involved, an expedition will be needed to ascertain the exact location. And, of course, establish a trade enterprise.' Fernão smiled. 'I will propose such a plan to the king.'

Fernão's request for an audience was granted once more, and he entered the Grand Hall. This time, Leonora, the dowager queen attended, along with many courtiers. Fernão approached the throne and handed the king's servant the letter of acquittal. Manuel read it over and then tore it up.

Fernão's face turned red. 'That is my acquittal.'

'I will be the judge,' Manuel replied.

'Very well. But I implore you to grant my moradia.'

Manuel turned his head to his courtiers with a smile and they returned the gesture. 'Hmm . . . denied.'

Queen Leonora frowned and gave her brother a scowl.

It occurred to Fernão that there may be a reason the king was so antagonistic. As a page in the court Manuel never liked him much. But complicating matters further, the courtiers exacted their own pressure by making demeaning insinuations against his country roots and short swarthy appearance. He realized that his prospects diminished for every appearance in the royal circles. Nevertheless, he pressed on. 'Well, if no moradia, then let me serve you again in the east. Francisco Serrão has discovered the Moluccas . . . the Spice Islands. It is far into the east. Perhaps we can establish a base before the Spaniards claim it. Perhaps we—'

'Enough! Serrão? I remember him. Your friend, the cook. Fitting he ends up in the land of *spices*.' Manuel laughed at his own joke and the court sycophants joined in. Manuel gestured for them to quiet and then continued. 'But I hear he is a troublemaker. He has not reported back to our base in Malacca. Perhaps he is a renegade?'

'I assure you, my king. He is honest—a warrior for the crown—an explorer, opening new trade for us. Please let me also serve you again.'

The courtiers rolled their eyes.

Manuel noticed their disapproval and turned back to Fernão. 'We shall no longer need your services.'

Fernão stared at the king in shock, his face paled, and a touch of nausea rose in his throat. He took a deep breath and composed himself. Fernão knew he had only one option, and he had to exercise it. 'If this is the case, then would you allow me to offer my service to a lord who would desire so?'

'Go as you please,' Manuel said coldly.

Fernão stepped forward to kiss his sovereign's ring. But Manuel withdrew it at the last second while turning his head toward one of his grinning courtiers. With this last humiliating rebuttal, Fernão turned and limped out the Grand Hall.

# 16

Fernão remained in his room for three days with only a pitcher of water and a loaf of bread. On the third morning, Enrique rapped lightly on his door. There was no answer. He continued to knock every quarter hour—until on the sixth attempt—Fernão answered, 'You never give up do you? Enter.'

Enrique peered into the dim lit room. A half-eaten loaf of bread lay upon a small table. Fernão seemed groggy but managed to slowly sit up on the edge of the bed. His body was gaunt, his eyes sunken.

'Please, come outside,' Enrique implored. 'It is a sunny day and there is a pleasant breeze on the balcony. I have some fresh fruits from the market.'

Fernão slowly rose, stumbled forward, and squinted his eyes upon leaving the dark bedroom. After taking a seat at the balcony table he found a fruit basket and began to pick at the skin of a ripe orange.

Meanwhile, Enrique retrieved a bronze astrolabe from a cabinet and brought it outside. 'I found this while cleaning. What is this? It looks like some sort of measuring instrument.'

Fernão stared at it blankly. His thoughts turned to his many adventures at sea. Like a sail finally catching a breeze, his mind and spirit began to flutter to life. The passionate drive of nautical science and exploration came back to remembrance. He wondered if perhaps the Good Lord was using Enrique to bring him out of the doldrums. Fernão took it as a sort of divine intervention.

He turned to Enrique, fully aware. 'I will show you the first procedure.' Fernão demonstrated to Enrique how to set the date and time on the astrolabe and adjust the movable pinhole sight to line up with the sun. 'We need to construct a tripod before taking measurements,' he said, setting the astrolabe down. He thought for a moment, then smiled. 'We can go now and locate some materials.'

Enrique was quite astonished at Fernão's sudden recovery.

The following day they constructed a tripod and commenced daily instruction on the basic operation of the astrolabe.

Some days later, after some careful thought, Fernão penned a letter to his friend Serrão. He told him of the latest events and closed with:

> God willing, I will soon be seeing you, whether by way of Portugal or Castile, for that is the way my affairs have been leaning: You must wait for me there, because we already know that it will be some time before we can expect things to get better for us.

Over the next year, Fernão made frequent visits to the India House to follow up in his quest to ascertain the longitude of the Moluccas and the optimal sailing route to find them. Fernão's passionate drive combined with his practical navigational acumen drew many like-minded individuals into his personal quest. He conversed with famous cartographers, such as Pedro and Jorge Reinel as well as Diogo Ribera. Fernão also discussed maps and shipping routes with Lopo Homem. Fernão found this to be quite beneficial, for Homem had privy information, due to his assignment by King Manuel to compile all the existing charts for creating a world atlas.

Approaching the end of 1516, Fernão kept his mind occupied and tried to ignore the passage of time. He was 36 years of age, and still without prospects for commanding an expedition. He kept faith that his opportunity would come, and his faith was finally rewarded. One day, as he was poring over the latest western sea charts in the India House, a voice called out his name, 'Magalhães!' He turned to find Captain João Lisboa facing him with a big smile.

'You know me?' Fernão said, wondering how the famous commander and explorer recognized him.

'Of course. You led the cavalry charge in Azamor. I was chief pilot of the fleet back then. You seem to enjoy the thrill of combat.'

'If it achieves an honorable victory.'

'Indeed,' Lisboa said, approvingly. 'So now you are buried in books and charts.'

'Yes sir, best to be prepared with the latest navigational innovations and discoveries.' Fernão thought now would be an opportune time to inject some sincere flattery. 'I read your recent publications on seamanship and the nautical needle. I found them very insightful.'

'You have read them?' Lisboa replied with pleasant surprise. 'Perhaps it will be of some use to you one day.' He looked over the chart spread out on the desk depicting the continents of the New World. Fernão had left a ruler lined up along the coast of the southern continent. Lisboa traced his finger near the indicated positional alignment. 'So, you are interested in the lands south of Brazil?'

'Actually, I am looking for the optimal route west to the Moluccas. My friend Francisco Serrão resides there now. We have plans to start up a trading enterprise.'

'I see. Do you know of the Haros?'

'Of course, the international trading financiers. They have a headquarters, here in Lisbon.'

Precisely. I sailed under an expedition financed by Christóbal Haro a few years ago. We sailed past the mouth of a wide river, what the Spaniards now name—Rio de la Plata. After sailing some distance beyond, we encountered foul weather and turned back. It was regrettable we could not sail further south. I have heard rumors of a strait leading to the great ocean in the west.'

Fernão knew Lisboa was an esteemed veteran pilot and any information he divulged would be invaluable. He listened carefully as he continued. 'Well, as you may have noticed, Spain has been sending out exploratory missions with urgency. They have discovered that the sailing route below Brazil turns westward and will now claim these lands are in their jurisdiction based on the Treaty of Tordesillas. Furthermore, they seek for a strait passing through the continent to the great ocean beyond.'

'I heard reports,' Fernão said. 'A Spaniard named Vasco Núñez de Balboa has seen a great ocean to the other side of the continent. He viewed it from a ridge they call—the Darién Highlands.'

'Exactly. He has confirmed its existence, named it the South Sea.'

'Why the South Sea?' Fernão asked. 'Why not the Western Sea?'

'Insightful question,' Lisboa replied. 'It is believed, based on the latest navigational charts of Balboa, that the narrow isthmus in this region runs east to west, and therefore the great sea would indeed be south.

'I see. But the remainder of the continent generally runs north to south?'

'Correct. Balboa eventually crossed the isthmus and explored the coastline in canoes. He is the first of us to explore the opposite side of the New World.'

'Incredible.'

'But whoever finds a navigable strait will secure even greater fame in the annals of exploration. Of course, the quest has its dangers; for mighty tempests, frigid cold, and dangerous natives, all await those who dare to seek the path. Have you heard the news on the Solis expedition?'

Fernão shook his head.

'Well, a Spanish fleet of 3 ships and 70 men sailed from San Lucár, Spain, on October 8, 1515. The commander, Juan Diaz de Solis, had served in our India armadas and eventually had enlisted with the Spaniards. They were sent to explore the coastline south of Brazil. Upon reaching the Rio de la Plata, Solis commanded a small crew to explore on shore. Soon after landing, they were attacked and torn apart by giants—human giants. On the beach, the natives roasted them and ate their flesh in full view of the fleet. With no time to render assistance, their comrades could only watch in horror. The mission was abandoned, and the fleet returned to Seville in September.'

'Man-eaters . . . giants. I have heard of similar accounts from Vespucci,' Fernão said.

'You knew Amerigo Vespucci?' Lisboa asked.

'I met him here in the India House.'

'Indeed. A well-traveled fellow. He died in Seville a few years back. I hear that a young German cartographer has honored him by naming part of Brazil—America. We will miss his navigational genius.'

Fernão and Lisboa nodded to each other in agreement.

'So, have you requested a command to lead an expedition to the Moluccas?' Lisboa asked. 'Everyone knows you are an experienced navigator and soldier.'

'I have, but I was quickly denied. It seems the king has an ill disposition to me.'

'A shame. But you are not alone in that. As a matter of fact, the Haro's had—'

A heated argument escalated on the opposite side of the chamber. A short man with disheveled hair tossed a book at a young cleric. 'Idiots! How do they allow you people in this study? They should require an intelligence exam.' The crazed man stormed down the center aisle of bookshelves toward Fernão and Lisboa.

'Ah, Ruy Faleiro,' Lisboa remarked. 'What has irked you so much this fine day?'

Ruy scanned over the two men. His hands shook in agitation. 'I only made a simple query to locate the latest ephemerides publication and the imbecile just stared at me blankly, obviously ignorant of what I was even asking. I need to adjust my calculations on longitude but must have the latest data.' Ruy sized up Fernão. 'And who is this?'

'Forgive me, this is Fernão Magalhães. He fought with us in Azamor and served many years in the Indies, even as far as Malacca. A fine navigator from what I have been told.'

'And you are here with charts and books because you are to embark on a new mission?' Ruy asked.

'Well, I was researching for a route to the west, to the Moluccas . . . trying to calculate the distance and location to these islands.'

'Sounds like a longitudinal study, is it not?' Ruy asked with a smile, his mood lightened.

'I suppose so. I need to know if the Moluccas are in the domain of Portugal or Spain. Of course, it may be of little use to me.'

'And why is that?'

'The king has denied me any command, ever.'

'Regrettable. It appears the king denies much talent these days. Denied myself for the chair of astronomy at the University of Coimbra . . . passed over by court scheming and prejudice. The king's courtiers especially despise those of us from the northern highlands.'

Fernão's eyes opened wide.

Ruy took notice. 'So, you are from the north?'

Fernão nodded.

'That explains much. You know they are so jealous of my abilities . . . even claim my knowledge must come from the dark arts . . . accuse me of making a pact with the devil.' Ruy shook his head in disgust. 'Pitiful scoundrels.'

'I see you two have much in common,' Lisboa said. 'I must take my leave now.' On the way out he turned for a moment. 'Let you know if I speak with the Haros. Maybe they have some plans.'

'Funny he mentions the Haros,' Ruy said.

'Why is that?' Fernão asked.

'They have also been disparaged by the king. Apparently, a Portuguese privateer, Estevão Yusarte, had plundered their 16-ship fleet in the Gulf of Guinea. Seven of the vessels sank. They sued the king for damages, but all claims were denied. Even with intercessions from the Netherlands and Spain, Manuel has stubbornly refused to give any recompense for damages. I believe it is only a matter of time before the Haros transfer their holdings to Spain.'

Ruy suddenly changed the topic. 'You know, there is a small publication we have received from

Poland called, the *Commentariolus*. Have you heard of this?'

Fernão shook his head.

'Well, the author, Nicolaus Copernicus, has carefully postulated a theory on how the planetary spheres revolve around the sun which is itself located near the center of our universe. A clever astronomer he is, and his mathematics are sound.' Ruy Faleiro continued rambling on about astronomy, cartography, and navigational devices. Fernão listened and added comments based upon his own first-hand experience acquired during many years at sea. They continued for hours until the India House staff forced their departure, for it was late.

A few days later, Fernão was strolling along the wharf and found an old acquaintance making a sketch of a carrack under construction. 'Duarte!'

The young man looked up from his writing pad. 'Magalhães! What a coincidence meeting you here.'

'Yes, a long time since Cannanore. I see you are still with pen in hand. Did you ever finish your travel journal?'

'Just published this year!' Duarte Barbosa replied with a big smile. 'I was thinking of adding a cover drawing, of this vessel here.'

Fernão looked at the sketch, then at the ship. 'Nice!'

'Enough about me,' Barbosa said. 'What have you been doing?'

'Spending a lot of time in the India House. Researching for an expedition to the Moluccas.'

'You know, I never quite reached that far east. For those places, I had to use testimony from Varthema and other merchants for my book.'

Fernão nodded at the mention of Varthema. Then he said, 'You remember Francisco Serrão?'

'Of course, your friend.'

'He made it to the Moluccas. Claims there is such an abundance of quality cloves, nutmeg and mace, that one could become quite wealthy.'

'I always wanted to go there and see for myself. And the riches only add to the drive.'

'I am planning to take a western route . . . compiling notes.'

'Any chance to lead an expedition?'

'The king denied me. No opportunity in Portugal anymore. But maybe that is no longer relevant, because Serrão believes the Moluccas reside in Spanish territory.'

'You know my father is a Portuguese expatriate living in Seville and has connections. Perhaps he can arrange some introductions with the Spanish court. He serves as the *Alcaide's* second in command at the Alcazar fortress. If you like, I can let him know your intentions.'

'Thank you, my friend.'


On November 24, 1516, Fernão had finally received his 200 cruzados owed from the Abraldez suit. However, the king never paid the ten percent interest due, which further exasperated the antagonism between Fernão and King Manuel. But now, he at least had enough to travel abroad if needed.

Over the next months, Fernão and Ruy bonded over their love of cosmography. They collaborated to formulate a new approach to the enigma of longitude. Fernão's practical experience complemented Ruy's theoretical knowledge. The two personalities could not have contrasted more, for Fernão was taciturn and a man of action while Ruy was a lover of books and theories with a passion often accompanied by sudden fits of rage. But Fernão realized the partnership was worth the inconveniences of their oddly matched personalities and forged ahead with their joint studies.

After establishing in his mind that Ruy could be trusted, he proposed how they could apply these insights for an expedition to the Moluccas via a western route. One day, Fernão revealed the secret map Behaim had given him depicting the strait near the *Dragon's Tail* of the New World—a strait leading to the great ocean beyond. The two pledged they would not divulge their secret route to any other, until they had claimed victory in their mission. They were to be equals. If anything should happen to either, regarding the enterprise, they were to inform the other within six hours. Of course, Fernão only regarded divulging their specific route as the obligation to inform, not the general mission. Over the next days, Ruy continued to apply his scientific knowledge to their proposed route and Fernão made careful annotations on the charts.

João Lisboa eventually introduced Fernão and Ruy to the Haro brothers. Apparently, King Manuel had threatened Cristóbal de Haro with imprisonment for unpaid taxes. All knew this was a ruse and that Manuel, in fact, owed them. The Haros carefully listened to Fernão and Ruy propose their plans for an exploratory mission to the fabled Spice Islands. Satisfied with their navigational acumen, the Haros divulged their plans to relocate their headquarters to Seville and promised them sponsorship if they would expatriate to Spain. Fernão and Ruy had already prepared for this scenario and pledged to join forces with the Haros.

In the autumn of 1517, Fernão paid several visits to his cartographer friends and discussed his plans for an expedition to the Moluccas. All were greatly inspired by the idea and the prospects to further the science of cartography. Without hesitation they all pledged their support and would plan to meet him in Seville. Fernão was ecstatic upon their heartfelt response and set his mind to the task at hand.

In October 1517, Fernão departed Lisbon and sailed west on the wide Tejo River to Belém. Looking toward the shoreline, he watched construction crews working feverishly upon two great projects.

In the background, a magnificent structure was taking shape. This edifice—The Jerónimos Monastery, had now encompassed the original church of Santa Maria de Belem. King Manuel had purposed it to house his mausoleum. It was to be built in gratitude to God for opening the vast spice trade ushered in by the pioneering voyage of Vasco da Gama to India. Fernão had learned the construction had begun in January of 1501. It was financed by taxes levied on the lucrative African and Indian commercial enterprises. The Saint Jerome monks secluded in this great monastery were commissioned to pray for the king's soul and provide spiritual aid to sailors embarking on new voyages of discovery.

In the forefront and a little to the west stood the mighty new Tower of Belém. The work had begun in 1514 and was over half complete. The fortress was constructed upon rocks in the water near the shore. Once completed, it would tower four levels and serve as a formidable deterrent against encroaching enemy fleets.

Fernão watched the early sunlight reflecting off the stronghold's white stones and the fields along the hills of Lisbon. He embraced the morning, knowing this was surely his last farewell to his homeland.

# The Magellan Chronicles: Sources

Albuquerque, Afonso de. *The Commentaries of the Great Alfonso de Albuquerque*. Translated by Walter de Gray Birch. 4 vols. New York: Cambridge University Press, 2010. (London: Hakluyt Society, 1875).

Arciniegas, Germán. *Amerigo and the New World: The Life and Times of Amerigo Vespucci*. Translated by Harriet de Onís. New York: Alfred A Knoff, 1955.

Barbosa, Duarte. *A Description of the Coasts of East Africa and Malabar in the Beginning of the Sixteenth Century*. Translated by Henry E.J. Stanley. Kentucky: n.p., 2014.

Bergreen, Laurence. *Over the Edge of the World: Magellan's Terrifying Circumnavigation of the Globe*. New York: Harper Collins Publishers, 2003.

Blackburn, Graham. *The Overlook Illustrated Dictionary of Nautical Terms*. Woodstock, NY: The Overlook Press, 1981.

Bridgeman, Keith and Tahira Arsham, eds. *Magellan*. England: Viartis, 2008.

Camerota, Filippo, ed. *Museo Galileo: A Guide to the Treasures of the Collection*. Firenze, Italy: Gionti, 2010.

Caruncho, Daniel R. *Royal Alcazar of Seville: More than a Thousand Years of Art and Architecture*. Translated by Cerys Giordano Jones. Barcelona: Dos de Arte Ediciones, S.L., 2016.

Castanheda, Fernão Lopes de. *Historia do descobrimento e conquista de India pelos Portugueses*. 2 vols. Lisboa: Typographia Rollandiana, 1833.

Corrêa, Gaspar. *Lendas de India*. 2 vols. Lisboa: Academia Real das Sciencies de Lisboa, 1858.

Cliff, Nigel. *Holy War: How Vasco da Gama's Epic Voyages Turned the Tide in a Centuries-Old Clash of Civilizations*. New York: Harper Collins, 2011.

Cribb, Joe, Barrie Cook, and Ian Carradice. *A Comprehensive View of the Coins of the World Throughout History*. London: Little, Brown & Co., 1999.

Crowley, Roger. *Conquerors: How Portugal Forged the First Global Empire*. New York: Random House, 2015.

Danvers, Frederick Charles. *The Portuguese in India*. 2 vols. London: Elibron, 2007.

Delagado, Francisco Gil. *Seville Cathedral*. Spain: Escudo de Oro, n.d.

Diffie, Bailey W. and George D. Winius. *Foundations of the Portuguese Empire 1415-1580*. 10 vols.

Minneapolis, MN: University of Minnesota Press, 1977.

Edwards, Charles Lester and Amerigo Vespucci. *Amerigo Vespucci*. Edited by Keith Bridgeman and Tahira Arsham. England: Viartis, 2009.

Fernándo-Armesto, Felipe. *Amerigo: The Man Who Gave his Name to America*. New York: Random House Publishing Group, 2007.

Gibbons, Tony, ed. *The Encyclopedia of Ships: Over 1,500 Military and Civilian Ships from 5000 B.C. to the Present Day*. San Diego: Thunder Bay Press, 2001.

Góis, Damião de. *Lisbon in the Renaissance*. Translated by Jeffrey S. Ruth. New York: Italica Press, 1996.

Green, Toby. *Inquistion: The Reign of Fear*. New York: St. Martin's Press, 2007.

——. *The Rise of the Trans-Atlantic Slave trade in Western Africa, 1300-1589*. New York: Cambridge University Press, 2012.

Guillemard, Francis Henry Hill. *The Life of Ferdinand Magellan and the First Circumnavigation of the Globe: 1480-1521*. London: George Philip & Son, 1890.

Hargrave, Catherine Perry. *A History of Playing Cards*. New York: Dover Publications Inc., 2014.

Hazard, Henry W. and Kenneth Setton, eds. *A History of the Crusades: Volume III: The Fourteenth and Fifteenth Centuries*. 6 vols. Madison, WI: The University of Wisconsin Press, 1975.

Johnson, Donald S., Tapio Markkanen Juha Nurminen, and Pär-Henrik Sjöström. *The History of Seafaring: Navigating the World's Oceans*. London: Conway Maritime Press, 2007.

Joyner, Tim. *Magellan*. Camden, ME: International marine Publishing, 1992.

Kemp, Peter, ed. *The Oxford Companion to Ships and the Sea*. Oxford: Oxford University Press, 1988.

Konstam, Angus. *Historical Atlas of Exploration 1492-1600*. London: Mercury Books, 2006.

Krondl, Michael. *The Taste of Conquest: The Rise and Fall of the Three Great Cities of Spice*. New York: Balantine Books, 2007.

Lavery, Brian. *Ship: The Epic Story of Maritime Adventure*. New York: DK Publishing, 2010.

Major, Richard Henry, ed. *India in the Fifteenth Century*. New York: Cambridge University Press, 2010. (London: Hakluyt Societ, 1857).

Mandeville, Sir John. *The Book of Marvels and Travels*. Translated by Anthony Bale. Oxford: Oxford University Press, 2012.

Martyr, Peter. *The Discovery of the new World in the Writings of Peter Martyr of Anghiera*. Edited by

Ernesto Lunari, Elisa Magioncalda, and Rosanna Mazzacane. Rome: Istituto Poligrafica, 1992.

Menzies, Gavin. *1421 The Year China Discovered America*. New York: Harper Collins Publishers, 2003.

Monteiro, Saturnino. *Portuguese Sea Battles Volume I: The First World Sea Power 1139-1521*. 8 vols. Translated by Maria do Céu Barreto. Oeiras, Portugal: Saturnino Monteiro, 2014.

Morris, John Gottlieb. *Martin Behaim the German Astronomer and Cosmographer of the Times of Columbus*. Baltimore: John Murphy and Co., 1855.

Morrison, Samuel Eliot. *Admiral of the Ocean Sea: A Life of Christopher Columbus*. Toronto: Little, Brown & Co., 1970.

Newitt, Malyn, ed. *The Portuguese in West Africa, 1415-1670*. New York: Cambridge University Press, 2010.

Nicolle, David. *The Portuguese in the Age of Discovery c. 1340-1665*. Oxford: Osprey Publishing Ltd., 2012.

Nielsen Jr., Niels C., Norvin Hein, Frank E. Reynolds, Alan L. Miller, Samuel E. Karff, Alice C. Cochran, and Paul McClean, eds. *Religions of the World*. New York: St. Martin's Press, Inc., 1983.

O'Bryan, John. *A History of Weapons*. San Francisco: Chronicle Books, 2013.

Passos, John Dos. *The Portugal Story: Three Centuries of Exploration and Discovery*. Lexington: Doubleday, 1969.

Pearsen, Michael. *Port Cities and Invaders: The Swahili oast, India, and Portugal in the Early Modern Era*. Baltimore: The John Hopkins University Press, 1998.

Perreira, Duarte Pacheco. *Esmeraldo de Situ Orbis*. Translated and Edited by Geroge H.T. Kimble. New York: Routledge, 2016.

Pigafetta, Antonio. *Magellan's Voyage: A Narrative Account of the First Circumnavigation*. Translated and edited by R.A. Skelton. New York: Dover Publications Inc., 1969.

——. *The First Voyage Round the World by Magellan*. Edited by Henry John Stanly. New York: Cambridge University Press, 2010.

Pires, Tomé. *The Summa Oriental of Tomé Pires*. 2 vols. Surrey, UK: Ashgate Publishing Ltd., 2010.

Preto, Luis. *Jogo do Pau: The Ancient Art and Modern Science of Portuguese Stick Fighting*. n.p. 2013.

Rossfelder, André. *In Pursuit of Longitude: Magellan and the Antimeridian*. La Jolla, CA: Starboard Books, 2010.

Sanceau, Elaine. *The Reign of the Fortunate King 1495-1521*. USA: Archon Books, 1970.

Stephens, H. Morse. *Albuquerque*. Oxford: Clarendon Press, 1897.

Theal, George McCall. *History and Ethnography of Africa South of the Zambesi 1505-1795*. 3 vols. New York: Cambridge University Press, 2010. (London: Swan Sonnenschein & Co., 1910).

Thomas, Hugh. *The Slave Trade: The Story of the Atlantic Slave Trade 1440-1870*. New York: Simon and Schuster, 1997.

Webster, Roderick and Marjorie. *Western Astrolabes: Historic Scientific Instruments of the Adler Planetarium & Astronomy Museum*. 2 vols. Chicago: Adler Planetarium & Astronomy Museum, 1998.

Weinstein, Donald. *Ambassador from Venice: Pietro Pasqualigo in Lisbon, 1501*. Minneapolis, MN: University of Minnesota Press, 1960.

Whiteway, Richard Stephen. *The Rise of Portuguese Power in India. A.D. 1497-A.D. 1550*. Columbia, SC: n.p., 2018.

Varthema, Ludovico di. *The Travels of Ludovico di Varthema in Egypt, Syria, Arabia Deserta and Arabia Felix in Persia, India, and Ethiopia, 1503 to 1508*. Lexington, KY: Forgotten Books, 2014. (London: Hakluyt Society, 1863).

Vicente, Gil. *Four Plays of Gil Vicente*. Translated by Aubrey F. G. Bell. San Bernardino, CA: Forgotten Books, 2015.

Zweig, Stefen. *Magellan*. London: Pushkin Press, 2011.

# About the Author

Brett Stortroen has authored the biographical novel, *Night of the Dragon: The Saga of Saint George* and the non-fiction book, now sold in over thirty countries, *Mecca, Muhammad & the Moon God: A Candid Investigation into the Origins of Islam.* With a BA and MA in Theological and Historical Studies, he also publishes articles on his web site, bigfaithministries.com. Traveling the world as a telecommunication engineer in the cruise industry, he has been able to incorporate his maritime experiences and historical research into the latest biographical novel series, *The Magellan Chronicles.*

www.ingramcontent.com/pod-product-compliance
Lightning Source LLC
Chambersburg PA
CBHW031948240626
47153CB00003B/904